Sparrow Song

The Rohendra Complex, Book 2

Georgina Makalani

Cover Design by Deranged Doctor Designs

(www.derangeddoctordesign.com/)

ISBN: 978-0-6453956-7-9

Also by Georgina Makalani

The Last Dragon Skin Chronicles
The Legend of Iski Flare
The Magics of Rei-Een
The Mark of Oldra
The Raven Crown

The Rohendra Complex:
The Dragonfly
Sparrow Song
Shimmering Bear
Rohendra Queen

One

Isla stood at the large window and looked over the glittering city spread out before her. It appeared clean, ordered and beautiful. She tugged again at the binds around her wrists. She had been testing them intermittently since she had arrived, but the thick plastic was beyond her. She had only succeeded in causing the sharp edges to cut further into her skin.

Her reflection in the window was more distinct than the world beyond, and she looked a mess. She tried not to flinch as her focus rested on the reflection of the man standing behind her.

"Where did you find E'anah?" he asked, as though noticing that she had seen him. She wasn't sure how to refer to him. He was her Kalli, and yet he wasn't. Colonel Calder was something very different from the man she had known. "Come now, Little Dragonfly." His voice was soft, familiar and far too close. "Tell me."

"He found me," she said, trying to keep her breathing level. How many times had she dreamt that he had returned? How many times as she'd drifted to sleep, fearing the dark would take her, had she hoped he would appear and make it all better?

Despite her concerns as to whom Gray truly worked for, the moment she'd seen him in that dark room as the dusters had lit up the space, she knew she had made a mistake. He hadn't known Kalli was still alive, and it saddened her that she had now gotten him killed. They had been dragged in different directions the moment they had landed at Hendra Central in the expansive hangar. Too many men had dragged him away, Calder's hand too tight around her neck to even turn and guess where he might have been taken.

Isla knew Calder well enough to understand what would have happened next. She straightened her shoulders and tried to remind herself why she had agreed to go along with this. The benefit Ebberah was so sure she could bring to the Complex, the need to learn just what the Hendra was doing with the Rohen and why they were mining it. Then she would be free to go where she should have in the first place—a quiet death. Although, it would likely be public and bloody. She was almost looking forward to that as well.

"Was he looking for you?" Calder asked, his voice jarring her from her thoughts.

"No, I don't think so. He was doing something else—looking for something else—when our paths crossed at a racetrack."

"You were a good racer, I heard."

Isla tried to hold her pose, but she turned from the window with a sigh and looked up into his face, searching his eyes for the man she had once known behind them. She couldn't see him. "I have a way with ships."

"You always liked to tinker with the grease monkeys."

"They were people too, knowledgeable people. You never appreciated that."

He shrugged and walked across the room. It was far larger than she would have expected to be given, but it wasn't clear yet if this was her space or she was waiting for someone else. She hadn't been given any indication that she would be released from her bonds. Calder might have moved away, but he hadn't taken his eyes from her. Isla didn't know what she could do as she sensed the metal flowing through every surface around her.

The door opened, and Isla stared at the blonde woman who entered. She was beautiful and dressed impeccably; Isla was sure that even Ebberah would have been impressed. "Colonel," the woman said as though surprised to see him there. "Are you still here?"

"I am waiting for Hendra," he said casually.

Isla bowed her head as the woman turned her gaze to her. The First Wife—someone Isla would love the chance to talk to if she could get her alone. Although she doubted the woman would share anything worthwhile with her.

"You should refer to her as *the* Hendra. And I believe I have a title or similar that you should be using as well."

Calder rolled his eyes and sat down on the couch.

The woman opened her mouth and stared as the Hendra entered the room. Despite the leader of the entire system standing before her, Isla remained fixed to the spot. The Hendra looked just as formidable as she had the last time Isla had seen her. She didn't seem quite so impressive on screen.

"Brute," the First Wife muttered, not too quietly.

"Calder." The Hendra's firm voice carried, and Isla felt the power of it wash over the room.

He looked up at her, and only as she glared at him did he climb back to his feet. Isla wondered what power he had within this world.

"She is not someone I can leave you alone with," he said.

"But you will."

He opened his mouth and then closed it, glancing at the other woman in the room, who was watching Isla more than the conversation between the others.

"I am telling you she is not to be underestimated."

"Telling me?" the Hendra asked, her voice dangerous. The First Wife stopped and looked back before raising her eyebrows, as though surprised the Hendra would raise her voice—or was it that she hadn't thought she would need to? She inched closer to Isla. "I don't need you to tell me anything," the Hendra continued.

Calder shook his head and turned back to Isla, his face serious. He took a step forward as the First Wife did the same.

"You are very beautiful," she said softly. "I had heard you were scarred, and yet... Oh, your arms. Can we remove these?" She turned back to the others.

"Alice, I don't think..."

"Thank you," Isla said kindly, holding her hands out. The Hendra indicated to Calder with a slight tip of her head.

He stomped across the room and took Isla's arm too tightly. He pulled a large knife from his belt as Alice let out a noise of surprise. He sliced through the bands quickly, and Isla let out a soft cry as he sliced into her skin.

"Colonel!" Alice chastised, reaching for her immediately to put herself between Isla and the soldier.

"Your Grace," Isla said, looking up as she wrapped her hand tightly around the fresh wound. "You will get bloody."

"I have seen worse," Alice said, surprisingly calm. "Fetch the first aid kit." The other two watched rather than acted until the Hendra nodded. Alice led Isla to the couch and directed her to sit down, her hand still tight over the wound. "She needs help," she repeated.

The Hendra cleared her throat, and Calder moved too slowly towards the door. When it opened, he said something to the man outside. Isla tried but couldn't hear the conversation, and then he turned back to the room.

"I think you can leave now," Alice said to him.

He raised his eyebrows in surprise and looked to Hendra. She nodded once. "We will talk later. I have things to do here."

He left without another word, but Isla was surprised at the lack of respect and ease with which he spoke to the leader of the Rohendra Complex.

She wondered what relationship they had. She wanted to let them know that she knew who he was, but she wasn't sure if both of the women in the room knew the truth, and he might have already shared with the Hendra that Isla had guessed his identity.

"I think you could go, Alice," the Hendra said. But the other woman gave her a look like she wouldn't be told anything. Instead of pushing the point, the Hendra sat on the opposite couch and looked her over.

They remained in silence, Alice holding Isla's arm tight enough that she started to lose feeling in her hand, the Hendra staring at her as though trying to read her thoughts. Isla tried not to stare back.

A servant entered without knocking and sat an intricately carved wooden box before the First Wife. She nodded her head and the man left. With one hand still tight around Isla's wrist, she opened the box with the other and moved her fingers quickly over the small vials within. Isla leaned forward and looked them over. She could smell the forest within the wood and the contents of the vials. Alice selected one, and Isla felt no fear that this woman would do her harm.

"Is this really necessary?" the Hendra asked, clearly bored.

"We invite the great war hero into our home, and she is attacked by *your man*. What will people think?"

"I'm no war hero," Isla muttered.

"Of course you are, dear," Alice said, sounding motherly and older than she appeared. Isla would have been surprised if the woman was any older than she was herself. But then, they had access to far more than the average man in terms of health care and enhancements; she might be very much mistaken.

"Alice," the Hendra said, drawing the woman's attention. "She is hardly a guest."

"I don't believe the newsflashes," Alice said, leaning in a little towards Isla. As she lifted her hand slowly, Isla saw that her arm was already healing.

Alice wiped quickly with an ointment from the vial that tingled, and Isla thought she could taste something earthy despite the fact it was placed on her arm. "Let's wrap this. Such a slice will take days to heal." Alice quickly pulled a white silk from the box and wrapped it carefully around Isla's wrist, not too tightly. "Is that better?" she asked kindly, but there was something in the way she looked when Isla met her gaze. As though she had a secret to keep.

Isla pulled her arm in. "I'm sure it will be," she muttered. "Thank you, Your Grace."

The woman beamed and turned back to the Hendra, her eyebrows raised as though she had proven a point.

"We have business, Alice," the Hendra said kindly. The woman nodded, closed her box of goods and stood.

"It was lovely to meet you," she said, bowing her head to Isla, and then she walked gracefully from the room with the box in her arms.

The Hendra cleared her throat.

"Your guard dog didn't think this safe," Isla said before the woman could say anything.

"You don't scare me," the Hendra said. "Nothing scares me."

"Nothing?" Isla asked, looking back towards the door.

"I don't need to fear, and Colonel Calder is not my guard dog. He is Elite. They do as they must for the good of the Complex. But you know that, don't you? You were Elite. Once."

"I'm not sure it goes away," Isla said, leaning back into the soft cushions. She was ready for some sleep, although she wouldn't admit it. "I am a wanted criminal now, even if I didn't commit any crime."

The Hendra waved her hand as though that wasn't important. "You are a hummer, and for the moment that is what I need from you."

Isla sighed and sat forward.

"You survived the mine," the Hendra continued.

"I am not what you need me to be," Isla said, standing and brushing at her dusty, damaged clothes. Did she look as messy as when she had studied her reflection in the window? She ran her hand through her hair and found it half loose.

"You will be, even if I have to torture your little sparrow to make you hum."

Isla kept her face neutral, but the relief to learn that Gray wasn't dead helped her to straighten her shoulders. "Go ahead," Isla said. "I am no hummer—and Rohen is illegal, as is the mining of it. What do you think I could do?"

The Hendra grinned. The likeness to the cold Calder was frightening, and again Isla wondered just what their relationship was. Or could be. The leader of the Rohendra Complex was pregnant with her first child and heir. There should be much that she feared. Isla didn't think for a moment, no matter what the Hendra had promised Kalli or Calder or whatever he was called, that he would not betray her if there was a better offer.

"I always wondered about the meshing," Isla said casually, looking at the Hendra's abdomen rather than her face. "Is that difficult? Costly?"

The woman took a deep breath, and Isla could see that she was trying her hardest not to react. She didn't have the same skill in keeping her thoughts from her face, although Isla was sure she usually did. Maybe it was that she couldn't keep such fear hidden. The heir was her weakness.

"Have you struggled with your pregnancy?" Isla asked conversationally. "I have never had a child of my own, obviously," she added with a smile as though they were old friends, "but you look so pale—or is it that your image is touched up on the flashes?"

The woman's face creased easily into a scowl.

"You should look after yourself," Isla said, taking a step toward her seat. "It wouldn't be good for the baby if you were stressed."

The door opened, and Calder's solid form filled it.

"Take her over to the facility. We can work on what we need later."

"What do you need?" Isla asked.

The Hendra looked away, the conversation over as Calder grabbed her arm. He gave the silk bandage a look, then looked to Hendra as though she would explain it. She simply waved her hand for them to leave the room. He walked quickly from the room, dragging Isla with him.

Hendra watched the woman at the other end of the table, fussing over the food on her plate but not eating any of it.

"How did you know she was here?"

"Who?" Alice asked absently. Looking up from her plate, she focused on the cup before Hendra and looked disappointed. "You haven't had your juice."

"I thought I didn't have to anymore." Hendra tried not to sound like she was whining, but for the last few days, she had been free of the hideous vegetable beverages her wife insisted she drink.

"Of course you do, and you don't look yourself. You're too pale. I'm worried."

"You don't have to worry; the doctors aren't worried."

Alice held up her hands in a sign of defeat, but she sighed before she went back to moving her food around.

"Island Tarle," Hendra said slowly.

Alice looked up then, appearing confused.

"The woman you met."

Alice appeared to be waiting for more. Her hand had stopped mid-movement as she'd been moving her fork through the food on her plate, and she gave no indication of understanding the question.

"How did you know she was here?" Hendra asked, not as kindly as she could have.

Alice sat down her fork. "Very little occurs within this house without my knowledge," she said, her chin held high. "It is my own little domain, my own little..." She shook her head. "Servants talk, Hen."

Hendra blinked slowly, taking in the woman at the end of the table. She had underestimated Alice, thought her blind to what went on.

"Her face is all over the newsflashes, across every planet in the Complex. As soon as that shuttle landed, the news was all over the house."

As much business was conducted in their house as it was throughout the entire Hendra Central building, confidential meetings mostly. If news spread so quickly through the staff, knowledge of these meetings might be all over the Complex. She knew that wasn't the case, though, because the staff knew how to behave. If they didn't, they didn't last, and getting a reference would be the least of their concerns.

"What do you not want me to know?" Alice asked, standing beside her. Hendra wondered when that had happened, when she had lost the edge she'd had. Could pregnancy addle the mind?

"Nothing," she said quickly, her hand on her belly. Then she reached out and gulped down the bitter liquid, unable to hide her grimace.

"I have told you it is easier to stomach when it is hot. And I don't care who fathered the child," Alice said, sitting in the chair closest to Hendra and taking her hand. "It will be my child. He will be looked upon as mine, and I shall love him as my own."

"If it is a girl?" Hendra asked.

"Oh Hen," Alice said, leaning in and kissing her softly. "As long as the baby is healthy, that is all that matters."

Hendra reached for Alice as she pulled away, holding her in place and kissing her more firmly, desperately almost. She hadn't taken the time for this woman in too long. Alice inched forward and sat on her lap, pushing her hands through Hendra's hair. Hendra pulled at the perfect blouse, running her hand over the smooth skin of the woman in her arms, but Alice pulled away and Hendra let out a frustrated sigh.

"It might not be good for the child," Alice said, her face flushed as she glanced around. But the room was empty, as though she'd known when to send the servants away. The doubts of earlier returned, and Hendra nodded once. "It isn't that I don't want to be with you," Alice said quickly, giving her a bright smile. "But it is still early, and my weight on you might be..."

Hendra nodded again and stood, straightening out her own clothing and wondering for a moment if she could find satisfaction elsewhere. But as the door opened and a servant entered to clear the table, she knew it wouldn't be here. Alice, still flushed, smiled as she left the room. Hendra wondered if she had mentioned the servants as a way to curb her actions. They knew the risks of working for the Hendra and what would happen to them if they divulged anything that went on within the house. Would they really risk that to tell Alice what she did or who was there?

It didn't matter now—the girl was gone, and the Sparrow had barely landed at Hendra Central. She wondered if she would get the chance to talk to him. Not that she was terribly interested, but he had managed to evade the colonel for far too long, and she wondered if there was more to their history than Calder wasn't telling her.

She marched quickly back to her office and closed the door. She half expected the colonel to be leaning against her desk as he too often did, and part of her longed for his firm body. But she shook off the idea and searched newsflashes on the Sparrow. There was little of the group except the main one, Gray E'anah. A handsome man, and in some ways similar to the Calder she'd known before making him Calder.

She searched through his history, his schools, home planet. There was more than just a similarity with Calder; they had been friends. Someone he'd known from a past long before becoming a soldier.

When Calder didn't appear over the next hour, she assumed he was busy at the facility. She was desperate to see what the girl could do, hoping someone could make her show them even if she wasn't keen to help. And Hendra didn't want to give away what she had planned. She hadn't told a soul—not Alice, and certainly not Calder—why she was storing the rohen or what she needed the hummer for. Once she was sure and she had control of the mines, she would lift the ban.

A smaller news story caught her eye as she was dreaming of the future. It mentioned the Sparrow, but there was no mention of Gray E'anah. There was an image of a man lying face down in the dust. She wondered if they had killed someone. But then it said the dead man was from the Sparrow, and she assumed his shady activities had caught up with him.

At least Calder appeared to be working on cleaning up the mess the Sparrow had become. They were only enforcers, according to Calder, and not particularly good ones, and therefore should have been easy enough to deal with.

As Hendra moved her hand over the panel to close the screens, she caught an image of Alice. She was dressed immaculately, shopping. Something she used to do, but not of late. Then the name of the shop leapt from the screen. Alice was shopping for baby items. Several servants followed her, carrying bags and boxes. Odd that she hadn't mentioned it at dinner, but the conversation had quickly turned to the wanted criminal she had entertained.

Again, Hendra realised she had selected the perfect wife. That hadn't been her intention, but Alice had slipped into the role so well. She was the perfect caring host, the loving wife and parent-to-be. No matter what Alice thought, or even understood, of what Hendra had done, she would stand by her, and Hendra was thankful.

Two

Gray leaned back against the wall. His eye had swollen shut, and the blindingly white room made him squint with the other at the man sitting on the only chair. Calder didn't want to look at him directly, or so it appeared through his blurred vision. Instead, he stared at something above Gray's head, a mark perhaps. He couldn't guess. The only hope he had was that they needed Isla and so she would be alive, somewhere.

"Hendra knows our connection," Gray mumbled, putting a hand to his jaw to find his wrist was still tethered to the other. He wondered why his tongue felt so thick, and if the words he had tried to say had made any sense.

"She sent me in," Calder said, his focus still above Gray.

"And before that, when you were Kalli, did she send you in then?"

The large man's gaze shifted. He hadn't reacted when Isla had repeatedly called him Kalli, other than to knock her to the floor, fighting her as though she were a soldier of the same standing. Gray had understood that she had been then, that he was right to fear her—although he had the feeling she was on the right side, whatever that might be.

"Don't believe the girl's lies."

"I knew you. I know you." Gray hoped he sounded as insistent as he wanted, but the room was blurring further around him. As Calder stood, his vision disappeared altogether.

The room was empty when he woke; even the chair had been taken. Gray hoped he had put some fear into the man, although he doubted it. If this was Kalli, as Isla was so certain of, then he had a connection to both of them. The fact that they lived and had hidden would be enough to give the Hendra concern. At least it would if he were the Hendra. Maybe she wasn't the leader he had hoped she was.

He looked down over the wide, bloody bands around his wrist and groaned. Even if he could get out of here, he had no idea where Isla was, no plan, and he was fairly sure he wouldn't be any use.

He breathed out slowly, looking up at the stark white wall, and his breath caught in his throat as something moved across it. "Help her," a voice whispered.

"I can't," he returned.

The door opened. He looked up at a guard he didn't know, half expecting Calder. Gray glanced around the small space. What he'd thought was there was gone, and he was no longer sure he had seen it. The door closed with a loud click, and he was alone. Gray didn't do well being alone. He needed people, and a plan, and something to do. Something like clearing his name, finding the girl and working out what the Hendra wanted with the metal that appeared to run through every part of the Rohendra Complex.

Something brushed over his shoulder, unnerving as he was leaning against the wall. If he could find a way out of the room, he might have a slim chance of finding Isla. Although, he was starting to think that this was it—he had no hope of finding her, and if he did, they wouldn't be able to get off the planet.

There had been something between Kalli and Isla, not just that they were colleagues. There was something else between them. The realisation was odd, as though Gray wouldn't have expected his friend could have formed a relationship with someone like her. Although she would have been something different then, somewhat scarier. He was trying to imagine them together when a blade moved before his face, and he pressed himself into the wall.

A child stood before him, lost, pale. The metal moved oddly across the blade she held. Her silver eyes, like the metal, focused on him as she waited, her knife reaching out. He held his hands up to her.

The metal moved between the cuffs and his skin, warm and silken, and the bands fell away. He looked over his wrists and then to the girl, but she was gone. He pushed himself against the wall to help himself stand. He wasn't really in a fit state to be doing anything. Was there any chance that Isla would still have her magic cream if he managed to find her?

The door clicked but didn't open. Gray looked around the blank space again before staggering the short distance across the room and pressed his palm to the smooth, white surface of the door. It slid a small way, and he saw no one on the other side. He breathed slowly, trying to level his panic and formulate some action. When the door slid open all the way, he staggered out into the empty hallway. The door was quick to close behind him in a whoosh, and he heard the click as it locked in place.

He looked one way and then the other, unsure where he was going or how he was going to get out. The wall rippled partway down the corridor. He headed in that direction. The Rohen might be something he did not understand, but it understood Isla—or was it that she understood it? Either way, they seemed to have some understanding, and he had to trust that it was helping him. He stopped, his hand on the wall. When he lifted it, a trail of blood marked his travels from the room he'd been held in.

It disappeared as he watched, but he held his hand away from the surface and tried to maintain his feet. Everything ached, and his head swam with every step. Was the child part of the metal, or was she another hummer trying in some way to help Isla? How many of them were there?

Footsteps echoed along the clean corridors. He pressed against the next door he passed, and it opened, surprisingly. Maybe the metal was helping him. The door closed silently behind him as he turned to take in the room. It was identical to the one he had just left. As he took in the cramped space, the air left his lungs. He bit down on his lip and fell to his knees.

Reilly. Or at least it had been. The battered body was barely recognisable, and the grey pallor of his skin indicated that he was gone. Gray reached out a hand and then pulled it back, forming it into a tight fist. He had done this. He had dragged Reilly into this. The man had wanted a quiet life, not that they would ever have truly had that after they'd been betrayed by the Elite. But he'd had a family—he'd had a chance.

The rage building in his chest threatened to explode, and he climbed to his feet, the adrenalin pushing him on. He put his hand to the door without hesitation, and it opened. Calder had done this. Calder had done whatever he could to find Isla, but Gray would be damned if he was going to let him have her.

Or at least keep her, he assured himself as the startled face of a soldier focused on him when the door opened.

"I thought you were dead," he stammered, as though Reilly had returned.

"Doesn't look like it," Gray growled. He reached out swiftly and knocked the unsuspecting man out. Then he shook out his already sore hand, the punch taking more than he'd expected, and grabbed the duster from his belt. The movement of bending and collecting it nearly caused him to black out as dizziness overtook him, and he leaned heavily into the wall.

It seemed to hold him steady as he found his feet and looked over the weapon in his hand. It was set to stun, but he flicked easily through the settings to its deadliest mark. Calder wouldn't have his set to stun, he thought, remembering the soldier Calder had disintegrated in the dark depths of Oric's capital. He hesitated a moment, wondering if he could kill

Calder if it came to that, but he left the setting where it was. He might be lucky and any other soldiers he came across carried dusters also set to stun.

"Thank you," he whispered to the walls as he pushed himself along the corridor. Maybe the Rohen was working with him, or maybe it was helping him reach where Calder needed him to be. He rolled his aching shoulders and then looked back at the soldier still unconscious in the middle of the floor. Maybe he should have moved the man, but they would know soon enough that he was out. Gray didn't have the time to waste—he had a girl to rescue. Again.

He moved through the hallways, finding it odd that there were no soldiers. He wondered if the man he had managed to knock out had been on some sort of round. When he reached a dead end, he sighed, leaning into the wall again. This was hard. He was exhausted and hungry, and his limited vision was still not quite as well focused as he would wish. Then he saw the screen imbedded into the wall. He looked around and listened for approaching footsteps, of which there were still surprisingly none, before pressing his hand against the screen.

Then he looked at his bloody hand, the imprint clear on the screen that now shone blue. The Rohendra Complex star lit up the screen. He squinted and looked away. "Where am I?" he muttered, putting a finger to the screen again as a floor plan appeared. He smiled, and it hurt, although the number of small rooms off a labyrinth of corridors soon wiped it away. Who else were they holding down here and why? He pressed on a cell, but it didn't give him any more information or zoom in closer. If Isla was in one of these cells, it could take him days to go through them all trying to find her.

"Other levels?" he wondered aloud as he swiped. To his surprise, another floor plan appeared, different, open. He swiped again, but it returned to the golden star. He swiped the other way, and the other floor plan reappeared. He pressed on it, but nothing was clear. Then he noted the foyer area and quickly returned to the plan of the floor he hoped he was on. Somewhere near where he thought he was standing was a lift. All he had to do was find it.

"Hey!" a voice called behind him. The sound of boots running echoed loudly. Gray fired, then cursed as the smooth, white wall exploded in shards of sharp stone. He cringed away from it. The boots stopped.

A buzzing, crackling noise made him duck as an energy bolt hit the screen behind him. The image disappeared as the screen faded to black and then crackled again, sparking. Gray lifted the duster and fired through the dust, his aim steady.

Silence filled the corridor. There was nothing remaining of the soldier. Then part of the wall dropped to the floor, echoing and making him jump, and another spark flared from the screen behind him. He had to go up. There was no indication that there was a lift or exit to the floor he was on anywhere close. He ran along the corridor, the adrenalin keeping him on his feet. He stopped and leaned against the wall. Other than branching corridors, the same bright light and the same white walls, there was nothing. He was starting to get disoriented. He had no idea how long until someone else found him or he fell over from the threatening exhaustion.

He glanced back, wondering if he could find the way he had come, if he had left any sign for others to work out where he might be. But there was nothing except the unending white walls. Something moved, but it wasn't someone in the corridor; it was something in the wall. He stepped forward again, moving towards it as quickly as he could. Something moved from the wall, and he wondered if it was the girl he had seen earlier. The idea that she was Rohen rather than a girl seemed to make more sense. Although how that could be, he couldn't understand. As far as he knew, the Rohen was liquid metal. But then, he had seen a lot he didn't understand since he had found Isla.

The girl turned and walked along the corridor, and he raced after her. Then she turned a corner and, when he reached the intersection, she had disappeared. But it was another blind corridor. Short, no rooms coming from it. He tried to picture the map he had seen, but he couldn't. Then something moved along the wall, and a door opened. Gray, standing in the middle of the corridor, faced directly into the lift space and at the soldier looking at him as though he didn't belong there. Gray raised his duster before the soldier could grasp why he was so out of place, and he was gone. There was a time Gray would have felt bad about such a loss, but he had run out of options. He had to get out of this building, or he would be there f orever.

Three

Isla sat on the hard, narrow medical platform in the middle of a room. There was very little else inside it other than a table, which would be wheeled over the bed when samples were brought in. It currently contained a small, sealed glass cylinder with a small amount of Rohen. There was enough Rohen to fill her palm, if she could work out how to get it out of the cylinder, and she had tried.

She glanced up at the air lock that led between the room and the rest of the laboratory, but she couldn't see beyond it. Despite the room being mostly made of glass, the windows surrounding her were tinted. She knew they were watching her—she could feel it, despite not being able to see out. She huffed and looked back to the metal in the jar. It didn't move.

The first time, the Rohen had moved as soon as they'd wheeled the table closer, but she hadn't been able to do whatever it was those on the other side of the glass wanted. She had spent hours reaching for the Rohen, trying to understand what it wanted, what they wanted, but it was as though she couldn't quite reach it.

Her head ached. She knew the Rohen was frustrated. It was crying out to her, but she didn't know how to reach it and she was starting to think there was something preventing their connecting.

She had thrown one cylinder at the floor, attempting to free it, but it didn't even crack. They had given her a break then, although she wasn't sure for how long. She wasn't really sleeping, and when she did drift off someone soon appeared with another sample. Each cylinder they carried in contained a different amount of Rohen, a different size and a different sample from what she had seen before. She wasn't sure how she knew that, but she was certain. How much Rohen did they have stored here?

A small ripple moved across the lower section of the wall. Isla blinked slowly, wondering if she had really seen it happen. She wanted to put her hand to it and let the Rohen take her away, but she had a job to do. She had to find out, if she could, what the Hendra was up to—why they needed her to work with the Rohen.

In the time this Hendra had been in rule, very little had changed. Her father's legacy of trade, collaboration, it all went on as it had. The only real difference she had made was to ban the mining of Rohen, and it was not clear why. The mining was a dangerous undertaking—it always had been. The use of the metal had varied across the ages, and yet the mining had changed very little.

Isla couldn't remember when the ban had first been announced. But it was odd, as though it was something of significance she hadn't picked up. Maybe she had been too young to understand at the time.

The child came to mind, white, bedraggled, in some ways more metal than human as she moved with the wall and the Rohen. Isla had been left in the bright lights too long, trying to reach the Rohen through glass. She wasn't any use to anyone, and she doubted she would be much use to Hendra. She glanced at the window, wondering what they would have her do next.

Isla had no idea what a hummer was, other than myth. Although she had been gifted as a child, she had fought that to some degree, wanting more from her life. Now she wanted nothing more than to be in the forest with her family, learning and talking with the master.

She ran her hands over her face before the tears could form. She wouldn't give them the satisfaction of knowing the situation had gotten to her. She had put herself here. She needed to know, needed to understand herself more than she needed to learn what the Hendra was trying to do. But perhaps she could learn both at the same time.

The pale face of the girl she had just been thinking of swirled across the wall. Isla's heart beat fast at the idea she might not be trapped here much longer. But then she might become something very different, like the girl appeared to be. Lost to the Rohen. They did say it was poisonous, toxic to the touch, and that was why the mining was so dangerous—the gasses, the liquid, the unpredictability of it.

Isla wasn't afraid of the Rohen. She closed her eyes, sitting on the edge of the bed with her feet dangling down, so far from the cool floor she sensed beneath it. The smock, she knew, exposed her perfect skin. Her hand moved absently to her collarbone and the small nick she thought was there, although she no longer knew if it was all in her mind.

When she had slept last, she had dreamt of the swords again. None of her questions had been answered, nor her memories returned of why they'd been there and who was responsible. Just that there had been swords. It seemed that had been her connection to the Rohen. That attack had awakened something. Would she remember more if she allowed it to take hold? She didn't want to become some strange mix of woman and Rohen as the girl appeared to be.

Closing her eyes, Isla felt it pulsing around the room, running through the walls and the floor. Then something banged, followed by a loud crash and a moan. The glass flickered. The reflection changed, and she could see the expanse of a laboratory on the other side. Turning slowly from her hard seat, she could now see through all the windows. Beyond her glass cage was a control panel, a woman lying face down against it. Gray stood over her, his hand on the back of her head as he looked around. He was a mess. When he locked eyes with her, she smiled. More soldiers ran through the room towards him. He raised a duster and shot two without hesitation. As they disappeared in an instant, the third ducked behind some equipment.

Isla slipped down from the bed, her feet burning against the cold tile. Her body still ached from the beating it had taken, yet she didn't appear to have received the same treatment as Gray, whose outstretched arm dripped blood onto the back of the woman against the controls. His face was swollen and purple, his lip cut, one eye closed.

Isla ran her fingers around the marks already disappearing at her wrist. Even the cut from Calder's knife had disappeared. The First Wife was something unexpected, and if she had been willing to help Isla while standing in front of the Hendra, she might do the same for Gray.

Isla banged on the glass as two more soldiers entered the space. Something hard passed over Gray's face, and she wondered what had changed for him. He shot towards the approaching soldiers, then twisted around as a shot grazed his shoulder. She gasped, but it appeared they had their dusters set to lower firepower. His sleeve had already been damaged; maybe they were trying to wing him instead of kill him. They might also have instructions to be careful, considering the lab was full of equipment and containers with varying amounts of Rohen. As the other soldier stood from behind his barrier, Gray shot him without hesitation.

Another bolt of energy hit Gray in the leg. Isla banged her fist against the glass, hard, and felt the shift in it. She looked around for an option and picked up the top of the table that had sat beside the bed. She smacked it into the window. Other than a tinny echo around her cell, there was no impact or mark on the glass. She turned around, trying to find a way to get to him as he dropped below the panel and out of her sight.

The two soldiers at the doorway advanced, and then one also dropped out of sight. The other moved forward slowly, weapon raised. Isla banged again at the glass, trying to draw his attention, but he had reached the counter and lifted Gray up to his feet. The soldier grinned and pressed the comms device at his throat. Then Gray swung a surprisingly strong hook that connected with the soldier's jaw, and they both dropped out of sight again.

Isla banged the glass with the flat of her hand. She moved from window to window, trying to find any sign of life, but there was none. She stopped at the air-locked door. She had thought they were worried about the metal; they all dressed in hazmat suits when handling it. She wondered about the miners and their lack of sophisticated equipment.

The door opened, and she turned to find Gray just standing in the inner chamber reaching for the other door.

"Stop!" She held up her hands.

He looked lost for a moment, the blood running down his arm and leg from separate wounds. One whole side of his face, puffy and purple, looked much worse closer than it had from across the room.

"It's a double lock," she called, unsure how much he could hear. "It's controlled from the outside."

He shook his head, groaned something to himself and backed out of the small space. Moving back to the control panel, he pushed the woman's lifeless form to the floor and pressed something. The windows changed; Isla could no longer see out. She banged against the glass, sudden panic closing in around her again.

Then the door clicked, and she was racing through it. She moved from foot to foot, trying to wait as one door closed for the other to open. Purified air rushed over her, and she gulped under the pressure. When the door clicked, she fell out into the lab proper and into Gray's bloody arms. She clung to him as he groaned, and then he was pulling her along.

"Great to see you alive too," he croaked, "but there will be more, and soon. Any idea how to get out?"

"No," she replied, thankful for his warm hand. "I'm sorry," she murmured, but he didn't turn to face her, just pulled her between the desks and containers. She stopped. His fingers were pulled from her hold as he continued, and then he leaned against something as he looked back at her.

In a large glass container was a puddle of Rohen. As she stepped closer, it rippled and then rose up to meet her. She put her hand on the glass. It moved forward and touched the other side, and then it was a puddle again as a distant door clicked open.

"Come on," Gray mumbled, pulling her away from the container and the still Rohen. She had a sense she had to save it—she needed to save it all—but she wasn't sure what from.

Another door opened in the distance, and she could see Calder. Gray dropped to the floor, pulling her with him. He looked her over for a moment, a flush covering his one pale cheek. She wasn't dressed for this. Calder walked right past their hiding spot and then started to run across the lab. Isla heard but didn't see the outer door of the room open. She had heard it so many times before, but she didn't hold the same dread.

She stood slowly as Calder entered what had been her holding cell to find she was gone. He looked around, probably wondering why there was no one else there, and she waved. When he didn't respond, she remembered that the windows had been tinted. Gray yanked her into motion again. They disappeared through the same door he had entered through, and she was instantly lost in a dark corridor.

She held more tightly to Gray's hand, but she couldn't make her feet move. It was difficult to breathe.

"Focus," Gray whispered, giving her hand a squeeze. "Don't fall apart now."

"As if I were the sort to fall apart," she returned.

She was sure she heard his eyebrows rise.

"What happened?" she asked.

There was no response. He felt his way noisily along the corridor, and then they were standing in an office. Clean and organised. She wondered if this was Calder's or he just had right of way through it. She was reminded of how he had behaved with the Hendra. He had far more power than she would have liked.

"We have to find Alice," Isla said, heading for the door, but Gray held her hand tight and prevented her from moving. "What is it?" she asked, looking into his face. He was hard to read. "You're scaring me," she whispered.

He looked as though he were just realising she was there. "You scare me," he said, his face still neutral, his hand still tight around hers. "Reilly." He looked back to the door.

He didn't have to say anything else. She understood what he meant, and the words she'd heard earlier from Calder made sense. "It's my fault," she said.

He shook his head quickly. "Mine." He gave her a sad smile. "Who is Alice?"

"The First Wife," Isla said, trying to sound casual.

He blinked at her as though he didn't understand, or as though she'd lost her mind. "Why?"

She turned her hand in his, exposing her wrist, the smallest pink line still visible. "I think she might have some skills we could use."

An alarm sounded in the distance.

"We're going to die anyway," he muttered, pulling her towards the office door. Then, noticing something, he diverted towards a shelf.

"Do we have time for this?"

"This man doesn't walk from office to office," he murmured, looking over the shelf. An old metal toy caught his eye. As he went to lift it from the shelf, something clicked, and the shelf swung outwards to reveal a dark cavity behind it. "Told you."

"We don't know where it goes," she whispered as he led her into the space. The door closed with an inaudible click behind her.

In the dark, he let go of her hand. Before she could say anything, she heard him slump loudly against the wall. Her first instinct was to shush him as he moved, but she feared she wouldn't be able to lift him if he ended up on the floor.

She leaned against him, pressing her body into his and keeping him upright. "Gray," she whispered. "We need to keep moving."

"Can't move anywhere with you..." he whispered, his voice catching in his throat.

Isla didn't know where to go. Would they be safe in the dark behind a hidden door? Maybe, until Calder wanted to use the passage to reach someone or somewhere. If he managed to get out of the cell she had spent far too long in. She grinned, remembering the pure anger that had filled his features, and was very pleased she had escaped him.

"Maybe I can call the Rohen."

"No," Gray breathed, clutching at her. There was no strength to his hold. "We'll find a way."

"Ok," she agreed softly, slipping her arm around him and pulling him towards her. "But we have to keep moving."

She half supported, half dragged him through the dark corridor as he ran a hand along the wall. She closed her eyes against the dark, but it wasn't going to help her. The smell of blood filled her senses as they hobbled along, and she realised he was hurt more badly than she had thought.

"You are really good at getting shot," she murmured, stopping him. She allowed him to lean against the wall as she ran her hand over his arm and then his leg.

"It's a new skill," he murmured, "and it seems to work for the ladies."

"I'm looking for wounds," she grumbled.

"I can tell you where they are. Somewhere around the point where my leg is a mad mix of burning and numb." His hand took hers and dragged it down to a warm, wet patch on his leg.

If only she had her ointment. "Keep it there," she said, pulling her hand from beneath his and lifting the smock to her teeth. She tried to guess how far she had nicked the thin material, but it didn't matter in the dark. It tore easily. She ripped it all the way around and then reached for his hand again.

"Told you it was good with the ladies," he muttered, but his speech was becoming slurred. "Good thing I saved you," he whispered as his hand found her shoulder. She wrapped the strip of cloth around his leg a couple times, then tied it tightly. He grunted.

"That should help," she said.

"I caught it twice in the arm," he added as she draped the arm around her shoulders, and they continued.

"I might not have enough smock."

"I've seen it all before." There was something light in his voice, but not as it had been before.

"I'm sorry," she said.

"Don't be; it was nice."

She stopped, trying to make sense of the words, and then continued on. She knew full well what he had seen had been far from nice. It was a red, puckered, scarred body. Now that it was smooth, she wondered if she would feel any differently about it—and what Gray would think of it. She refocused ahead, sure she could see a light.

She heard the hum of the duster, faint but something she was attuned to.

"Do you want to carry it?" he asked.

She shook her head. She had her hands full with Gray. As they drew closer to the light, there was a small box on the wall. She wasn't sure if it was a sensor or something else. Although she looked to Gray, he was focused on her. She leaned him against the wall again, the weapon in his hand. She stepped up to the panel and put her hand beside it. Closing her eyes, she could feel the Rohen. It flowed through the wall, through the panel, surrounding them. She moved her hand to the panel. Hoping Gray was ready if there was something on the other side, she asked with everything she had for it to open.

Isla raised her arm to shield her eyes from the blue light. Despite only being dim, it was too much after the dark of the corridor. She looked back along where they had come from as the light lit up the corridor. There was no one following them. Gray, standing opposite the door, looked even worse than she'd imagined. The pale side of his face was getting paler.

She dragged him into the room and waved her hand over the panel to close the door. She directed him into a chair, soft and lush, and for only a moment thought the blood that would seep into the fabric would give them away. She ran a bloody hand through her hair, trying to encourage the wispy curls to stay out of her face. Then she turned to the screens that covered the wall before her. There were no controls, only screens, lots and lots of screens. They showed her different parts of the city, but there were rooms as well. She stepped closer, wondering where they might be.

She placed a hand on one that looked like an office as Calder raced into the room. "Hendra Office" flashed across the bottom of the screen.

"Can we get sound?" Gray asked.

"I don't know," she said, looking around for some control. She placed her hand back on the screen and lifted a finger.

"You are useless," the Hendra chastised as Calder sat back against the edge of her desk, his back to her, his arms crossed. "I made you," she spat, coming around the desk.

"As I did you," he returned, his voice level.

"Hardly," she scoffed.

His hands were on her—he moved so fast she jumped, and Isla wondered just what he was capable of. But the touch was tender as he ran his hands gently over her belly.

"Wow," Gray breathed.

Something sharp cut through Isla's chest. Something like jealousy. A wet hand slipped into hers, and she turned to find Gray watching the screen.

It took too long before the Hendra stepped back out of Calder's reach. "This is my child. We might have had some fun, but that doesn't mean it is yours."

Calder laughed, and the hairs on the back of Isla's neck stood at attention. She knew that laugh, and yet it frightened her more than she could say. She was thankful Gray still held her hand, although she was frustrated that she needed it. That she was not as strong as she had been.

A movement caught her eye. While the silent stand-off continued in the office, a blonde woman stood to the side of another room, as though listening. Isla tapped the screen. "Private Lounge" flashed across.

"Where is that room in relation to this room?" Isla asked, pointing from one room to the other.

"Who is that?" Gray asked, squinting at the screen.

"Alice."

The woman turned as though hearing her name, and Isla chewed her lip. Another man entered the space, and Alice instantly held up a finger. He bowed his head and retreated. Then Alice raised her eyes to the camera.

"Can you hear me?" Isla whispered.

The woman lowered her eyes again and then, smiling, she left the room through a door beneath the camera and appeared in the office.

"Alice darling, we are working."

"You are always working," Alice said sweetly. She had a cup in her hand that Isla hadn't noticed when she had stepped through the doorway. "You aren't looking after yourself well enough. The colonel makes too many demands on your time."

"It is what we do," Calder said, bowing his head just enough to be seen as showing respect for the woman's position. "Running the Complex takes a lot of work."

Alice snaked an arm around the Hendra and slipped the glass into her hand. "And my wife is pregnant. The heir of the Rohendra Complex is just as important as the universe itself," she said, her voice clipped. "If she is overdoing it because of you, Colonel, I will hold you responsible should something happen."

"What might happen?" he asked.

"Hush now," the Hendra said, sipping from the cup and then grimacing. "You worry too much, my dear."

"It is my place to do so."

The Hendra smiled, and Isla wondered for the first time if she might actually care for the woman, although she doubted the Hendra knew just what Alice was and just how much she knew.

"Run along, Colonel," Alice said politely.

"We have an issue that needs dealing with."

Alice made a show of looking at an old timepiece on her wrist. "In the middle of the night?"

"Escaped prisoners don't wait for daybreak."

"Unless they are a threat to the entire solar system, I'm sure you can deal with a few convicts on the run. Does it really need the Hendra's attention?"

"We will be finished shortly, Alice." She held out the glass, but Alice only looked at it. With a sigh, the Hendra drank it down and then handed back the empty glass.

The Hendra grimaced as Alice left the room, hovering in the neighbouring room for a time before she headed out.

Isla looked over the screens, but she couldn't see where Alice might have gone.

"That is vile stuff," the Hendra muttered.

"Better to hide poison in."

"Stop that," she snapped, and Calder sighed. "I trust her."

"Yet not me," he said, his hand on his heart as though her words had wounded him.

"I don't trust anyone," the Hendra said. "Now find my hummer, turn that bloody alarm off and..." She studied him for a time. "Who else escaped?" she asked carefully.

"The Sparrow," he said with a sigh.

The Hendra studied him for too long.

"I told him she wouldn't trust him," Gray murmured, and he then groaned, putting his hand to his leg. Isla noticed that the blood had already soaked through the makeshift bandage, despite its tightness.

"Why?" Isla asked.

"He is Kalli, isn't he?" Gray asked, something sad in his voice that she hadn't expected. She nodded without meeting his eyes. "And we both have a history with Kalli, some of us stronger than others." There was nothing playful in his voice. "We have escaped him, repeatedly. She will begin to think he is helping us, or not as invested in ending us as she hoped. And any moment..."

"Get out," the Hendra said, her voice level, calm. Isla shivered. Calder opened his mouth to say something, but the Hendra turned away from him, moving back behind her desk. "Don't return until you have them, or *you* might have to be reassigned."

Isla saw his lips move but didn't hear what he said. He stood slowly and bowed to the Hendra, who didn't even raise her eyes from her desk, and then sauntered from the room.

"I think we should find somewhere else to hide," Isla whispered.

Looking over the screens, it was impossible to tell where Calder had gone.

"It's not really a good spy hub," Gray muttered. Again, Isla thought his words were slurred. She needed to find him help, only she wasn't sure where it might come from. "We need to go," he said, his hand heavy on her shoulder. She nodded. "What about the wall thing?"

She looked up at him studying her too intently. "What?"

"Open the wall," he whispered.

"I didn't do that," she admitted, looking around the little space and wondering what they were between. "The colonel's office at one end—what is at the other?"

"What do you mean, you didn't do that?"

"I thought it was an option, but I didn't ask it to send me anywhere. Just hide us."

He nodded.

"I didn't think you would believe me."

Gray smiled, his hand heavy. She locked her arms around him as he started to sway. "You like me," he said. "But this not the time."

"I don't like you," she returned, but she did.

"Isla," he whispered when she hadn't let him go. "We have to find a way out."

"Thanks for coming to find me," she whispered.

"It was my fault you were in that tank."

"Let's not do this again," she said, guiding him towards the door. She took a deep breath and headed out into the corridor. It was still dark, and there was no sign of anyone else. Hoping they were doing the right thing, she continued along it, one arm around Gray and his arm around her shoulder. He was leaning on her more heavily than he had before as she ran her fingers along the wall. She could feel the metal beneath them, but it stayed where it was. She didn't call it to the surface, as she wasn't sure what that would mean. She stopped when her fingers caught a dip.

There was no light, and she had no idea what she was doing or where they were going. They just couldn't go back. The door opened, a gentle breeze brushing over her skin. The man leaning into her shivered. Her footsteps echoed through the space, and she stopped, aware that she was in bare feet and still underdressed.

She wondered at the duster still clutched in Gray's hand. Where had he managed to find it? She opened her mouth to ask the question when she heard a noise, and a man appeared in the dull light of an opening. Gray raised the weapon. The man waited, then motioned them forward.

Something about him was familiar, but Isla couldn't quite place what that was. They had no idea where they were or who their allies might be in this. Everyone seemed to be working against everyone else.

Four

G ray tried to hold Isla back, but she was headed in either way. And they were in the middle of the enemy camp here; they couldn't trust random men at doors. Yet he was longing to sit down. His leg was killing him, he was getting weaker by the moment and, despite his best efforts, he knew he was relying on Isla to keep him upright. He squeezed his hand around the duster. When they entered the room of soft, warm greens, he immediately thought of the forest.

A blonde woman was curled in a dark chair, her light skin accentuated by the contrast. Isla bowed her head. But the woman waved her in.

"You are very close to Colonel Calder's secret here," Isla said.

"Which means it is the last place he would look for me," she said. "You may go." She waved the man towards the door, although he stood for too long watching her. It was only as she nodded once more that he turned and left them. She stood then as Isla tightened her hold on him, and he wondered what she knew.

"Sit him down, my dear."

Isla looked to the couch the woman had indicated and then twisted her hands in Gray's clothes. There was a nervousness here that unnerved him.

"Island," the woman said, stepping closer. "You must let him go."

Isla helped him towards the chair and lowered him down. The leg, when he looked, was worse than he'd thought. That explained his dizziness. They had trekked blood through the room and had likely left a trail of it for Calder to find. He sat forward.

"My man will take care of it," the woman said, her face familiar. As she stepped closer, Gray felt the world spin out around him.

"Alice," he breathed.

"Hello," she said politely.

Isla nudged him from the side. "I don't think we can call the First Wife by her first name," she whispered.

"You did," he chastised, aware that his voice was too loud. "You said we had to find her."

"You know what I am," Alice said, her eyes on Isla, her voice calm. "The gifted find each other."

"You have different gifts," Isla said quickly, her hand running over her wrist.

"You also have a gift for healing. I have seen it." Alice smiled as she looked Isla over. Gray reached out for the back of her smock and dragged her closer.

"What do you want? Where are you from?" he asked.

"Draroh," she said, bowing her head. "The forests of Draroh."

Gray looked up at Isla, who stood still and stiff, his bloody hand still tight around the back of her smock. Draroh was the most distant planet from the sun, larger than Oric but in some ways equally mysterious. Few went to Draroh, and even fewer left it.

"How?" he asked.

"How am I the wife of the Hendra?"

He nodded slowly.

"It was a love match," she said, raising her shoulder.

Gray dragged Isla closer.

The First Wife put her hand to his leg then, the movement swift and it startled him. It burnt as she pressed down, harder and harder. He cried out, clutching tighter at Isla's smock. He only noticed the ornate box on the low table between his chair and the one she had been sitting on when she reached into it, small bottles clinking loudly together. Isla leaned forward, her hands clenched as though to prevent her from touching what was not hers. She seemed to sniff at the air above the box.

Sitting the duster in his lap, Gray ran his hand over his leg.

"Don't touch it," Alice said kindly. He nodded and wrapped his fingers around the duster. The bleeding had stopped. She wiped a small amount of grey cream across it, and he wondered if it was made in a way similar to Isla's creams.

"His shoulder," Isla whispered, then pulled at the remains of his shirt to expose his shoulder. Twice, nearly, at the same mark. Alice wiped the same ointment over them, and the stinging, burning sensation died down. "And I don't suppose you could do something for his face."

"A lost cause," Alice said sweetly, but as he focused on her through the one working eye he had, she was grinning. She nodded, put the vial back in the box and rummaged through the other bottles, looking for something else. "There is a bathroom through there. Perhaps you could get a cloth, and we'll see what damage has been done."

Isla nodded, and he found it very hard to let her go.

"Gray," Isla said softly, her hand on his arm. He willed his fingers to release her. She disappeared from his view quickly and returned with a soft, warm cloth. She hesitated, hovering near his face, but he closed his eyes and nodded. She wiped very carefully across his tender skin. He winced, wondering if Calder had managed to actually break his cheekbone.

"Here," Alice said as the movement across his skin stopped. He couldn't open his eyes. The exhaustion was taking over, and he wasn't sure he could ever open them again, let alone stand up.

A gentle touch moved across his skin. He opened his eyes to Isla's intense gaze as she applied whatever cream the other woman had presented her with. He only hoped it wasn't some poison.

"Why?" he asked as she sat the bottle back in with the others. Isla sat on the arm of the chair.

"Why would I help?" Alice asked, holding her hands out. He noted that they were covered in blood, although she hadn't managed to get any on her light-coloured clothing.

"Gray," Isla warned, and he realised that his fingers had worked back into the back of her gown, as though it was the only way to be sure she was safe.

"It is right to ask. My wife hunts you out," Alice said, her voice sweet as she stood. She moved across to a small kitchenette and began to wash her hands in the sink. If water had been so close, why had she sent Isla from the room? Some form of a test?

"You might want to keep us here for the Hendra."

"I wouldn't have wasted my time patching you up," Alice said as the servant appeared with a tray. "Tea?"

The sweet, hot scent filled the room, but Gray pressed his lips closed. Isla leant forward, although his hold prevented her moving very far. "It smells like home," she whispered, and he let her go.

"My favourite," Alice said, indicating the tray as it was set on the table. "Please."

Isla sat forward and poured tea into a fine cup. She inhaled and then turned to hand it to Gray. A warm smile he didn't think he had seen before flashed across her face as she let it go, and his hands shook. The hot liquid splashed over his fingers. Isla pressed her hands around his, concern creasing her brow, and then she looked back at Alice who was working her way around the table towards him.

Alice pressed her hand against his forehead, another part of him that ached, and he bit back a groan. The world still wasn't quite in focus. She leaned in and peered closer into his eye, which no longer felt quite so tight. "Tea and sleep," she whispered.

Isla lifted his hand and the cup towards his mouth, then stopped and gently blew across it. If he didn't know this woman, he might have thought she cared. Then she raised it up, her eyes on the cup, and tipped carefully. The tea was sweet, and he gulped at it.

"Slowly," Isla coaxed.

He nodded again, felt the room swim and let the duster fall to the floor, clutching at her arm.

"It is ok," Alice said. "Slowly now, drink it all down."

He focused again on the cup, Isla's careful movement, and sipped as slowly as he could at the tea. Isla gave him a tight smile when he was finished. Then the man was there trying to move her out of the way, but he wasn't letting her go.

"I'll help," Isla said, and the man gave her a nod as she lifted Gray out of the chair. How was she so strong? Then he was leaning on her again, her shoulder and the smock smeared with blood. Her wayward curls brushing against her exposed skin and for the first time he noticed freckles dotted her nose.

They moved through a door to the side of the room, a light glowing dimly above them. It was small but contained a wide bed. Isla helped lower him to the edge, then stepped back. Sleep would help. He knew it would, and yet he couldn't leave her alone with this woman. The words wouldn't come; his tongue felt heavy. He reached out, just grabbing her fingers, and shook his head. She surprised him by brushing his shaggy hair from his eyes and then helping him to lie down. She removed his boots and, despite the state of him, she pulled fresh white sheets up and over him before she sat on the edge of the bed.

"I'll stay," she reassured him. He didn't want to lose her, not again. He couldn't find her if they took her to the mines, and the fear that accompanied that thought confused him. Despite his best efforts, his eyes pulled closed.

He dreamt of the forest, of the trees, and large cats and children pressed into crevices. He woke scared. Sitting up, gasping for breath and then looking around the strange white room. Or at least it would have been white except for the blood smeared across the wall and the sheet—and there beside him, too still and also covered in blood, was Isla.

"No," he gasped, reaching out for her. She sat in a rush, her hands looking for a weapon she didn't have. She leapt out the other side, looking between him and the door. He could only look at her battered body, her exposed legs, the blood around her neck, and he was crawling across the bed towards her, needing to shield her from he wasn't sure what.

He stopped at the look on her face as he climbed to his feet, a mere step from her pressed into the wall. He looked up, waiting for the ripple that didn't come. Maybe his mind had been playing tricks. He raised his hands to show he meant no harm and sat back on the edge of the bed.

"I thought..."

She took a breath, and he wondered if she had been holding it. "What did you think?" she asked too quietly.

"You usually yell, 'What the Hell, Gray!' when I wake up in a bed beside you."

"What did you think?" she asked again, her voice firm, no hint of frustration or tolerance.

He looked down at his hands, still grubby and bloody, and then back to her neck and the blood smeared across her. She had carried him, supported him. Found a way for them to survive another day.

He shook his head, not sure what he had thought, what he had felt.

She took a step forward. He had the overwhelming urge to hold on to her, ensure she didn't get away, didn't fall into trouble. But instead, he balled his hands into fists, focused on the dried blood and her bare feet. Her dirty bare feet. How far had they run?

"Was it a dream?" she asked, her voice soft, coaxing. A feeling of distrust pulled at the corner of his memories, but he couldn't hold on to it. "Gray?"

He looked up as she tried to brush her curls behind her ears, but they escaped as quickly as she tucked them away.

"Readers," he whispered, the word strange in his mouth.

She stepped away then, moving around the wall towards the door, but he sprang to his feet with his hand around her arm, stopping her. Although he was well aware that she would get out of his hold if she wanted to.

"I do hope I am not interrupting," a soft voice called from the doorway, and they both turned to take in the First Wife.

"She's hurt," Gray blurted.

"I'm fine," Isla said, but she made no attempt to move. "We're fine. We'll be out soon."

The woman at the door bowed her head as though Isla were of higher rank. "There are fresh clothes in the bathroom."

She disappeared as quickly and quietly as she had appeared. Gray wondered where she gone and what she was about. The image of her on the screen returned. The man who had come to talk to her was the man from the evening before—or was it the middle of the night? He had no idea anymore.

"Gray, what did you see?" Isla asked, a hint of desperation in her voice.

"I thought I'd killed you," he said, the same panic filling his lungs. He squeezed tighter at her arm. "I can't let you out of my sight. We can't be separated; they play on that."

"I trust Alice," she said, her voice soft.

He shook his head. It still ached, but the world didn't spin like it had. "I can't trust anyone."

She raised her eyebrows.

"You," he said, pulling her forward as he sat back down on the bed. She stumbled. He wrapped an arm around her, pulling her close and down to the bed with him. "I trust you," he whispered into her hair, and she relaxed against his body.

Isla was allowing herself to become more to this man than she should, and he meant more to her than he should. She pushed out of his hold. She had spent too much of the night watching him sleep, worried that his injuries were worse than she had first thought. He had lost a lot of blood and was unable to support himself. But when she'd woken to find him leaning over her, he had scared her more than she'd thought she could be scared.

She had fallen into a deep sleep and not dreamed. As she made her way into the small bathroom, peeling the remains of the smock from her body, the shower started. Steam quickly filled the room. He had mentioned the forest and the children again. And the Readers. That worried her. She wondered, as she allowed the hot water to wash away the blood and grime, if the Readers had taken some of her memories and placed them in Gray. It didn't make any sense that he saw what he did.

As she placed her hand under the outlet and a small amount of creamy liquid filled it, she knew he had dreamt of the forest. She could picture those faces as she had returned home. They were her memories. And other than the certainty of the Rohen, and that the memories she did have of the attack were implanted and not true, there was nothing else she had been able to remember.

She scrubbed at her body, which looked unnatural in the soft light of the room, the lack of scars somehow unnerving. Although she had lived with them gone for days already, it still surprised her that they weren't there. She wondered if she would ever get used to it.

She allowed the air to dry her, sure her hair was a frizzy mess as she stepped out into the middle of the small bathroom and looked around for the clothes Alice had mentioned. Isla had felt a connection with the First Wife the moment the woman put her hands on her, yet despite what she had told Gray, she wasn't confident they could trust her. She was the wife of the Hendra, after all, and she was the second most powerful person in the Complex.

A complete outfit was piled neatly on the bench. She was sure it hadn't been there when she had entered the room. Looking about, she wondered who else had been in the room while she was showering. She dressed quickly, thankful for the sturdy trousers after being exposed in the medical-style gown for too long. Beneath the bench were two pairs of quality boots. Gray still had his, but she had nothing left. She pulled on the smaller pair to find them a perfect fit. Just how much did this woman know about them? Had she guessed that they would search her out? Hendra also likely knew a great deal, and Isla had no idea what they might have learnt from or about her in her time in the glass tank.

A distant sound buzzed, and Isla looked herself over in the mirror. She wondered if there was anything she could do for her hair. Fearing there wasn't, she simply pulled it back into a low bun, wound it as tightly around itself as she could and, with a wide band of material also left on the bench, secured it in place.

A knock sounded twice on the door, and she opened it to find Gray looking relieved. "What is it with you today?" she asked.

"You sound more like yourself," he said, looking her over. She had the same sensation she had worried about in the shower, that he was looking at her differently. "What do you think she has planned for us?"

"I don't know. I'll ask," Isla said, heading past him and to the door. She was sure she caught the movement of his hand towards her from the corner of her eye, but it didn't make contact.

"She's gone."

Isla stopped and turned back to him. "Gone?"

"Got a call, left."

That might have been the sound she had heard. "Wash up and let's work out what we're doing next."

He disappeared into the bathroom without a second glance. Isla moved slowly around the main living area. It was simple and comfortable. There were no windows to the outside world, and she had no idea where they were. She took her time looking through cupboards and behind furniture.

At the sound of soft footsteps, she turned and found the manservant behind her, although she was sure that he was far more than that. He looked her over openly rather than stare beyond her as the servants of Ebberah seemed to do.

"Where on Rennet are we?" she asked.

"The capital. The buildings themselves are not important."

"No," Isla murmured. But she had an idea they were close to Hendra Central, if not inside it somewhere, especially if the First Wife could come and go with ease. "Your mistress takes quite a risk."

He raised his eyebrows as though it was insanity to voice such concerns. Gray appeared behind him. "Will she return?" he asked. He wore a fitted t-shirt, with a vest and cargo pants that made Isla's heart leap with jealousy at the pockets. And they looked roomy and comfortable. Not that her clothing wasn't comfortable, but it was well fitted.

"Are we to wait?" Isla asked as the man turned slowly, taking in Gray's question. He had yet to answer either of them.

Someone cleared their throat, and Isla turned to find the Hendra standing too close to Gray. She wanted to pull him out of her reach, but she waited as the woman looked them both over, taking her time. Then she walked confidently through the small space and sat on the couch.

"I'm somewhat disappointed," she said.

"That we escaped?" Gray asked. "Or that your man could be the reason?"

The Hendra looked at him as though he'd said something she hadn't considered. Then she turned her gaze to Isla, looking her up and down, and sighed. "In Alice," she said.

Isla looked towards the door as though Alice might have reappeared and they were wrong to trust her, that she had only kept them there for the Hendra. Perhaps she'd been working for the Hendra all along. It didn't really surprise Isla that it could be true. She was married to the leader of the Complex, after all. They were expecting a child. She would never have gotten away with working against her.

"What about Alice?" Gray asked, and Isla looked at him as though he was not following what was happening here.

"That she would hide you away." The Hendra sighed.

"Hide us?" Gray asked, and Isla wondered if his blundering could protect the woman. The Hendra clearly understood that this was Alice's space.

"It looks like you should sit down with that leg," the Hendra said. He stepped forward, surprisingly stable after the night before, and sat carefully in a chair opposite her. She raised her eyes to Isla, who remained where she was. This woman could have anything planned.

"It seems there are many within the Complex trying to work against me or find ways to show that I'm not doing as I should." Isla wondered if she meant Alice or Ebberah—or were there a range of others?

"What are you doing?" Isla asked.

"What I need to for the good of the Rohendra Complex."

"Does Alice support that?" Gray asked.

"Of course she does. She is the First Wife, after all. It is her place to be supportive. And we are having a child. It is a busy time."

"And that is why she hides out here."

"She is far from the forest," the Hendra said, her focus on Isla. "It can be hard for her at times when she is far from the trees."

"She uses her skills to look after you," Isla said. The woman sighed and folded her hands in her lap. "What are you trying to do that people don't understand?"

"Much," she said, her focus on Gray. "I could give you back to the soldier."

"He might have been the one to let us go," Gray said.

"He wasn't. I've seen the footage." Gray opened his mouth and then closed it. "Yes," she said, her grin frightening, "all of it."

Gray was out of the chair too fast. Isla just managed to grab at his arm, and yet the woman opposite didn't even flinch.

"Sacrifices need to be made for the good of the Complex. I have made many myself. You are just learning what they are." She turned to take in Isla, but her grin faltered.

"What do you think I can do?" Isla asked, gently pulling Gray back towards the chair. She remained beside him as he sat down, her hand on his shoulder.

"The Rohen responds to you."

Isla shrugged.

"In the lab…" The grin returned. "It is like it is drawn to you. There are many issues with the mining of the metal. Not just the danger to the miners, but to the structure of the planet around the mines."

"You aren't just mining in Urgway," Isla said.

The Hendra shook her head, but she wasn't going to share the information.

"Why?"

"I understand the connections," she said, smiling sweetly and standing up. "I understand what can be done with it."

"It has been used well enough for generations," Gray said. "Why would you want to do anything different?"

"Because..." Her face fell, and she bit down on her lip.

Isla waited as the Hendra's eyes appeared to become unfocused. Did she have some link to the metal? Did she have some skill, like her wife, that Isla didn't understand?

"Because," she started again, taking a deep breath and pushing to her feet, "I understand what it is. My father learnt of it but chose to do nothing about it. I can."

She moved quickly towards the door, her hand brushing against her belly. When the door opened, Alice was on the other side. She looked more angry than worried, and Calder stood behind her.

"Make sure they are well enough to travel," the Hendra said, pushing past her. "They will fly out tonight."

Alice stepped into the room. Calder was about to, but the Hendra put her hand to his chest. He looked at her as though confused for a moment, and then the door was closed. Isla had no idea of what was happening between them, although she wondered about the woman's pregnancy. Something wasn't as it should be.

Alice bowed her head. When the door opened, her man appeared, and there was no sign of the others. He placed dishes on the table and disappeared again.

"I apologise," Alice said, indicating the food. Although she was starving, Isla was in no hurry to taste what was served.

"You sent her?" Gray asked, climbing to his feet and looking over the table. Isla could hear his stomach calling for the food.

Alice shook her head. "But it seems she understands far more than I gave her credit for."

"She doesn't credit you with enough," Gray said, walking over to the table. "You are responsible for the pain she is in."

"Pain?" Alice asked, although her voice lacked the worry that there should be from a wife.

"Do you know what she wants the Rohen for?"

"She has banned the mining."

Isla walked away then, joining Gray at the table. They weren't going to get anything from her that would be of any use. Like Ebberah, Alice had a plan and wanted to use them for it; she just wasn't prepared to share exactly what that was.

"I think she wants to sacrifice us," Gray whispered, glancing over his shoulder at the woman still standing in the middle of the room.

"Maybe that is all you are good for," Alice said. "Eat—you'll need it. Calder will return too soon to take you to Urgway."

Gray grunted something, and she left. Isla opened her mouth to ask what he might know, and he gave her a look that told her she should keep whatever it was to herself. They weren't unseen here. This was not the safe haven the First Wife had thought she had discovered. Isla wondered if the manservant was something else.

Five

As Calder deposited her into the belly of the large vessel that would carry them to Urgway, Isla wasn't as worried as she thought she should be. Not about being dragged back to Urgway, and not about the man who seemed to want her dead. She needed to know what they wanted, what they planned and what they thought she could do. That need overrode any concerns she might have had for her safety. Not that she thought she could do much to prevent her death if Calder was determined.

She took her seat next to Gray, buckled in, glanced over his yellowing face and tried to ignore the almost overwhelming sense of Rohen that surrounded her. His wounds were healing, and although she was still a little stiff from the fight with Calder, she knew that Gray was feeling more than the bruise on his face. She couldn't even guess when they had managed to capture Reilly or what they had done with her Dragonfly.

The size of the ship they were in meant they were not trying to sneak onto Urgway. Anyone would see them coming, and everyone would see where they landed.

"What is the story?" Isla asked.

As he buckled in opposite her, Calder looked up with a smile.

"What story?" Gray asked.

"You can't go in blind with no story as to why you are there. The people will become angry, inflamed even, against the Hendra if she appears to have gone against her own edict. And Calder wouldn't want to upset the Hendra."

"I see," Gray said, looking across at Calder. "So, what is the story?"

"You two think you are some sort of team, don't you?"

"You don't understand what the word means," Isla said, surprised by the anger in her voice. Gray rested a hand on her knee.

"The enemy of my enemy is my friend. Is that what you're going for?" Calder laughed, and Gray gave Isla a slight squeeze before he lifted his hand. The more she looked at the man across from her, the less like Kalli he appeared. What had they done or offered him to make such a change? Or had the Kalli she'd thought she'd known been the plant, the con, all along?

"What do you need me to do?" she asked, trying to sound as bored by the event as she could.

"Hummer stuff," he spat, as though she were some creature they would have fought years before.

She nodded but looked down, waiting for an idea.

After several hours in silence, Calder released his belts and stood. It was a transport designed just for moving between planets, and it wasn't as smooth as other vessels could be. Again, Isla thought of the little dragonfly. "I thought you two would have been whispering plans and plots," Calder said, grinning at them.

Isla raised her eyes to his, wondering again just what this man gained from his relationship with the Hendra, or what he had given in return for the freedom to be what he wanted to be.

"We have a telepathic link," Gray said, his voice level and serious. "We don't need to include you in our plans."

The other man scoffed, but he looked a little too long between them before making his way to the cockpit and leaving them behind. This was a ship designed for a lot more than just the three of them. There were rows of empty chairs reaching out not only along each side of where they were sitting, but behind as well.

Gray startled Isla by taking her hand. In some ways, it was comforting; but it was also distracting, and despite the fact that this was all she had now, she had to put some distance between them. She pulled her hand from beneath his.

"Someone was listening in that room," Gray said. "It wasn't on the displays we saw, but it might be there were others, some that only the Hendra had access to. Alice may not be as safe as she thinks she is, or as we considered her. She was playing us."

"I don't think so," Isla said softly. "But there is far more going on here than I can understand. Why couldn't they continue to use the Rohen as they did before?"

He shook his head. "And if it is everywhere, as you claim, why do we need to go to the mine?"

"It is everywhere," Isla said, unsure why he wouldn't believe her. "There was more at the mine than the metal."

"The trees," he said.

She nodded. She now understood that the familiarity she felt in the trees on Rennet was the Rohen. Perhaps the same was true of the trees on Draroh. She looked over her hands, trying to work out just what she had, what gift the master had talked about and why she could manipulate things as she could. "How did you get out?" she asked, looking at Gray.

"Of where?" he asked, his focus on her hands.

"The facility, or wherever we were."

He chewed on his lip for a moment, and Isla's fear that he was involved in ways he hadn't explained returned for a moment. Then he was reaching out and taking her hand again. "There was something in the wall," he said quickly. "A girl?" It was like he wasn't sure of what he had seen.

Isla nodded. Ebberah's daughter. "I think there are more hummers in the world than the Hendra would care to know. Or she might have been searching for them."

"What if she has already used them up, or killed them trying to do whatever it is she needs?"

"Maybe they were lost to the Rohen. But I don't think that is quite what you imagine it to be."

Gray blew out a long breath and nodded slowly. "Either way, I'm no real use to them."

"Of course, you are," Isla said, giving his hand a squeeze. "You are the incentive to keep me doing whatever it is they need me to do." Although it hurt more than she expected that she had put him in that position.

Nothing else was said between them until they landed, and Calder was quick to guide them out. Surprisingly, they were not at the mine but a large city in the middle of Urgway somewhere. It looked vaguely familiar, but then Isla thought all cities on this planet looked the same. They entered a large building that was surprisingly clean, given the dust and sand of the desert planet.

They moved through a series of doors and, as Calder opened one more with a keypad, Isla followed him into the space and then stopped. The screaming was unbearable. She dropped instantly to her knees, her hands pressed over the sides of her skull. It wasn't that she could hear it—she could feel it moving through every part of her body. And Gray was crouching down over her, shielding her, but he couldn't block out what he couldn't see.

A strong hand closed around her arm and dragged her back to her feet. Another man moved forward; he had long, dark hair pulled back neatly in a low ponytail and small, round glasses. Although short, his scruffy beard was wayward, and she wondered why he didn't neaten it up or take it off. Very few men wore beards in the Complex other than the elderly or those in high office. The distraction eased Isla's head somewhat, but when she refocused on the lack of noise, it started again. Calder's hold on her stopped her falling to the ground while Gray had taken her other arm.

"It will ease," the man assured her in a voice that didn't seem to fit his body. It was deeper than she would have expected for someone so slender.

She tried to take in the space around her, but the sounds and the pain made her squint, and she couldn't focus. Then she was moving, more dragged than directed, as Calder pushed her along after the man, who turned and waved them forward.

"What is it?" Gray murmured in her ear, but she couldn't work out how to explain it to him.

They entered a small glass area, and the noise died down. As the door clicked closed, Isla felt as though she were locked in again like she had been in the lab, but the relief at the lack of noise allowed her to at least take in her surroundings. The room itself was small, only containing a desk and three simple chairs. The space beyond was a laboratory similar to what she had been held in before. Large, circular glass tanks were spaced around the room, each one surrounded by scientists. Large panels were covered in controls, some buttons or slides, some similar to what she had installed within the dragonfly.

Inside each cylinder was some amount of Rohen. All of it was raised up, stiff as though in pain, facing towards her. Isla stood slowly and walked to the glass. As she raised her hand, the pain dulled, but she could still feel it tugging at her soul. The metal relaxed. A noise level increased within the room, but it was the scientists, all wearing white uniforms. When nothing else happened and the screaming didn't resume, they all turned and looked at her.

Gray stood then, moving quickly to her side.

"That's interesting," the scientist with her mumbled. "What did you do?"

"Nothing," she said, wondering just what they were trying to do. What did they think the metal could do? She was reminded of the metal in the glass in the lab they had escaped, seeming as though it were asking to be taken along. To be saved. "It can't get through the glass," she whispered.

"Odd, isn't it?"

Isla turned to the scientist and took him in; he was clearly studying her. "What do you think I can do?"

"It doesn't react as we expect."

"What do you expect?" She turned away from the view to find that the room outside on the other side was similar, although one of the tubes appeared to be empty.

"It doesn't behave as metal should."

"How many other metals have you studied?"

"All of them. At least all that we can identify in the Complex. Beyond our stars, it is hard to know what else might be out there."

"What if it came from somewhere else?" Gray asked.

"It is found everywhere," the man said, turning his attention to Gray. "On every planet, in every setting."

"And yet you come here to mine it." Isla knew too well just how far spread the metal was, only she was sure she had no real understanding of what it was or how it had come to be that way.

"It is easier to find in the sandy rock. Here, at least. The sensors are confused in more built-up areas and planets due to the amount we have used over the years in ships and as conduit."

"It is more than that," Isla said, wondering if they would ever discover what it truly was, or if they would want to. The opening in the wall suddenly made more sense. Initially she had thought that Ebberah's child had done that, but it had been the metal itself. Only she wasn't going to voice that here, nor was she sure she should voice it ever.

A wave moved through the metal within the cylinders as one, starting at one end of the room and flowing across it. Something odd tugged at Isla, something like when she had felt the large cat in the tree before she had seen it, before she had realised it was a friend and not a foe. The metal stilled again. Taking a deep breath, Isla sat down.

"There is far more to you than I realised," Calder said, his voice soft. For a moment, he took her by surprise. When she looked up, the calculating man was studying her, and anything she might have felt for who he had been evaporated.

"I thought you knew she was a hummer," the other man said.

Isla raised her eyes to Gray, who gave the slightest shake of his head. He needn't worry; she wouldn't be telling them any more than she had to. She needed to work out what they were doing, although how she would report that back to Ebberah was beyond her. Looking at Gray and thinking of the girl he thought he'd seen, she wondered whether the girl could report to her mother well enough—or did she not know how far her daughter was travelling through the Rohen?

What would the Rohen allow? Isla looked out again into the room where the scientists moved around between cylinders and control panels. The metal remained unmoving.

"There seems to be different levels. Have you seen it do that before?" Calder asked.

The man shook his head. "But it reacts differently to different people, and not necessarily due to their level of skill."

"She survived being submerged in it," Calder said as though it was something he had tried before. Isla wondered how many hummers they had hunted down only to kill them in the process of testing them.

"Really?" the man asked, turning his full attention back to her. "Could we try that again?"

"I'd prefer you didn't. I don't really remember the experience, but I know it took far too long to recover from it."

"Why don't you remember?" the man asked, shuffling his chair closer. Isla was tempted to push back, but she was almost against the wall as it was.

"She was unconscious when she went in," Gray answered for her.

"You saw it." The man turned his full attention to Gray. "Fascinating. Tell me."

"She survived," Gray said, looking at Isla. Although she was curious herself what had happened, she was grateful he wasn't going to tell them what that was. Reilly had waved his hands in the air and described the metal floating. She turned and looked back out the window, but the Rohen was still. She hadn't seen it do that again—at least she didn't think she had.

"We'll try some things and see what we can discover." The man stood, and Calder dragged her to her feet.

"I thought you wanted to learn about her," Gray muttered.

"Oh, we will," he said, striding out into the space, and the sound of screaming started again.

For the first time, Isla looked scared. Not just worried or upset, but truly scared. Gray wasn't sure how he could stop what was happening, and he didn't know how he could free her and find out what they needed at the same time. She had willingly put herself here in many ways. As she stood in the glass cylinder, the scientists watched monitors and pressed various controls around her. The Rohen sloshed around in the other cylinders as

Isla's hands pressed over her ears. Gray wanted to smash the glass and save her
.

As he watched her struggle, he wondered if Alice was facing the same or if she had managed to talk her way out of whatever it was the Hendra thought she had done. Or had she been a part of Hendra's plan all along? He felt sorry for the woman, but he wasn't sure what for or if she even needed his pity. Still, he was blaming her for this all the same. All Isla had wanted to do was help him, save him, when he should have been saving her. Again.

"Please," he murmured, and a quiet came over the space as she stopped shaking. The Rohen in the other containers stilled.

Several scientists turned to him, including the odd man who had shown them in. Gray raised his hands slowly, and their attention returned to the woman in the glass jar. There had been moments when he had pleaded with the metal to give to him before, but he wasn't sure if the quiet had been his doing.

Isla locked eyes with him and tried to smile, but she wasn't fooling either of them. The noise of the men around them picked up as they looked over the monitors and various readings.

"Call it," the scientist said.

Isla blinked away from Gray to the scientist and then back. The same uncertainty covered her features, worrying Gray more than he would like to admit.

"Call it!" he demanded, reaching forward and banging on the glass.

Gray wondered if it might break. It might give her a chance if it did, but there was a lot of glass above her. If it shattered, he didn't think she would survive the experience.

Isla closed her eyes, pressed her hands to the glass and took a deep breath. Nothing happened.

Gray looked over his shoulder at the surrounding room and the lack of movement. The odd stillness in the metal.

"Tell it to leave the chambers," the man suggested, but she opened her eyes and looked at him. If it were that easy, surely the Rohen would have found a way out already. The stuff was more alive than he had imagined. He was reminded of the metal following Isla in the lab, appearing to plead with her to free it.

She squinted as though a pain had started in her head. The metal around the room hummed. The vibrations moved through the floor, through the equipment and along the glass. The fear that the glass would break took hold of Gray. Something moved in the controls surrounding Isla where the scientists stood. Lights flashed, and the vibration increased. Isla smiled in the cylinder. Was she was doing this? Or had the metal somehow communicated what it was doing? It might have been a strange thought previously, but Gray had no doubt the metal could do all manner of things without the interference of men. Or of any other species, for that matter.

Looking around the room, Gray was surprised by the lack of other species represented. There was the occasional tall, lanky Relec of Urgway, with their thick, weathered skin. But many of the original species of the Complex—who had travelled between the planets long before men had come, colonised and taken control—were usually equally represented between the planets and the various occupations. What might they know of the Rohen that they hadn't shared? Gray chewed on his lip, almost mentioning the Readers by name. Not that they were understood to exist by many, and even then, they were called memory collectors. At the idea of them, Isla opened her eyes and stared at him. The vibrations continued around them, increasing steadily. "Run," she mouthed. He glanced at Calder, confident the man would shoot him dead before letting him get to o far.

He shook his head, then ducked as the world around him shuddered. The metal was still in the cylinders, and he wondered at the metal they had just discussed being all around them. He looked down at the ground and then back to Isla. The look of fear had been replaced with resolution. Whatever was about to happen was going to be big, and she knew she might not survive it. Although, if the metal was doing this, Gray doubted it would allow her to die.

Across the room, he was sure he saw a man appear in the middle of the space as though from nowhere. It wasn't someone he recognised, not a species at least, and his skin shimmered. It might not have been male. The vibrations continued. The world shook. Before he could reach the cylinder and find a way to release Isla, something flashed within the glass and was gone along with her.

The air left his lungs as Calder turned his cold stare on him and the scientists yelled amongst themselves.

"What the hell happened?" Calder screamed.

"I think she called it."

As Gray tried to determine where she was, what was going on and how he was going to find her again, she reappeared on the other side of the room. She looked a little confused, dizzy as she leaned into the panel. The scientist beside her made to tell her off, then stepped back as he recognised her.

"Stop," she said, her voice carrying across the room. In the silence that followed, everyone turned to take her in. "You did this," she said, looking up at Calder. He took out his duster and held it up, levelling it across the room at her. Isla took a deep breath and stood taller. "Whatever you did to make that hideous day happen, when you thought killing us all was for some greater good. That day caused all of this."

She remained still, and Gray tried to grasp what she could mean. Calder must have been involved in the day she had survived, but he wasn't sure how it had happened. Isla hadn't remembered—unless she had now. Gray wondered what it would take for her to share that with him.

"You created the rift," she continued.

"What are you talking about?" Calder asked, voicing just what Gray himself would have liked to ask. He stomped towards her.

"Rohen."

"Has it got to you? Did you breathe in too much of the fumes in the mines, in the lab?"

She smiled then, that unnerving smile that made Calder falter and Gray want to take a step back. "Stop," she said again. The scientist beside her stepped back, hands raised. Isla reached across the panel towards the glass, although she couldn't quite touch it. The metal within rose in a soft wave, something he had seen before, and reached towards her. She looked back to the panel, holding her hands above the controls, and closed her eyes. Something made her tilt her head as she lowered her hand to just above the panel. A hum passed through the room again. The glass rose slowly. The metal remained just where it was, a small puddle as though still surrounded by glass. Isla tilted her head a little to the side, and all the cylinders in the room rose about three inches.

Nothing else happened. And then, as one, the metal ran like water from the pedestal over the controls. The scientists jumped back, some raising hands to their faces, as the metal disappeared.

"You wanted her to call it," Gray said.

Isla was shoved from behind to the floor, a soldier with a knee in her back. She lay still. A gun pressed into Gray's back as he made to step forward, the wide barrel making him raise his arms instead.

"Give it back," a whisper moved through the silence, firm, determined. "Give it back!" he demanded. Gray didn't move. The scientist moved past him, striding towards Isla and the soldier pinning her to the ground. "Give it back!" he shouted over her.

"I don't have it," she said.

"Where did it go?" He was more desperate now, looking around the lab.

Isla shrugged, and the soldier on her hummed the weapon to life. Her face pressed into the floor, she closed her eyes. For a moment, Gray was sure the floor around her rippled, but no one else moved or appeared to notice it. She blew out a slow breath. Then the soldier was hauling her to her feet, and she glanced at him for only a moment before her gaze settled on the scientist before her. He was white with anger, his hands clenched, his lip trembling. Gray took a slow step forward. This man was capable of anything, and he was likely to take that out on Isla.

"You said she would help me," he snapped, turning the anger on Calder.

"You wanted to see what she could do. She showed you."

"It wasn't me," Isla said, calm and reserved, her face twisting a little as the soldier twisted her arm. Despite his concerns, Gray knew she would be able to get out of such a hold if she really wanted to. He wondered then if she cared about her wellbeing. She might be helping the Rohen, but did she care what it cost her?

Helping the Rohen. The thought was odd, yet that was just what she was doing and what she had done in the mine—she had helped it to freedom. So many questions flooded Gray's mind, but he bit down on his lip lest he say anything he shouldn't. She glanced at him again, as though understanding what he was thinking, and then back to the scientist.

"It was you!" he screamed. "Do you know how hard it is to find enough Rohen to work with?"

"Did you need so much? And what was your work exactly?"

Gray expected her to put her hands on her hips, if she could have freed them from the man standing behind her. The man before her stammered as though looking for an answer, then remembered that he didn't have to answer to her. His face creased with an angry scowl.

"You were causing pain," she said, her voice soft. Several of the scientists still standing around glanced or whispered to each other.

Gray wondered if that was even possible. It was a metal, after all. What were they causing pain to? The thought of the shimmering image made him wonder if they understood the metal at all. But then, he guessed Hendra had a very good idea of what she was working with and why she had taken such steps to prohibit the mining and then started the tests.

"How did it get out?" the man snapped.

"It opened the glass," Isla said, as though that made perfect sense. "You were watching—what do you think just happened?"

He growled something that made Gray inch forward again and wonder what it would take to reach her. She looked up and gave a subtle shake of her head as a heavy hand rested on his shoulder. He breathed out slowly.

"How?" the scientist stammered, now more confused than angry. He moved over to a panel and ran his hands over the controls.

"Why did it wait so long?" Isla asked in return.

"It needed you," Gray said, and they all turned to him.

She smiled, but said nothing else.

"You opened it," the scientist insisted, but she only raised her eyebrows. Even Gray was starting to doubt. They needed her. It needed her, the Rohen. There was a connection, and whether that was because she was a hummer or for some other reason, he didn't know. But she helped in some way. They helped each other. He pressed his lips together to prevent his saying anything more. They needed her to help them help themselves. At what point had he started thinking of an inanimate object, a metal, as *them*?

Six

"Why can I see them?" Gray asked, and Isla lifted a finger to her lips. She didn't trust that there wasn't someone listening—there was always someone listening. And so far, they weren't safe no matter where they were, including with the First Wife.

Gray moved his fingers out in a rippling motion towards her. She put her hand on his and gently lowered it to his knee. They were sitting shoulder to shoulder in a small cell. The bench was cool beneath her, made of hard plastic, and the walls were wooden; she could smell the forest in them.

She stood and ran her hand over the wood, then pressed her nose to the grain and breathed in what it had been. Despite the lack of metal in the room, she could feel the Rohen beneath the surface. It truly was everywhere.

She leaned in, stretching out her mind through the wood, through the metal that ran past, felt it pause and then continue. There was nothing to indicate they were listening here.

"Them?" Gray repeated.

"I don't know," she admitted, turning slowly and leaning into the wall.

He stood up, and she held up a hand. She was tired, but she was ok.

"You don't think I'm a hummer?" Gray said, appearing somewhat worried by the idea. Isla took a deep breath, pushed off the wall and sat back beside him. She was sore, but they had been kinder this time.

"I think in some ways we have scared Calder," she whispered.

"That could explain some things," Gray admitted. "But not if I am a hummer."

"I'm not sure if I am the hummer they think, let alone what you might be."

He sighed and reached out for her hand, but he pulled back as his fingers brushed over her skin. She looked to the door first and then to him. He was right—they shouldn't get any more attached than they were. They were friends, and she cared. She didn't want to care anymore than that, and she was sure it had already done more harm for him that she cared at all.

"What do you think they will do?" he asked.

"With us?" She shrugged. "I wouldn't mind getting back inside that mine."

"Are you insane?" Gray snapped.

"Likely," she replied.

He opened and then closed his mouth as though not sure how to respond.

"There was something I would like to see again," she said, staring ahead of her.

"Mmm," he murmured.

Isla rested her head back against the wall. The wood was almost warm. There was more to the Rohen, something no one had explained yet, something maybe no one really understood. She had seen a glimpse of something more in the lab, unless it was the intensity of the cries behind the glass, somehow amplified. She shivered. Gray wrapped an arm around her shoulders and dragged her close.

"Cold?"

"Scared," she admitted, unsure where the word had come from or why she would share it with him. Even in the darkest moments as an Elite, she had never once shared her fears with Kalli. They might have been something more than soldiers to each other, but she had always known she couldn't share any weakness. Even outside the uniform.

He pulled her closer. "Me too," he whispered into her hair.

"I thought I was ready to die," she continued. "I don't know now."

"Well, that's a relief." A soft laugh tinged his voice, but there was worry there too, although she wasn't sure whether it was for her or for himself.

"Why?" she asked.

"I don't want you dragging me down with you. Do you know how many times I've been shot since I met you?"

There was laughter in his voice, but when she looked up, there was concern in his eyes. She looked away just as quickly. His intense gaze was getting to her, and she had promised herself not to let that happen.

"What if we offer to get more Rohen for the crazy scientist?" he suggested.

She looked back as he released his hold on her, instantly missing the heat of his body. He stood and started to pace the small space before her. "Go on," she prompted.

"We get dropped in a mine, you get the chance to do whatever it is you do, and we see if we can find the answers to this."

"And if they drop a group of soldiers with us?"

He stopped for a moment, his brow creasing as he studied the floor. "We have been around a lot of Rohen recently, but others are wary. It is dangerous and toxic. That was why the mines were supposedly closed in the first place, the danger the Rohen posed."

"Breathing apparatus," she stated.

He blew out a breath. "Would they still volunteer?"

She raised her eyebrows.

"Then we lose them. Those mines are easy to get lost in; the tunnels are crazy."

"As is the scientist who's determined to find more Rohen to experiment on. And what if they find the...?" Her voice petered out at the idea someone might be listening, lest she give away a secret hidden so well for so long. As Gray lifted his gaze to her from the floor, she touched her fingers to the wood panel.

"I think the Rohen has more control over who finds what than we would like to admit."

"And yet they managed to have vats of the stuff. Once they find a runoff, it runs."

Gray rubbed at the bridge of his nose and dragged his fingers across his eyes. "Your plan?"

She wanted to own up to something brilliant, something that would get them as far away from Calder as possible and stop the mining. But she had nothing. It was a very bad idea, but getting to the mine was the best they had. She nodded once. "We go to the mine."

"You sound so enthusiastic, but try to be a little more so when you tell them."

Isla looked at Gray seriously as he pounded on the door and then sat back down on the bench and gestured to it. When it opened, Calder was silhouetted in the doorway. Isla saw the similarity to Kalli. Her throat closed, preventing any words from forming. She raised her arm over her eyes to shield them from the bright light behind him and realised just how dim it was within the small cell.

"We'll help," she mumbled.

"Why?" he asked.

"Take it or leave it," she snapped, lowering her arm and trying to stare at him directly.

The door slid shut, and silence followed.

"Plan B?" she asked.

"We find a way into the mines ourselves."

"I am trying to appreciate how optimistic you are, and yet I can't see what you think we can do from here."

"There will be an opportunity," he mumbled, and Isla heard something at the door.

Gray started to push up from the wall as the door opened, but Isla reached out and put her hand to his arm. The movement was not enough to stop him, and the silhouette in the door was very different from the one she expected.

"I didn't think you would show yourself here," Isla said.

"My solar system, my job to get involved," the Hendra said, entering the room. She stayed by the door, which closed when she raised her hand despite the groan that came from the man standing outside.

"I have a feeling that much of the trouble is down to what you have been doing," Isla said.

"Really?" The Hendra crossed her arms. "I thought it was due to you and your stupid notion that you're doing some good."

Isla bit down on her tongue to prevent the words she wanted to say from escaping. That wasn't going to do them any good at this stage. She needed to get out of this space into the mine and find out exactly what was going on

.

"You had some skill before you discovered your hummer abilities," the Hendra said, looking her over too closely. Isla didn't want to mention what skills this woman's wife might have—she might not know. And although, like Gray, she wasn't sure if she could trust Alice, she didn't want to share what secrets Alice might have.

"I'm not sure I am a hummer," Isla said.

"I've seen how the metal moves to your will. We just need to bend that somewhat so it matches with mine."

Isla tried not to sigh. "What do you need?"

"I need it to do as I want. I need the metal to…" She paused. Then she smiled, a sickly smile that made Isla shiver. "Let's just get it doing as you ask first, and then we'll see just what you can do."

"Why do you think it will help you, that it will do as you need it to?" Isla asked.

"It is metal. It is not a battle of wills." She laughed. "It is just slippery. I once heard that it is something very different than the other metals we know."

"Surely your scientists can do whatever it is they do to make it something they could work with. Temperature?" Isla asked, thinking of the heating of metal she had done to mould it to her needs within a spaceship. The mechanics she had worked with were capable of similar. Yet the metal they worked with was hard, and this was already liquid. Could they make it hard? Would it work to lower the temperature instead of raise it?

"It has been tried, with little success. It was originally considered that it would be easier and safer to mine if the mines were cooled."

"But the mines were hot," Isla said.

"It was difficult to maintain. There were areas that were cooler, but not cold enough."

Isla remembered shaking in the cold air of the mine as the warm liquid metal surrounded her. It would have to be very cold. She looked beyond the woman back to the door and wondered what other experiments they had tried on the metal within the lab. A heart-stopping idea occurred to her.

"How many labs like this are there in the Complex?"

"Many," the Hendra said with a shrug. Isla thought of the room she had been kept in, likely not that far from this laboratory, and that was just in the capital of Rennet. "In the cities, at least. The buildings are difficult to maintain in the outer areas. The trees grow through them, or the desert sands take them back."

Isla wondered if it was nature working back over the buildings or the metal in some way reclaiming what was theirs. It might be harder in the cities for them to take one building without bringing destruction to others.

"Clearly, keeping you locked away to work on this is not the way forward," the Hendra said with a sigh. "Alice assures me that you will work with us."

Isla glanced at Gray as he made a strange noise in the back of his throat. She nodded once.

"Lovely," the Hendra crooned, the same sickly-sweet smile returning as Isla noticed her hand clench. She stood from the hard plastic bench and stepped forward, and the Hendra scowled.

"You are in pain," Isla whispered.

"It is nothing," the Hendra said, knocking on the door. It slid open without hesitation; whoever was waiting on the other side was ready. "I will send for you when it is time to leave," she said, and the door slid shut behind her.

"Are we free or not?" Gray asked.

"I think that depends on who you ask," Isla muttered, sitting back down on the long bench and wondering just what it was she had seen in the Hendra's eyes. Something was wrong. Something was very wrong.

Hendra sat slowly at the desk. Her whole body ached in ways she had never expected. The doctors claimed that she was like any other expectant mother, but she knew something wasn't right. Something hadn't been right for a while. They had scanned and tested and assured her all was well, but she didn't feel well. And then the look on the girl's face in that cell, as though she had seen something in her, seen her pain through the careful construct she had created. It scared her more than she would like to admit.

She needed the girl, but she didn't trust her with information. Island had been just another soldier, chosen at random from the bodies to bring back from the dead. She had been the least dead of what remained. There had been no choice in it and Calder, as he was now, had given no indication that she was anything special. But she had shown herself to be stronger than they had anticipated when she'd survived the treatment and surgeries followed by the long days of the hearing; listening to the recordings as she relived the horror of that day.

Hendra had not expected her to survive. And not only had she survived, she had turned out to be something much stronger than Hendra could have expected. Something that she might be able to use. If Calder had taken the time to get to know her better in the first place, he might have been able to hand her over sooner, and that day might have been something else.

Calder wasn't as careful as he should be. She blamed him for the loss they had endured, the men and women wasted that day. It was hard work to produce a real Elite team that would do her bidding without question. Especially when she had started well before her father's death. Long before she'd had the power to ensure it happened the way she wanted.

She groaned and clutched at her side as a sharp wave of pain rippled across her torso. It was too early to feel the connection to the child within. It was something Alice had talked of, and yet she didn't have that. Not that she was sure she wanted it. It would do her no good to become emotionally attached. This child was far more than that. This child was the future of the Rohendra Complex. It would be many things; it would grow and develop to be strong and clever, but it didn't need her to do that. It didn't need her to care. The only thing Hendra had to care about was the continued state of the Rohendra Complex. This child was key to that, but so was her work with the rohen.

She sucked in a deep breath. Alice had assured her that once the child was moving within her, she would want for the contact. She wanted the child—she needed the child—she just didn't feel the bond that Alice was so sure would come.

The pain subsided and Hendra sighed and blinked in the dull light, reaching for a light on the desk to find it already on. She would need to ensure that Alice had a key role with the child, although she didn't want her wife getting soft and ruining her. Not that her own mother had that chance, and Hendra had not missed it.

As though on cue, Alice arrived in the office with another green liquid in a glass, although it looked different. How that could be, Hendra wasn't sure. She was given so many green liquids, and yet she was starting to see a subtle difference in them. They were all bitter, though; she had yet to distinguish any difference in flavour. As the glass was set before her, she thought of Calder and his warning. She looked up into the smiling face of the woman before her, the only one she had allowed herself to care for.

"Are you alright, Hen? You seem a bit distant."

She rubbed at her eyes and lifted the glass, sniffing at it before she put it down. The bitter taste she knew was coming made her stomach twist.

"I'm working over a difficulty, that is all."

"Drink up," Alice said lightly.

"Are you upset that I found your hideaway?" Hendra asked, closing her hand around the cool glass, but not lifting it from the desk.

"As though you would not know the entire planet. I knew it wasn't secret. But there are times I need a little space," Alice said with a shrug as Hendra looked up. Her smile was sad.

"Alice," Hendra said, but she wasn't sure what she wanted to say.

"It can be hard in the spotlight all the time," she said. "I knew that was what I was getting myself into when we met, when we married." Her smile lifted a little. "But it is unrelenting, and at times I need a little space that reminds me of the trees."

"Would you like to go home?" Hendra asked, wondering what she would do if the woman said yes.

Alice smiled again, sad. "I am home," she said, reaching out and running her fingers down Hendra's cheek. Hendra leaned into them, although they were withdrawn quite quickly.

Hendra moved the glass in her hand. "Were you going to tell me they were there?"

"Of course," Alice said quickly. "I thought that if I won some trust, they would stay and that would be easier, but..." She paused, looking at the glass in Hendra's hand. "I was a little reluctant to give up my quiet space."

Hendra lifted the glass and gulped at the bitter liquid until it was gone. She slammed the glass back on the desk and wiped at her mouth. Alice beamed at her and reached to take it back. Hendra caught her wrist, and Alice raised a wary glance from the glass to Hendra. She ran her thumb gently over Alice's soft, pale skin. "We should find you somewhere quiet," she said.

"Thank you," Alice said, pulling from her hold. "Don't work too late."

"Alice," Hendra called after her.

She turned, glass in hand, her face expectant.

"Do you think I look well?"

"Of course," she said with a smile. "You are the picture of a glowing expectant mother." As she left Hendra rubbed again at her eyes, trying to clear the fog that seemed to be filling the room around her.

Seven

The transport was tight, smaller than Gray had been on previously, yet the tension that filled the space seemed to be just as palpable. The crazy scientist had come along, looking even more manic as they landed. He bounced about in the seat like an excited child, and the large soldier beside him appeared to want to take him by the throat and throw him out long before they landed.

Gray had half expected the Hendra to join them. She seemed to be the one with the vested interest here. He was still trying to work out just what she thought they could do and what benefit that would be to her. She claimed it was all for the good of the Complex, yet Gray knew full well that whatever she wanted from them had nothing to do with the Complex at all.

The craft landed smoothly, and the manic scientist leapt to his feet. He was out the door before the soldier had even unbuckled. Not for the first time, Gray wondered where Calder was. He doubted that there were many as trusted with this as Calder was, and yet the man across from them appeared to be just as in control as Calder usually did—until Isla reached for her buckles, when he flinched towards the duster holstered at his side.

Isla smiled, that sweet smile that unnerved Gray, and the soldier tilted his head towards the door. They unbuckled, then moved out onto the tarmac and stopped. This was not where they had thought they were being taken.

They were still on Urgway, yet in the middle of nowhere, and there was no sign of the desert sand. Gray felt somewhat uneasy in the unnatural setting. He wanted to take Isla by the hand, but she strode ahead, following the scientist as he leapt about rather than walked across the large, smooth, and far too white surface towards a low building.

He glanced up at the bright sun and was surprised by a tinted forcefield. It didn't appear to do much to block the light, only the heat from the sun. It must have opened to allow them to land. Gray wondered if it also worked to shield them from view if anyone happened to fly overhead.

"Any ideas?" he muttered, but Isla was too far ahead. A sharp shove pushed him from behind, and he trotted after her, wondering just how many soldiers were stationed around the building. Would they have a chance to get inside the mine and find what they thought was important rather than what Hendra wanted them to go after?

The scientist disappeared inside. Gray made a mental note to find out what his name was, or he was going to end up calling him Crazy. Not that it mattered. Other than the odd grunt, no one in the group was actually talking to them. The Hendra, when he thought back to the other night in the cell, had been far too talkative, although she still wasn't willing to tell them just what she needed from them.

Isla paused at the door and looked back. It only took a few steps to reach her, but she looked like she wasn't sure what he was up to. Did she have a plan that he didn't? Other than getting her into the mine somewhere near the Rohen to see what she could do for them.

Them, he thought again. He should be thinking of the Rohen as *it*, but he couldn't. It was something living, something more than just metal, and although he couldn't articulate, even for himself, what that was, it frightened him more than it put him at ease.

He indicated the door and longed for a chance to hold a duster himself, unsure what he might find beyond the white space. Isla walked in ahead of him just as the soldier behind him gave him another not-so-friendly nudge. A jet of air caught him by surprise, the high pressure taking his breath away. And then he was standing in the strangest space. It was white, spotless and, as he was pushed forward and his boots echoed in the space, completely empty.

"What is this?" he asked, looking about and finding Isla doing the same.

"This is not a mine," she whispered.

The scientist was across the space and waving them forward. One whole wall of the building was mostly window, and he was looking out into the world beyond. Gray moved forward slowly, footsteps echoing through the space. The guard remained by the door; his hand too tight on his duster. Was he scared? What might he be scared of? Gray reached for Isla, but she strode ahead, and then he stopped.

Through the window was a strange world of silver metal. It glimmered in the sunlight, but he would have seen this as they'd landed or when they'd crossed the ground. Silver trees stretched high above the height of the building.

Gray could feel a hum, but he couldn't determine whether it was in the building or outside. Isla was pressed against the glass. He moved slowly to stand close behind her, as though protecting her from something, and yet the strangeness was beyond them.

It looked as though someone had created a garden in metal. Fluid and smooth, yet not liquid like the metal usually was.

"It is beautiful," Isla whispered, leaning back against him. "How?"

"We found it like this—just out in the sun, no one around. Trees growing towards the sun like any other, but not. See how solid they appear?" The scientist moved along the window, taking in the detail.

"When?" Isla asked.

The crazy man smiled. "You know so much, and yet you seem to share so little."

"When?" she repeated, and Gray could feel the tension in her back as she stiffened. "This wasn't always here."

"No," the man admitted, taking a step back. He cleared his throat and stopped. "Around the time the Hendra died."

"The last Hendra—this Hendra's father?" Isla asked.

He nodded again.

"That is why she banned the mining."

"It was one of the reasons. She knew there was more to the metal, something connected to the Complex."

Gray raised his eyebrows at the idea, and the man pressed his lips together. He was telling them more than he should.

"Why are we here?" Gray asked.

"I want to go out," Isla said.

He wanted to hold her back, but he knew this was why they had agreed to come, that she needed to get close to the Rohen to discover what it was, and what she could do.

"That is not part of the agreement."

"Isn't it?" she asked, stepping towards the scientist. There didn't appear to be any doors from the building into the silver forest.

"You tried to bring it in," Gray said.

The scientist looked down at his feet and then back out the window. "We cut a branch, but it reverted into liquid form when it came out of the sun."

"What happened?"

"The fumes of the liquid in confined spaces can be... odd," he said, as though searching for a word. Gray looked back out the window, wondering just what this was. "We confined it."

Isla looked around and then scowled as she returned her gaze to the scientist.

"We have a lot of labs," he mumbled.

"I want to go out," she said again.

"You can't," he said. "We don't have access to the space, and…"

"The glass," Isla interrupted. "What is it about the glass?"

"It is made from sand not found here. We don't know why, but it prevents the Rohen crossing it."

"To stop it coming inside," she said.

He nodded and glanced back out into the garden beyond them. "It is magical, but the few that found it and tried to move through it… were…"

She stared him down as he gulped.

"Consumed," he said.

"What?" Gray asked, moving over and pressing himself to the window. He had seen the Rohen consume and carry Isla away, but she hadn't been hurt. "Did you find them?"

At the silence, he turned back to find the man staring.

"Did you?" he repeated.

He sucked in a large breath and nodded.

Gray had been around a lot of Rohen of late himself. The large vats had scared him initially, but then he had been carried away and hidden. He had thought Isla had been in control of that, but she hadn't. It had chosen not to harm him. Was that because of Isla? He didn't know. "Open a window," he said.

"Are you insane?"

"Possibly, but we both know it won't hurt her."

"I wasn't worried about it hurting her."

"Why couldn't we see it from the sky?" Gray asked.

"It somehow hides itself. The shimmer that we see from here—from above it deflects the light, making it impossible to focus on. We've spent time in the air, sent up different people, hummers when we can find them, and cameras, but nothing."

"What sensors have you used?" Isla asked.

"All of them."

"What are you thinking?" Gray asked.

"Even in my racer, I had a range of sensors for other ships, heat. Either way, I can't see why this would only be discovered from the ground, unless it wanted to be found."

"Wanted to be found? You make it sound as though the metal can think for itself."

She looked at him seriously. He turned back to the garden and then to her. "It responds to stimuli," he said carefully, slowly, as though a new idea were forming in his head. "It is not alive."

Isla smiled then, and Gray thought he saw movement in the garden. He stepped closer to the windows, but it was Isla who took his arm and pulled him back. A subtle shake of her head.

"We can access it from outside," he said, looking beyond the garden at the fence that had been erected. "Who is that going to stop?"

"The metal cannot cross that either."

"It doesn't just travel across the sand," Gray snapped. They'd had the stuff in tanks, studied it for years, watched it recently run and disappear in the very circuits they had used to study it. Mines were underground; the metal he had seen was underground. "It has grown up from the ground," he said, holding out his hand. Then he grabbed Isla by the hand and dragged her back towards the door.

The soldier stepped forward, his hand rested on the duster in its holster, but it was a threat all the same.

"The Hendra sent us here to find out about the Rohen," Gray said.

"I don't have a problem if you die in the sun. But others might," the soldier added under his breath as he moved to the wall. He put his hand against it, and a panel slid open to reveal suits and tinted helmets.

Isla stared too long at the suits and then nodded. If it was how they could get outside, then so be it. He remembered too well the hot sun burning his skin as though he were being cooked.

"Is this a good idea?" Isla asked as he dragged her around the side of the building. It was larger than it appeared and when he found the fence, it was as tall as the building. He should have been able to see the trees over the top of it, but he couldn't.

As he tried to look beyond what was too high to see over, Isla pressed her hand against it and closed her eyes.

"What is it?"

"I've come across this before?"

"Where?"

"I don't remember."

He waited in silence, watching her trying to read a wall. What if this was something she had found before? What if this was one of the memories she was searching for? "Here?"

"What?" she asked, looking up.

"Have you been *here* before?"

She shook her head and then looked back to the wall. "I don't think so."

"How do we get in?"

"Are you sure about this?"

"Not at all," he said confidently, standing straighter. "But I know you need to get in there, and they will either accept me with you or not. Either way, you must get into that forest."

She gave him a small smile and, with her hand still flat against it, she walked along the length of the wall. He walked with her, looking up and still seeing nothing of the great silver trees that lived beyond it.

Isla could feel the thrumming through the wall. She wasn't sure what it meant, but she knew she had to find a way through, and Gray was willing to help. She hadn't really thought about the risk to him. The metal seemed to work with her, even at times protect her, and yet she had no real understanding of what she was or what that meant.

Gray and Reilly appeared untouched in the mines, despite the effect on the others there. Or was it a choice thing? Like the scientist had said, it seemed to be selecting whom it interacted with, and when it did harm. Was it self-preservation?

Something changed in the wall beneath her fingers. It wasn't like the Rohen she could sense everywhere, although she could feel the pull beyond the wall. This was something else.

"What is it?" She could hear the concern in Gray's voice, the worry, and yet he was the one sure that they needed to be here, or at least with the Rohen.

"What do you think might happen?" she asked.

"Sorry?"

"Why are you so sure we need to be here?"

He smiled then—that too-relaxed, *I know what I'm doing* smile that he got, usually when he had no idea at all. Isla tried not to smile back. She was worried. He should be worried, and he was keen to drag her into a mine or into the thick of a Rohen forest when he had no idea what that would mean. His smile slipped.

"You don't trust me," he said, clearing his throat. "Fair enough."

"It isn't that I don't trust you," she said quickly. "I'm nervous."

"You?" He relaxed a little, looking at the wall. "You are fearless."

If only that were true, she thought, looking back to the wall as her fingers found a crease. When she ran her finger over it, it clicked and opened. Beyond was the forest of silver trees. Growing amongst them were smaller plants, shrubs, bushes, small flowers. Some she thought she recognised; this could have been a forest growing anywhere, but for the silver metal.

"You saw something?" she said then, standing in the doorway, unsure if she should enter even as she so desperately wanted to.

He looked more unsure of himself as he nodded, then shook his head.

"Gray?"

"I thought I saw something," he said quickly, "but I don't know. Like someone was out here."

"Someone?"

He shrugged and looked back to the opening. Then he glanced behind her and she turned around. A soldier watched in the distance, but he wasn't trying to stop them. She wasn't sure what orders he had, but if they were not to go into the forest, then he wouldn't allow it.

Gray nudged her inside, and the gate—if that was what it was—closed behind them with a gentle click. Isla wanted to see if they could leave the same way, but her panic subsided as they stepped amongst the trees. The main difference between this and the forests she knew was the ground. It was still the fine, crimson Urgway sand. The plants appeared as though they were real plants, but shining silver in the sun. When she stepped closer, they glimmered as they had from her view behind the glass.

She reached out but hesitated. The shimmer seemed to reflect the hot sun, but no heat radiated from the metal. She could see the building but not the windows, as though they were on a further side of the forest. She wondered if the scientist was there watching, recording notes, experimenting with her although she had thought it was her choice.

"Is it Rohen?" Gray asked, too close behind her, breaking into her thoughts.

"What do you think it could be?"

"I'm beginning to think there is much to the universe that I don't understand or know about," he said honestly, reaching past her. "Odd," he mumbled, but his fingers didn't quite reach the trunk of the tree before them.

Others had cut it, and therefore they had touched it in some way, although Isla was sure they would have been suited up. In the shade of the trees, she removed her helmet and reached out. She pulled Gray's hand back from the tree to discover he had removed his gloves.

"We have a relationship," he whispered, pulling away from her. Was he pouting?

"What?"

"The Rohen," he said, indicating the tree. "We talk."

"You talk to the Rohen?"

"Well, I've asked, and it kind of provided."

"What did you ask?" She crossed her arms.

He opened his mouth and then closed it, looking around rather than at her.

"This is why you think you are a hummer," she said, trying to get him to look at her again.

He shook his head. "I think they help."

"They?"

"Them."

"Gray, what are you talking about?" she asked, frustrated by his confusing explanation.

"That," he said, his face paling. She turned to follow his line of sight and the figure moving through the trees towards them, but as she blinked it was gone. It was as though it were metal and not at the same time. She couldn't tell if it was human, but it had a humanoid shape, although much taller.

"I saw that in the lab," she whispered.

"What?" Gray asked, his focus on her again, his hand tight around her arm. "They were there?"

"Who are *they*?" she asked. Gray glanced around and then surprised her by leaning in very close.

"Rohen," he whispered, so softly she wasn't sure she heard.

"The fumes," she said, glancing around. "The fumes are getting to you. I can't detect them, but maybe that is what being a hummer is."

Gray looked hurt as he stepped away from her. But he nodded once. He looked back towards the gate, and she felt uncomfortable, like she was sending him away. She didn't want to do that.

"I'm sorry," she muttered, but he was looking out around the garden, backing up towards the wall. "What if you're right?" He blew out a soft laugh, but it was sad. She hadn't wanted to hurt him. She was worried about him again, and she didn't want to be. She backed up, then stopped as her body made contact with the tree. Gray froze.

It felt as firm as any tree she had climbed as a child, and she turned to run her hand over it. Despite the feeling of firmness, the tree seemed to ripple with her touch. "What are you?" she whispered.

"Isla," Gray said softly, and he looked nervous when she looked from the tree to him. With a subtle movement of his fingers, he indicated she move towards him.

"It's fine," she said. The calm of the forest washed over her, and she too removed her gloves. He was looking more and more unsettled. She shouldn't have sent him away, although maybe the fumes of the metal were a problem. When had he removed his helmet? Something soft and warm closed around her. She looked down at the shimmering skin.

Gray reached out towards her, shouting, but she couldn't hear him—only the calm of the forest, and then she was lost to the dark. Gray's voice rang out around her, echoing off the shadows of she wasn't sure what. It was dark and cool, but she wasn't worried or scared, and she wasn't sure if she should be or not. The world settled to an uneasy silence. She stepped forward carefully, slowly, almost shuffling her feet. But the echo had ceased, and there was nothing before her. It felt like sand beneath her feet, as though she were in the forest but not.

"I don't really like the dark," she whispered. A soft glow lit up the world around her. The same trees and plants she had seen in the sun appeared to be replicated here. Where the trees had glistened in the sun, they now seemed to produce their own light. She thought she saw a figure amongst them, but when she drew closer it was Gray curled on the forest floor.

"It isn't safe for you here," she whispered, leaning over him. Had he been dragged here with her or because of her?

"Isla is lost," he whispered, as though he might be talking to someone else.

"Gray." She gave him a shake. He remained still. "Gray!"

He sat up with a deep inhale, as though woken from a dream. He stared at her a moment and then pulled her into his arms, unbalancing her. She stumbled into him, ending up on the forest floor. She allowed it for a moment and then gently pushed at him. "I'm not good with..." she said.

He nodded, brushed himself off and climbed to his feet. He held out a hand to help her back to her feet, although he wasn't as steady as he should be. As she stood, she put her arms around him.

"I thought you didn't like this," he said.

"I don't want you to fall over. Do you know how often I have to hold you up?"

"I'm fine," he mumbled, pushing her away. He staggered a little and leant into a tree. It appeared solid, and it took a moment of her staring before he realised what he had done.

He lifted his hands and held them out. "I told you, we have a relationship."

She shook her head. "Why here?"

"It looks like up," he said, raising his finger. Her eyes travelled up, but there was nothing but black above them. "Are we down?" he asked, moving his finger to point at his feet.

"You tell me," she said with a shrug. "Any idea how we got here?"

"They took you," he whispered.

"The tree?"

He shook his head.

"The Rohen," she said, although she was sure the trees and plants were Rohen, formed for some reason like the natural world. Of all the planets, Urgway was the only one without any real vegetation of its own. They had introduced it—some other species had managed to cultivate different forms of food—but there were no natural forests or the like. It was too close to the sun to be anything but desert. "You saw it," she said, and he nodded slowly.

"They were different."

"Will you stop with the *them*!"

He looked to the floor. Did he feel something different than she did? Was there a connection between him and the Rohen? And why did she not like that idea?

"Our goal was to get to the Rohen, and we are there. I don't know what the Hendra thinks we can do, and I'm not sure what we want to do."

Gray remained focused on the ground before him.

"What can you sense?" she asked, stepping in closer, but he backed away from her.

He shook his head.

"Gray," she said slowly as the world around them glowed brighter.

"I don't know," he said, looking beyond her to the trees. He stepped around her and up to a tree, rubbing a leaf between his fingers. Then he raised his nose to it, and she wondered if she had appeared the same way when she had sniffed at the wood panelling. She opened her mouth to ask again, but he held a finger up without looking at her.

She sighed. "Why are we here?"

"Why did you want to be here?" Gray asked, his eyes closed and his fingers working over the metal texture of the tree.

"You are scaring me," Isla said, but when he looked at her his expression was serious.

"You wanted to see the Rohen. You wanted to know what it was about, what we could do for them. We are here. Learn." He squatted down before another bush and reached forward as though to pluck a leaf or flower, but again he gently closed his fingers around the metal and shut his eyes.

"*I* wanted to?" she asked, suddenly unsure, like her memory wasn't her own. Was he telling her what she'd wanted? Was he planting the memory? She felt unsure of him and the situation, and she couldn't remember why she was struggling.

The shimmering stopped as the cavern slipped into darkness. Isla saw the metal, in its familiar liquid form, slip away into the ground.

"Why are you so much more comfortable with liquid Rohen?" Gray whispered in the dark, the sound of his voice off, different. She shivered, afraid again of the dark and what it might be hiding.

She wasn't sure what she could say, and the memory of cold, sharp metal slicing through the air towards her made her scream. Firm arms closed around her. Despite the dark, she was safe, and yet the tight hold wasn't right.

"Gray!" she screamed into the dark, but there was no response. The hold around her was calming in an odd way, warm and comfortable, but there was no heartbeat, no indication that it was Gray or any other man.

The hold loosened, and she stepped back. Something shimmered in the distance, but it wasn't Rohen; it was a figure like she had seen in the lab, something unnatural and yet fully known to her at the same time.

It motioned her forward, and she followed after the dim light. She had followed several steps before she realised she didn't know where Gray was. The figure stopped and motioned to her again. She glanced behind her and saw nothing but the dark. As the figure moved further ahead, she raced after it, finding the path smooth. Her confidence returned a little as she followed it further and further into the unknown.

Eight

Hendra blinked into the bright sunlight pouring into the room through the large window, blocked only in part by the shadow of a large man. "Calder?" Her voice wasn't her own.

He turned then, concern on his features that she didn't think she had seen before, and she wondered if it was for her or for himself. She had built him up—without her, his life might have been very different. He might actually have had to face some consequences and live without the free reign he enjoyed.

She tried to sit up and groaned at the pain that radiated down her side. Her hand moved over her belly, and he was beside the bed in a moment. This wasn't her room, she realised as she focused on the equipment and the sterile smell.

"Where is Alice?" she asked.

"She was here, but you were sleeping more comfortably; the doctors sent her away to rest as well."

She nodded slowly, the odd burning sensation still travelling up and down her side.

"Call them," she demanded.

"Who?"

"The doctors!" she growled at him. "I'm not being told of my welfare by you, although I'm sure you are privy to far more than you should be."

He raised an eyebrow before he left the room, although the door was still ajar and she could hear him speaking quietly with someone on the other side. She took the moment alone to lift herself a little higher in the bed, but she didn't get anywhere before her arms gave way under the pressure.

Calder reappeared instantly beside, his finger on some control behind her, and then she was slowly sitting up. When she nodded, he stepped back and two neat little men entered the room.

They glanced at Calder and then bowed in unison to Hendra.

"I'm sure he knows it all," she said. The one closest to Calder glanced again at him, and the other man nodded slowly. "What happened?" she asked.

The doctor closest cleared his throat. "Stone" was printed neatly on the name badge, but she wasn't sure if she had met him previously. There were several doctors who rotated at times amongst the core group that monitored her health. With her pregnancy, several changes to staff had been made.

"You have picked up some form of infection."

"Treatable?"

He nodded once, but it was slow. She wondered what they weren't telling her.

"The child?"

"It is hard to say, Your Grace."

She sat forward quickly, reaching for his coat and instantly regretting the movement as her side burned. "Why is it hard to say?" she asked, lying back against the bed.

"The infection is interrupting our scans."

"Interrupting?"

He waved a hand, and a screen appeared in the air behind him with the overlay of a body. He took a small wand from his pocket and waved it over his arm. The vessels, the bones, and the structure of the man appeared clearly on the monitor. Readings ran across the bottom of the image, indicating his vital signs. Hendra nodded as he held it out towards her. He ran it over the side of her body that seemed to ache the most.

The image was an odd, distorted, angry red. "Do you know what it is?" she asked, trying to keep her voice level as she studied the blurry image.

"Not something we have seen before."

"Something new?" Her hand clutched at her side as she tried to sit up again. Then she sighed and leaned back. "Something foreign?"

"We can't be sure."

He waved the wand over the rest of her body, starting with her head, which didn't feel as fuzzy as it had the night before—or had it been longer? He continued down over her torso to her toes. The image changed, but it was hard to read, as though distorted in some way. The text along the bottom of the screen made no sense. "What language is that?" she asked.

"It isn't a language," the second doctor said. "It appears to be a corruption in the system. It appears that the infection in your body affects the equipment as well. But only when we try to scan you."

She ran her hand over her midsection. She didn't feel any different, but maybe they were mistaken. She looked to Calder standing too still at the end of the bed. Had he done this?

Stone waved his hand again, and the image was replaced with one she had seen before. "This was our last scan, only several weeks ago. There was no sign of the infection at that point."

This was the scan she remembered, the blood moving slowly around her system, the small, hot heartbeat in the centre of her abdomen.

"Do you think they are connected?"

"No," Stone was quick to respond. "If meshing had been involved, perhaps there might have been a risk of an introduced infection. The foetus is strong. Or at least it was when we were last able to check."

She took a shaky breath. Where had she been and what had she been exposed to? "How long do you think this infection has been working through me?"

"Weeks," the second doctor said. Hendra couldn't quite focus on his name tag.

She gulped down her fears of the lab. She had stayed away from them until just the last few days. That girl, she was behind this in some way. But then, Hendra hadn't really seen her, not weeks ago—at least, she hadn't been close enough. She looked again at Calder. He stood too tall, too straight, too focused, and that unnerved her more than she wanted to a dmit.

"What do we do?"

"Wait and see if it works from your body as we try to find a way to analyse it."

"Using old-fashioned methods that don't involve our current technology, I assume," Calder said calmly.

"We took a small sample of your blood, Your Grace, but we couldn't find anything."

"If it were an infection, it would be present throughout my system."

"We would expect that," the man said, almost apologetically.

"Calder?"

"I have increased the security around you. My fear is that someone has done this deliberately, with a form of virus that we cannot treat or reach."

She blinked at him in surprise.

"We have not seen the like before," Stone said. "It might be a technology we don't understand."

"Or a poison we don't know." Calder cleared his throat.

"Leave," Hendra said with a wave of her hand. "I need rest."

They bowed as one and left. She could hear them murmuring in the hallway outside the door. She wondered if they had an idea of what it was or if Calder had given them something else to think about.

"You too," she said.

"I won't leave you," he said, walking back to the window.

"I am directing you," she insisted.

"I don't care," he returned too quickly, although he was still looking out into the bright sun.

"Where is she?" Hendra asked, longing for the bed to lower again.

"Alice?"

"The hummer."

"She went out to the garden with Michaels."

"Do you think she'll work with us?"

"No," he said too easily. And with a sigh, he was beside her again. She waved her hand behind her, although it ached to do so, and he pressed something that lowered her back down. "She might pretend to help us, but I think she has other ideas."

"It listens to her," Hendra mumbled, finding it hard to keep her eyes open.

"Or she listens to it," Calder replied, giving her hand a gentle squeeze before he wandered back to the window.

Hendra had a strange dream that her brother was plotting to overthrow her and Alice was helping. It seemed so clear, and when the room came into hazy focus, she wondered if it was a dream after all. The two of them were in the room, her brother standing by the window and her wife sitting at her bedside.

"Good morning," Alice said sweetly, noticing Hendra awake.

She gave Alice a small smile and watched as Solon turned slowly from the window. His eyes fell to Alice first before he took a step forward.

"You had us worried," he said.

"I'm sure," Hendra muttered. "Alice, be a dear and lift me up?"

Alice nodded, then looked over the panels behind her and put her hand to something that raised her slowly to a sitting position.

"I've talked to them about your nutrition, but I don't think they are as serious as they should be."

Hendra took a deep breath and then closed her eyes as the pain waved down her side again. Whatever they were doing was having little impact on her health. But she wasn't going to stomach that green muck on top of it.

"They are still trying to isolate the infection, and they don't even understand what it reacts to. As much as I want you to be able to have an input here, you can't."

Alice seemed a little hurt, and she looked to Solon still standing at the end of the bed.

"I can help," he said.

"No, thank you," Hendra added quickly. She knew the kind of help he was keen to give. Despite all his talk of not wanting power, she was very sure he did. "Did I hear you talking of the council?"

He nodded slowly. "They are concerned. But I don't want to hamper your recovery."

"That might be some time off," she muttered as another wave of pain moved across her chest. Was it spreading? They had no idea what it was or how it had started; they certainly weren't keeping it at bay, and it wasn't going away on its own.

Alice leant forward as Hendra grimaced.

"I am still the Hendra," she murmured. "It is still my Complex."

Solon nodded slowly, sighing dramatically, and she longed for Calder to slap him. "Where is Calder?"

Alice cleared her throat. "He is out on some business or other. He has left two men at the door."

Hendra nodded slowly, finding her neck stiffening. She wondered if that was just because she was confined to the bed.

"Tell the council I will see them when they can gather."

"Is that wise?" Alice asked, but again her gaze flew to the man at the end of the bed. It made Hendra very uncomfortable.

"Alice, give us a moment."

She opened her mouth to protest, then thought better of it and headed out into the corridor. Hendra noticed that her eyes went to Solon, again, as she closed the door.

"Are you sleeping with my wife or just plotting together against me?"

Solon smiled as though the world was his. Hendra sat forward despite the pain that rippled through her body.

"I am the Hendra," she repeated. "What do you think the two of you could do that I wouldn't discover, or that couldn't be stopped? Calder has been watching her for months."

"Calder is your problem, sister, not Alice."

She scoffed and leaned back slowly.

"And if you appear before your council as you are, they will not only smell the weakness, you will be gone before whatever is eating at your body can finish you."

"Poison," she whispered.

Something shifted on his face, something she couldn't quite read. He surprised her by coming around and taking Alice's seat beside the bed. "The doctors think it is an infection."

"Calder feared poison," she repeated, looking towards the door. "Something advanced, perhaps. Something someone with medical knowledge could manufacture."

"You think *Alice* poisoned you?" he asked incredulously. "I have never seen a more devoted wife."

"Who has looked at you more than me since I have woken."

"She is worried," he said, leaning forward. "She cares—although how anyone could is beyond me."

She glared at him.

"You appreciate my honesty," he said, sitting back in the chair.

"I doubt that anything you say is based on honesty, little brother. I'm sure you are working your way through my allies, sowing the seeds of poison amongst them, trying to tell them I am too ill to rule."

"You are," he said matter-of-factly. "But it doesn't follow that I would want your seat on that council. I have enough to deal with on my own little part of the Complex."

Hendra cleared her throat and tried not to clench her teeth as another wave of pain rippled through her body. She closed her eyes and took a deep breath. "Send in Stone," she muttered, glancing at him from the corner of her eye, "and prepare for a meeting."

He stood slowly, reminding her of just how tall he was. Then he bowed, although she was sure it wasn't with any respect, and strode from the room.

She was struggling to breathe by the time Stone arrived a short time later.

"Your Grace?" he asked, rushing over and checking the panel.

She put her hand to her throat. If she lost her voice in this, she would be even more lost with the council. Although if she struggled to breathe, it would be worse, she supposed. "Rohen," she whispered.

"Rohen?"

"Is it rohen?"

He looked confused for a moment and then followed her hand as it rested gingerly on her side. His eyes widened.

"What if someone has been feeding me small amounts of rohen?"

"How?"

The thick green juices and odd-tasting tea seemed to be an option. But how would Alice accomplish such a thing? She was watched too closely; even when she thought she had a quiet little hideaway. *Why* Alice would try such a thing was the bigger question. And one that made her heart ache and her stomach turn.

Nine

Isla stumbled against the wall, the rough rock catching at her arm. The gentle glow of the figure ahead kept her walking, but she was tiring. It had been so long since she'd had the chance to really walk, but the constant dark was draining, and she wasn't sure of the last time she'd eaten.

She sighed. She used to be stronger than this; she used to be able to do anything. And she had lost Gray again. The figure stopped and turned, then beckoned her forward once more. She shook her head. "I can't," she murmured, sinking to the floor.

Come. It echoed through her bones, vibrating through the wall she leant against. She climbed back to her feet. Rohen was involved in this. She thought of Gray. Maybe he did feel something more, something different than she did. He had called the Rohen *them*. Like he knew it was more than just metal.

She knew it was something more as well—she had felt it flowing through the universe like blood through veins. Through the forest, through the walls, and through the very fabric of everything they had created. But then, had they? What if all of this had been created by something else, and that was why they were so infused throughout it?

The being in front of her stopped and then disappeared. Was she getting closer to what it truly was? She stepped forward despite the dark, bumping again against the stone walls, and then the smell of a forest filled her senses. She was home.

A gentle glow lit a cavern similar to the first one she had found underground, but not the same. It was similar to the garden they had found aboveground and the one she had lost Gray in. She rushed forward, seeing him curled beneath the branches. What were they doing? Was the Rohen playing with her in some way? It could move them through solid stone and drag them across the solar system. Were they still on Urgway, or had they been transported across the solar system? They had made her walk through the dark while they carried Gray here.

He didn't move as she approached. She knelt beside him, her hand to his shoulder. He was still, too still, and she suddenly understood his fear when he had woken to find her sleeping beside him. They wouldn't have bothered to carry him all this way if he were dead. Or perhaps it was the carrying that had finished him. He wasn't a hummer; he was someone who could be affected by the fumes and the metal. She gently placed her fingers on his neck, then breathed with relief as the throb of his pulse moved steadily.

She leant into him then, curling against his still form, and closed her eyes. She pretended she was far away in a forest she knew better than her own body on Rennet. Just her and the trees. It didn't quite smell the same, but her memories took her back there.

She was sure she was dreaming. The forest around her was silent. Nothing moved, no leaves murmured in the wind, no bird called, no animal growled or cried out. Her hands were tight around the branch. The solidness of it helped keep her grounded, no matter that she was high in the branches. Even her feet, when she looked down, were bare, and she could feel the texture of the bark.

Something moved in the distance, between the branches. She saw a flash of silver. It could have been the sun reflecting from something, although she wasn't sure what. She moved through the branches quickly, practiced, searching again for what she had seen. But there was nothing. As she dropped lightly from the branches, landing in the soft grass with familiar fungi growing around the base of the trees, she looked up to see a man.

Not a man—he wore the form of a man, but it was something very different.

"I know you," she said, something familiar in the way he tilted his head as though looking her over. "We've met."

He bowed his head.

He was like the form she had followed in the caves, but not; he was something different, someone different. And yet just the same.

She was struck with sudden panic. "You are not safe," she blurted, stepping forward. He remained where he was. She wanted to reach him, wanted to warn them.

Them.

Something in Isla stopped her reaching out. Something scared her. She worried for these people, although she wasn't sure why, and suddenly she was more scared of them. Her hand moved slowly to her collarbone. Her fingers found the dip, and the metal creature before her bowed his head once more. She backed up, her body hitting a tree. She wanted to be safe, she wanted to be sure. But the Rohen within the fibre of the tree called out to her, and she flinched away. Nothing was safe—nowhere was safe.

She blinked into the dim light of the cavern. Gray was wrapped tight around her, his soft breath in her ear. She slept on his arm, which had snaked up around her, and his fingers moved softly over her collarbone.

The silver flashed in the dark. She blinked. The swords—the sharp metal that had cut through her skin—was Rohen. Not just that the swords were Rohen—the Rohen had been responsible. She leapt to her feet. "What do you want from me!" she screamed into the forest. The leaves shimmered and whispered as though she had started a breeze to wake them.

"Isla?" Gray asked groggily. She spun, and then the movement in the trees started. She released her hold, stepped back and tried to fight the overwhelming urge that this had happened before, that she had been here before.

"We have to go," she said, pulling at him, trying to calm the panic that was growing in her chest. She couldn't think clearly here.

"Why?" he asked, taking hold of her fingers but not standing.

She shook her head, trying to remove the memories that were flooding in and threatening to overwhelm her. "Hendra is working with the Rohen," she whispered through gritted teeth. "They are..." She wasn't quite sure what they were. A threat? An enemy?

No, whispered through the cavern. Gray let go of her hand, looking around the dim space as he climbed to his feet. The trees fell silent.

"What the...?" he stammered.

"You aren't working with Hendra?" Isla asked shakily into the cavern. There was a long pause before the same whispered word echoed around her.

Gray looked at her with wide eyes.

"You are sharp," Isla whispered, her finger finding the dip in the bone once more.

Only when we need to be. The sound rustled through the trees and vibrated through the rocks.

"Tell me why they would need to be," Gray whispered, leaning in close as he held out his hand.

"I don't know." Isla's voice was just as quiet as she took the offered hold. His warm hand closed around hers, and she felt a comfort she hadn't allowed herself for some time. She knew they could hear every whisper, every thought.

The glimmering image of a being stepped from the tree before them and, despite her best efforts, Isla stepped back. But it was Gray who held her steady, his feet unmoving.

She sucked in a breath, which was surprisingly shaky. Gray turned to take her in, concern creasing his brow.

"I remember," she whispered.

The figure ahead of them bowed his head.

"Is this what Rohen looks like?" Gray asked.

The head leant a little to the side as though the creature, or being, or whatever it was, considered what he was asking. Then it held out a hand, indicating the trees around them.

"You are the trees?" he asked.

The creature repeated the movement.

"You are everything," Isla said.

"What?" Gray asked as the creature bowed its head once more.

"Why did you kill them?" she asked, her voice betraying the walls she had built around herself and the loss of that day.

The figure moved a hand in a similar motion.

"Don't you remember?" Gray asked.

She blinked at him. She remembered the silver and the flash of metal, the glimmers in the dark, the forms coming from nowhere to cut them down. But had she known that there was a risk? Had she understood why they were there? The same feeling of fear for the creature returned.

"They were trying to destroy you," she whispered.

The creature stepped forward then, arms outstretched. Without fear, Isla stepped forward, released Gray's hand and wrapped her arms around the entity before her.

Fragmented images flashed through her mind—Kalli, others, whispered words. She knew in her bones it was wrong, that it would destroy them all. Yet there was no way to destroy the Rohen. She stepped back, still unsure of what she had known, what they had planned, why anyone would send them in to face those creatures. Did they think they could really destroy them?

She shook her head.

"What do you need us to do?" Gray asked, startling her from the jumble of thoughts swirling around her head.

It was as though the being sighed.

"Is there nothing?" he asked.

"Maybe you are a hummer," Isla whispered.

The sparrow's song is true.

Isla raised her eyebrows.

"I just ask," Gray said, shrugging.

The sparrow's heart is strong.

"You assist because he cares?"

Another being, similarly shaped, appeared beside the first. Despite her wanting to help, Isla felt her nerves increasing. "Did you do this?" she asked Gray.

"I'm following you," he said.

"But they listen to you," she insisted.

"We listen to you both, but that does not mean we cannot act for ourselves." The second entity spoke clearly, a deep rumbling sound that flowed like liquid across the airwaves between them. The shimmering metal façade didn't change at all during the speech. "You have both helped us. We are grateful. We wish to keep you safe."

"Here?" Isla asked, fearing the dark would consume her.

He bowed a head. "There is more at play, more dangers than the queen."

"Queen?" Gray asked. "Hendra?"

"She is a necessity."

"She's ill," Isla blurted, thinking of the odd feeling as the Hendra had stared into her eyes, the dull look, the pallor of her skin. Something was very wrong with her.

"She is what she is."

Isla wasn't sure what that meant, but she kept her mouth shut. She was here to learn, although it might be harder for her to understand what was happening than she would like.

"Do you have other helpers?"

The entity, the Rohen, tilted its head to the side as though trying to determine what she was saying.

"Alice is a hummer," she whispered.

"She is more," the Rohen returned.

"Is Rohen the right word?" Isla wondered aloud. "Are you Rohen?"

"We are Rohendra," he said, the words washing over her like warm water.

In the dim forest, the familiar fungi lit the world enough that Isla shouldn't be scared. She sat, her arms pulled in tight around her legs. She was scared. More than she had ever been in the dark, for she knew now what was there. What she had found when she closed her eyes and remembered. Only she couldn't remember the why.

"Queen," she whispered.

Gray sat back against a tree, and she didn't need to go over it again. Isla had sat and mumbled to herself since the glimmering figures had left them. Since the Rohendra had left them.

"Why would they call her the queen?" she asked.

Gray shrugged. She didn't know, and they weren't going to tell her. *Them.* Gray closed his eyes. He knew. He knew them. He couldn't explain how that was, but she knew he held a connection, something very different from hers. She wondered if she would ever learn what it was.

"How could they make her a queen?" Isla asked.

"Maybe they already see her as Queen."

Isla shook her head. No, it was something in the way they said it. There was more to come, something was changing, something... "She isn't pregnant."

"What?" he asked, sitting forward, his focus on her for the first time since they had been left alone.

"Hendra is not pregnant," Isla said slowly.

"Of course she is. She announced it to the universe."

"She thinks she is, but she isn't."

"You aren't making sense."

"Ok, maybe she is pregnant, or carrying something, but Calder is not the father."

"You thought he was?"

"Come on," Isla snapped, jumping to her feet. "You saw them—you saw him. There is something."

"Is there?" He was too calm. "Did you know when he was with you if it meant something?"

Isla clenched her fists at her side. She wanted to slap the words away. As he stood, she stepped back in the fear she might knock him back to the ground.

"He isn't what he pretends to be," Gray said, and she flinched at the idea. "He does what he can to survive, all the time, in every situation. You know this."

She nodded slowly. She did know that. She just wasn't ready to admit it to herself. She had been angry when she'd realised who he was, steaming angry and hurt, but there was still a small part of her that hoped he had cared in some way, no matter the reasons he had done what he had.

"He is close to Hendra because it helps him. It furthers his career or agenda, whatever that may be, and I don't think you should allow what you thought he was to cloud your judgement."

"I am not clouded," Isla muttered.

"You are not yourself."

"Nothing is as it should be. My connection with the world," she said, pointing at the forest, "with the metal—it is not what I thought it was, and they are not what I thought."

Gray studied her rather than saying anything.

"They are the reason I'm here."

"Alive."

"No, Gray. Alone."

He opened his mouth and then closed it.

"They killed the unit. They left me for dead. They are the reason the Hendra hunted me and the reason my family is gone. The Rohen—" She paused, not wanting to call them Rohendra. It seemed strange to give them power by saying the word. "They want us to work with them, but they have only worked to destroy me."

"Why?" he asked.

"I can't remember. I can't grasp what it was we learnt that they wanted us dead. But I'm sure Calder knows, and likely Hendra as he wasn't there. That day we all died, he wasn't there."

"You are sure."

She nodded. In the dark, as the sharp edges caught the light, she remembered everyone's face but his. He hadn't been there; she was sure of it. But she wasn't sure at what point he had disappeared. "I've been over this so many times. Now it is clearer, but it doesn't make any more sense than it did then."

"Isla," he said carefully, as though she were a frightened child. "We came here to help."

"That was before I knew what they were."

"You have always known," he said, stepping in closer. "You feel them everywhere. The pulse of the planet, running behind the walls, breathing life through the land." He looked over his shoulder at the plants behind him. At the world she knew.

She blew out a long breath, feeling the panic subside a little with his soft, steady voice. Although she wasn't sure if she could maintain it if they reappeared again.

"What do we do?" she asked.

"What they need us to."

"What happened on the Sparrow?" she asked. He stepped back, lowered his hands and shook his head. "You know my story," she prompted.

He gave her a sad look. "This isn't mine to tell," he said, moving back to the tree. "Tell me what you think we should do."

"I can't get my head around it," she said, watching him return to the ground and rest his head back. Her mind was racing, trying to turn around what she had seen, what she had learnt and what she remembered of that day to put it into something that made sense. Now that she had more answers, it seemed to make less sense.

"Why don't you sleep?" he suggested, patting the ground beside him. "Or would you rather sleep in the trees?" He looked into the branches above him. In some ways, she longed to go up, explore and see what about this forest was different from her own, what was the same. But she feared the dim light. Although the fungi glowed, she knew they were deep beneath the earth and she would not have the comfort of the sun.

She relented and sat beside Gray, resting her head back against the strong, thick trunk, breathing in the scent of the wood, her shoulder against his. "It is too quiet," she said. "There are no animals."

"I'm a little comforted by that. I'm somewhat nervous of the big cats."

"I'm worried about what I might see in my dreams," Isla admitted. Gray reached out and took her hand. It was becoming a comfort to be this close, but she pulled away, reminded of Kalli and how his holding her hand hadn't meant what she'd thought. He folded his hands in his lap and put his head back again.

This man was something very different, she had to remind herself. Although why he was so sure she was worth the effort, she didn't exactly know. She had worried when she'd thought she had lost him. But that was because she'd thought she had gotten him killed. He was following her into something neither of them fully understood.

She shifted as the silence closed around her. Her hand itched for something to be sure she was safe, but she would never be safe in the dark, no matter her training, no matter what she held. They were stronger—they had always been stronger—and they would become whatever they needed to survive.

She took a deep breath, closed her eyes and tried to remember. She shivered at the fear, the uncertainty and the adrenalin she remembered rushing through her veins. Before the screaming started... She had to think back further, remember before the day, before the attack. They had been sent out by whom?

Kalli stood grinning before her in his familiar worn t-shirt. Something about him made her smile. He was easy, comfortable; everyone loved him. She wondered for a fleeting moment if it had been hard for him to maintain that—or had that been who he was and something had changed? Something that had made him send them in that day and become the hard Colonel Calder instead.

There were differences in the bone structure of the face, the colour of his skin. He was a different man, and yet she knew in her bones it was him. Had he been there? Had he been dragged away by the Hendra and altered to hide in plain sight? But that was one clear memory she had—he wasn't there. He had been there, leading the unit, but then she couldn't remember him at all. She wondered what he had been doing after he'd sent the rest of his unit in to die.

She shook her head, trying to clear the jumble of thoughts and she laid down on the soft ground, a gentle hand ran through her hair. He had always laughed about how unruly her hair was, how she wasn't neat enough for a soldier. She had thought it in jest, but maybe those little moments she treasured were the lies she told herself.

She wondered what other lies she had told herself—where she should be, that leaving the forest was a good idea in the first place. She sighed and rolled onto her back. Something flashed in the dark. She sucked in a breath but kept still. She was no longer sure if she was inside her own head or if they had returned to the forest. Perhaps they thought she should die as wel l.

Kalli's voice echoed through the small space, and she pressed herself against a wall. The cool, hard surface seemed to hold her still as she looked down over her training uniform. She closed her eyes, and his words became clearer. "Are you sure we can destroy it?"

"Destroy is a strong word. I prefer contain," another voice whispered. Hendra. Isla's heart beat too fast in her chest. She was sure she would give herself away.

"How can you contain that much Rohen?" Kalli asked, his voice quiet. "It is used in so much."

"This is just step one. We make an impact here, and then we'll use your unit for step two."

"They might not comply."

"They will do as they are told. They are soldiers, after all."

Isla missed what came next. Some others from the unit rounded the corner and she was wrapped up in the noise, and when she crept forward later, they were gone.

Kalli had looked at her differently then, when she had asked about the next mission. She hadn't usually questioned the reason behind whatever they were sent in to do. Despite any concerns she might have had, she had been a good soldier who did as she was told.

Had she questioned as a child? She couldn't remember now, all those hours working and learning with the master while she did as she was told. She had always done as she was told. She should have thought more about what she was doing. Questioned why she was being directed as she was with the forest, with her skills with the plants, with her training as a soldier.

If it hadn't been for that day, she would have been one of those soldiers who directed the Sparrow to do whatever it was they had done to make them outlaws. She would have put others in danger. All the while believing she was doing the good of the Complex, the will of the Hendra.

She shifted uncomfortably, as though her realisations had impacted the world around her. And then she was being gently shaken. She opened her eyes to a brighter light within the cavern.

"You cried out in your sleep," Gray whispered over her, her head in his lap. As much as she wanted to move, she didn't have the energy.

"I didn't sleep," she murmured, rubbing at her eyes. She hadn't slept in too long.

"You snore," he said, and she looked up into his grinning face. She scowled, and he nodded.

She sat up slowly and stretched her neck.

"Any bright ideas?" she asked.

"I thought you might have an idea."

She shook her head, tensing at the stiffness in her shoulders. "I'm not sure I understand what is going on," she said. "Not even in the beginning."

"You called for Kalli," he said softly.

She rubbed at her eyes again rather than look at him. "Maybe he was there. Maybe that is why he looks like he does, remade by the Hendra."

"Why?"

"Why did she save him, or why did the Rohen do what it did?"

"Both," he murmured. "Did she understand what she was sending you into? Did she know he needed saving?"

"They were working together from the beginning. He was doing as she wanted him to, whether it was right or not. They were trying to contain the Rohen. It fought back. But I wonder if she knew it was a fight they couldn't win."

"It has been mined for centuries—why now?"

"Something changed. Not just mining, although that allowed it into everything we did, everything we built, ensured it knew what we were and what we were doing. But this was something else, like the Hendra had discovered what it was and wanted it stopped. Maybe she was threatened by it."

"But they said she was the queen."

"My punishment in all this was death; perhaps they had another in mind for her."

"Why wait so long?"

"What is time? How long have they existed before us, beyond us?"

"You have a connection. Would they really have meant to hurt you when you have the skills you do—when you are a hummer?"

"I think they are just willing to listen, or willing to talk. Maybe whatever they have planned is not enough and they..."

"Need us," Gray finished for her.

"I can't see why. They are the Rohendra Complex. What can an old soldier and a worn-out enforcer do?"

"Hey!" he chastised, but he was smiling. She looked away, reminded too easily of the way Kalli smiled and how that would give her something to cling to. She didn't think she had the right to cling to anything anymore. No matter her connections to the Rohen, if that was indeed what it was, there was still the fear that anyone she got close to was lost to her.

Ten

"Alice, tell me again of the forest," Hendra whispered, her voice scratchy and not her own.

"Are you in pain?" Alice asked, leaning forward. There was concern along with something else in her voice, and Hendra feared it was longing.

"Tell me," she said, her voice stronger.

Alice gave her a small smile and nodded. "We lived amongst the trees, in small huts built from the gifts of the forest. It was easy and hard at the same time. I was able to run free, learn and grow from the forest and the animals around me, climb and hide amongst the branches, play with the other children."

"School," Hendra prompted.

"My father was important, and I didn't realise how important he was when I was a child. Once I reached my teenage years, I was told I would leave the trees."

"You didn't want to go," Hendra said.

"No. It was my home, my life. I hadn't even seen the cities of Draroh. But I was to go further away from the trees, to Rennet and a school I had never heard of."

"You made friends," Hendra said.

Alice nodded.

Hendra had asked about her relationship, or at least friendship, with Solon. They had been in the same year group, but Alice had been a child of the forest. Despite who her father had been, she was not someone who would have made it to the inner circle of the Hendra's younger brother.

"Life was better once I met you," Alice whispered, leaning in closer and taking her hand.

Something in Hendra tightened. She clutched at the hand.

"The doctors want to do more scans," Alice said, wincing at the hold.

"They can't see anything," Hendra said, leaning back and closing her eyes.

"You do seem better, but I worry about the baby."

Hendra kept her eyes closed. She hadn't allowed herself to think of the child. She had started to feel less pain, but she wondered if Alice had been giving her something, poisoning her slowly with those horrid green drinks. Perhaps it wasn't deliberate. She might have tried to help—maybe she was helping—and yet there was something different about Hendra that prevented that or made it poison.

She rubbed at her face.

"Hen?"

"I wonder if we are made differently."

"Different how?"

"You are a child of the forest," she said, "and I am not."

"We are the same species, Hen."

"Are we?"

Alice pushed the chair back and moved to the window. "That is an odd thing to say." Hendra could hear the hurt in her voice.

"We have grown on different planets, in different regions. There are other species throughout the Complex, some we don't fully understand."

"Like who?" Alice asked. "Would you compare me to a Frangar?"

Hendra smiled. Her wife was furthest from the round, squat species with long ears. Alice was tall and blonde, lithe as though she had spent her life running through the forest. But then doubt filled her. She hadn't fully understood just what the universe was until her father's death. Until he had told her the final piece of the Rohendra Complex and sworn her to keep it until she passed it on to her own heir.

Unlike her father, she saw it for what it really was—not an ally but a danger. A threat.

She sucked in a deep breath and let it out. The pain ached in her side, but it no longer rippled through her like the metal she knew to be more. That was why she had stopped the mining, the reason she would use it for her own purposes. She wouldn't be dictated to; she was the Hendra.

Alice stood by the window. As tempted as Hendra was to get out of bed and comfort her wife, doubt prevented her from trying. She wasn't sure of the relationship between Alice and Solon, and she couldn't be sure Alice wasn't involved in this. She had a way with medicines, if only rudimentary. Hendra had allowed her to treat small illnesses over the years and to assist with those like Island Tarle when she had been in the house.

She watched Alice's back as she slowly moved to watch the view from the window.

"Do you want to go home to the forest?"

"I've visited."

"Recently?"

Alice shook her head.

"Alice," Hendra said softly. The woman turned and gave her a smile.

"I'm worried, Hen, so worried. I don't know what I would do if something happened to you."

Hendra waved her back towards the bed. She raced over, taking her hands and allowing a tear to run down her cheek.

"I can't..."

"I'll be fine," Hendra said, hoping she was right. "Send in the doctors to do their scan, and we'll see. I'm feeling better already. Whatever they are trying seems to be working."

Alice sniffed, rubbed her hand under her nose and rose to her feet. "You are sure?"

Hendra nodded, and Alice left the small room in search of the doctors who would not be far. She threw back the thin blanket and twisted around to sit on the edge of the bed. It might have been a bad idea to try this on her own, but she wasn't going to be beaten by an infection or whatever it was surging through her body.

She was stronger than that, she told herself as she shifted forward and her feet met the cool floor. Pins and needles surged up her legs as she leant forward and put her weight on them. It hurt, but she was standing. With a hand on the bed, she inched along, her legs heavy and her feet burning.

Then she was standing in the middle of the room. She let out the breath she had been holding, and no pain rippled through her.

"By the stars!" Calder called behind her, racing forward and then, too carefully, putting his hands on her arms. "What are you doing?"

"We have to stop them," she whispered.

"Back to bed," he said, turning her slowly and guiding her across the room. But she could do it on her own. She caught sight of her face in the reflection of the window and stopped. She wouldn't have recognised herself or even believed the reflection to be hers, but for Calder standing beside her. "Bed," he whispered, too close.

She nodded, then allowed him to not only direct her back to the bed but help her in and straighten out the blanket over her legs. She reached then, grabbing his arm, and he raised worried eyes. "Find me a mirror," she said.

He smirked. "Really, who are you going to see?"

"Mirror," she repeated.

He nodded and reached into a cabinet by the bed; there was a bag she hadn't seen before and a small mirror.

She snatched it from him, studying her face. She looked pale, too pale. Despite all Hendra's time indoors, she was usually the picture of health. There was something wrong with her eyes, but she wasn't sure what. "What do you see?" she asked, looking up at him as the doctors came into the r oom.

"Feeling better?" Stone asked, looking at the soldier leaning over her in the bed.

"Hendra?" Alice asked.

She put the mirror down and waved him away. "I didn't realise how ill I looked," she said.

"You have more colour than you did," Stone said, still eyeing the soldier. "We need to get you eating soon; that will help."

Calder moved to the end of the bed, his gaze intense and focused on Alice.

"Run your scans," she said.

Stone nodded once and pulled the wand from his pocket.

Hendra tried to be understanding and patient, but despite her feeling better, or at least different, the scans showed nothing. They were still the hazy red they had been before, only now it had spread throughout her body. She watched the scan, willing it to change and yet it didn't. The doctor mumbled something, and Alice covered her mouth with her hands. Hendra thought for a moment that her eyes were smiling behind them.

"Where is my brother?"

"I'm not sure," Alice answered.

"Has the council been called?" Hendra asked Calder. "I asked for them to come."

He nodded, bowed his head and left.

"This is not a good idea," Stone cautioned, but he dropped his gaze as she lifted hers.

"He's right," Alice whispered.

"Bring my dress uniform," Hendra said.

Alice paused only a moment before she too disappeared. Hendra leaned back into the bed. She could do this. She had to do this, or by the time she made it out of this room, she would find her universe already under someone else's control.

If it wasn't already.

Gray was far more worried than he would like to admit. He was somehow calmer about the Rohen now that he had an understanding of it, had seen it fully for himself and the strange ideas he had made sense. Although how he knew it was something more, he couldn't determine. But the woman who wouldn't settle worried him more than she had previously. She still managed to scare him, but in a whole new way.

Isla had slept against him the night before, if it was night. It was hard to tell where they were or how long they had been there. It was lighter now than it had been, and Gray wondered if it was the Rohen within the trees that allowed them to grow in such conditions.

Her sleep had been restless. She had moved around, called out, murmured and even shaken at one point. He longed for a blanket, or to have the chance to hold her closer. But she was not herself, and he didn't want to add any pressure to that. He wanted to help, but he didn't want to get too close.

He knew that after Kalli, she didn't want that risk. She might have even murmured, "No, Gray," in her sleep, a soft sound as though apologetic, and he had wondered what she had dreamt of. He didn't sleep. He felt as though he had already slept for days. Despite the fact that he sat still while she paced the trees around them, he was keen to get moving, find something outside of the grove to help them all.

"Why are we here?" he asked suddenly. She stopped, turning to him slowly. "They don't need us; they seem to be managing well enough. They have a plan and a queen. Why do they need us?"

"Is that why Hendra wanted me?"

"I don't know," Gray admitted. "I don't know anything."

"We came to help," Isla said, taking a step closer, and for the first time she seemed calmer.

"We did, but did we really know what we were doing? Are they looking for us?"

"Likely," Isla said. "Although, the Rohen know where we are."

He nodded. What did they seriously think they could do? He had seen it, the ripples across walls, and the Rohen had helped them. But why had they helped? They had been the ones to hurt Isla in the first place, try to kill her along with her unit. They must have known what she was the whole time.

"Did they know you were a hummer?" he asked.

"They just saw me as a soldier, but then…" She stopped and walked directly to him, and despite his being more scared for her than of her, he stepped back. "I thought I knew something."

"You did," he said.

"I did," she repeated.

"Do you remember?"

"A little, but I thought Hendra and Calder were behind the attack because of what I learnt. But it wasn't them—it was the Rohen."

"Working together?"

"I think Kalli became Calder after that."

"You said he wasn't there."

"Maybe he was. Maybe I just didn't see him. It was a crazy time, dark, odd lights. I might not have seen what I thought I did. I know the Rohen were there—I know they were sharp." She shuddered. "But I didn't see them, not like we did when they stood here. I can't work out who is working with w hom."

"Hendra?"

"She tried to destroy them, contain them—to contain the Rohen."

"You are sure?"

"No, but that is what I heard her say. Maybe she was talking about us, about the unit. Maybe she thought we knew more than we did."

"But they, Calder and Hendra, didn't know what you were?"

"No, they didn't. I didn't share what I had learnt. I could make things, but they didn't know the extent of my connection to the forest."

"You didn't tell him?" Gray asked, genuinely surprised. He thought Isla and Kalli had something special, or at least that she did, if Calder had been acting all along. If he had been something different than he pretended. But it was something, a connection between the two of them.

She watched him and then turned away.

"Isla," he said softly, "this is hard, I appreciate that."

"It is fine. It is what it is. I've spent the last six years trying to move past it, then trying to accept it and learn what really happened. I remember more, but I can't trust my memories."

"The memory collectors," he said, then pressed his lips closed as she shook her head.

"They didn't help me; they shared with you," she said, and he nodded. "They shared what was mine with you, but they didn't help me find what was lost."

Gray opened his mouth to apologise, but she held up her hand.

"They are connected to the Rohen, or they are the Rohen—I don't know, but there is far more to this universe than I understood. More than I think anyone understands."

"The Hendra knows, but how many of those who work with her might know is unclear." He was thinking about the scientists, but he noticed the tinge of red bloom across Isla's cheeks. He didn't want to keep reminding her of what she had lost, what she had never had in the first place. And he knew that although they were becoming dependent on each other for survival, she didn't want to owe him anything. "Where do we go?" he asked.

"You tell me," she returned, looking through the trees. He got to his feet and looked in the same direction, worried the Rohen had returned although he wasn't really worried about the Rohen. Something in her movement scared him.

Isla sighed.

"Why me?" he asked.

"You sensed them when I couldn't. You thought we could help, and that we should work with them. I think it should be your decision what we do next."

"I don't want that," he said.

"I don't know what to do." Her voice was soft, the confidence she exuded appearing to evaporate. "I can't trust myself."

"Can't you? You've survived this long."

She opened her mouth to say something, but then closed it without saying anything. There was too much this woman had lived through, and to come face to face with those who had caused the damage... Her reaction to it was scaring him.

"Ok, they helped in some way. The Rohen may have harmed you, but they healed you as well and called you here."

She sucked in a deep breath and nodded.

"I think we should help, see what we can do."

"What can we seriously do? Two little insignificant humans. Rohen is everywhere; it can do anything."

"But it wants us here. Whether we understand that now or not, I don't think it matters."

She stared at him for too long and then surprised him with a nod. "Fine."

"And we aren't insignificant," he said. "One of us is a hummer, and the other can talk to Rohen."

At his grin, she almost smiled. Almost. But he would take that.

Eleven

Isla didn't know which side was the right side to be on in this fight. And it wasn't just the scars she no longer carried. She felt it deep within her that this was bigger than all the Rohen that flowed through the universe, and there was far more of it than all the other creatures on the planets.

She didn't know what would happen or what she could expect. For the first time in days, she longed for the simple life of a racer. The focused hunt for a win, nothing but the track ahead and those around you. It had filled every emotion and sense she had and didn't allow her the opportunity to think about anything else. Now she was thinking of everything, every possibility for the future, for a past she had lost, and what that would mean for others, not just her. Not just her colony and the family she had lost.

In the overwhelming emotions, she couldn't find a way forward.

A branch creaked, and she looked up. Gray was working his way between the trees.

"What are you doing?" she asked.

"Looking."

"For what?"

"A way out."

"I think we might have to wait for our glimmering friends to show us the way."

"You are kidding," he called, lost amongst the trees, but he had stopped his forward movement.

"What did you find?"

"You," he muttered. "The bravest woman I have met in all the Complex, and you can't find your way through the trees."

She surged forward, following his path, finding him standing between two trees with his arms crossed as though he'd been waiting for her.

"You don't know me," she muttered, pushing past him.

"Oh, I do. You are much easier to read than I expected, Island Tarle."

"Don't call me that," she snapped, turning back. He looked taken aback. She wasn't even sure why she had snapped, and she turned back to work her way through the trees.

"Isla Dee," he whispered.

She smiled despite herself then, although she didn't turn back and let him know it. What would they do when they did find a way out? Thoughts of the Hendra ticked over at the back of her mind. She wasn't sure if the Rohen had done something or if it was someone else, but something had changed in her. At least Isla thought it had.

Until recently, Isla had never seen the Hendra in person. Maybe she hadn't really looked before; maybe that was what she was. There was something that had ensured their family remained the Hendra, to the point that they didn't even offer another name for the firstborn. They were Hendra from the moment they were conceived.

No one in all the history of the Complex had managed to displace a Hendra. They had enemies, sure enough, those working against them at times. Isla thought of Ebberah and wondered if it was only because of her daughter that she worked against the Hendra. But if she was working with or connected to the Rohen, then having a daughter who was a hummer might only do her good.

Something glimmered in the distance, and Isla waited for Gray to catch her up before she continued. If she was going to face the Rohen again, she wanted him beside her. She glanced at him, focused on his footing and where his hands pressed against the trees.

"I haven't seen many trees in my time," he said, almost keeping up with her. "You have. Are these like real trees?"

"They are real," she said, pausing to run her hand over the bark of one.

"Do you think the Rohen created the other forests?"

"Like the one in the other cavern?"

"No, like on Rennet and Draroh."

Isla stopped then, taking in the world around her—the scent, the leaf litter. "Maybe," she said. But she had no idea. She was becoming less and less sure of what she did know as they travelled on. "I'm not confident in anything," she admitted, "not even my own skill."

"Really?" he asked. He was puffing a little from trying to keep up with her. It wasn't that she was fast; she was just surer of her footing.

"Plan?" she asked, resting against a tree as she waited for him to catch his breath and to understand what he was really thinking. Did she want to know? Did she want to care what he thought, what his ideas were as to how they would live through this? Did she want to live through this?

Something shifted, not in Isla but beneath her. The whole forest creaked in a way that only old trees could. In the moment of fear that washed over her, as Gray clutched at her, she felt a familiarity that made her smile.

"You have a death wish," he muttered.

"I know home when I feel it."

"You are mad," he whispered, leaning in close, his hand too tight around her arm.

"Come on," she said, leading him towards a space ahead where the ground didn't dip and the trees didn't lean. "There," she said, pushing on when he leaned into her as a tree on the other side leaned towards him.

"Are you sure you are home?" he asked when they reached the solid ground. Although she could still feel the heaving back and forth within the cavern, she couldn't see it. "Did that just happen, or is the Rohen telling us it is time to leave?"

"I wonder if someone is trying to contain them. If this forest might be connected to others, to the forest above us. It is all connected," she repeated, certain of that now. That the Rohen had in some ways repeated the same patterns across the planets in the Complex. And here on Urgway, where the desert was too dry to maintain the trees and the sun too hot, it had grown beneath the ground.

"Is there forest on every planet?" Gray asked, his thoughts mirroring hers.

"I think so," she said. "Although I have never visited the forests of Draroh."

"Not many have," he said, watching the trees ahead of him, "and fewer talk of it."

"Have you?" she asked, looking around the edges of the cavern. The light had to come in somewhere. The Rohen had to flow in somewhere, and yet it could move through solid stone.

He shook his head. "The Sparrow was on its way to Draroh. We were diverted."

"From Rennet?"

He nodded.

Rennet is the centre of the Complex in more ways than one, Isla thought. And it might be that more than the Hendra had control there.

"We need to get back to the Rohen forest on the surface."

A small fissure opened in the wall, and she moved through it without hesitation. Gray murmured behind her that there might be some risk of the whole world collapsing on top of them. But then they were standing in the sun, in the middle of a forest of silver trees that glimmered in the light, and Isla looked up as a scientist with small, round glasses knocked on the window and waved.

Isla marched towards him, Gray still holding tight to her arm. Although the scientist watched them, he looked a little more wary the closer they got to the glass.

"You can't explain this," Gray said.

"Rohen," Isla said, which appeared to be the answer to everything, only she wasn't always sure what the question was.

The man stepped back from the glass.

"Do you know his name?" she asked.

"No. Do we need to?"

"Maybe," she said, stopping and tapping on the window he had tapped not so long ago. "Are you going to let us in?"

"You need decontaminating," the scientist called through the thick glass, looking back over his shoulder. "There is no door on this side."

"The man thinks we need doors?" Gray asked. "Does he not know who we are?"

Isla turned back then and took in the dishevelled man standing behind her. The protective visor and gloves were gone, the trees providing enough shade from the Urgway sun that they weren't burning. "How long have we been here?"

"No idea," Gray said, looking at the building rather than her.

"And who are we?"

"The hummer that the Rohen itself... themselves..." He shook his head as though unsure what word he should be using, and losing the thread of what he was saying. He cleared his throat. "The Rohen wants you, calls to you. I am the non-humming one who asks, and they give."

"Really?" she asked.

He nodded back towards the building as the glass peeled back from the frames and the wall beneath it disappeared. The scientist, who had looked somewhat nervous, now looked terrified. He raced across the room as they walked into it, and the wall righted itself behind them.

"Who knew you could know so much," Isla said with a smirk.

A sudden jet of air stole Gray's response as a thick blanket of air covered them. When it cleared, the scientist was standing before them, struggling to hold a wide hose, his glasses askew.

"I think we have been decontaminated. Although," Isla said to him, stepping closer as he shakily raised the hose again. "I don't think the Rohen is quite as poisonous as you would have us believe."

He lowered the hose in shock. "I've seen it," he said, as though that was enough for them to understand and believe him. "In the lab," he went on when neither of them spoke, "and in the mines, the stories are widespread. It is why they wear the suits."

"But we use it in everything. It was used in everything, and there were no effects from it then," Isla said.

The scientist shrugged as though he couldn't explain the difference. And he worked with it all the time.

"What do you know?" Isla asked.

The man looked down and gave them another quick burst of air. He lowered the hose, then jumped back as Gray emerged from the fog to wrench it from his hands. "I've seen it turn, try to work with someone as though communicating in some way, and then they..."

Isla waited as the man stopped and held his ground. "Gray," she said, and he stopped.

The man raised his small eyes to her. "It consumed them."

"Consumed them?" Gray asked. "Like it ate them?"

"More like it covered them, and then when it returned to a puddle, the person was gone."

"I've never heard of such a thing," Gray said.

"Of course you haven't—our work is secret."

Isla wondered if that were true. And if it was the case, what had the Rohen done? Or what was it trying to do? She had been cocooned in the metal several times herself, and it had yet to do her any damage—any she was aware of. She suddenly remembered the sharp in the dark, that they had hurt her, very nearly killed her. But that had been in retaliation for something else. They hadn't known her. Or had they? They would have known her from the forest, from the skill she had. Maybe they hadn't been trying to kill her and she had just been in the wrong place at the wrong time. Maybe that was why she had managed to survive when no one else had.

"Ms Tarle," the man broke through her thoughts. "Sergeant Tarle," he corrected himself.

"Isla," she said, and he seemed to breathe for the first time. "And you are?"

"Michaels." He held out his hand, which she looked at without taking, and he slowly lowered it. "Can you tell me what went on out in the garden?"

"It is pretty," Isla said, turning back towards it.

"They are back," a soldier stammered by the door. He was followed by several more, and she wondered what it was they would try to do.

"How long were we gone?" she asked.

"An hour or two," Michaels said, "maybe more. I find it hard to judge time. I can get easily lost in my work and spend days standing here looking out on the wonder of the garden."

"It's creepy," the soldier said. Isla raised her eyebrows. It wasn't for a soldier to be giving an opinion, and this man was Elite. An Elite standing guard over a forest. It didn't really seem fitting, but as she looked back over her shoulder, she was sure the Hendra didn't want too many people learning about this.

"How long?" Isla asked him more forcefully, suddenly unsure why it was so important that she find out.

"Hours," he muttered. "Three or four." He looked at the scientist as though the man were an idiot.

Gray made an odd noise beside her but didn't say anything else. She was sure they had been gone overnight, but perhaps time travelled differently. Maybe they hadn't been on the inner crust of the planet as she had thought.

"What did you learn?" Michaels asked, his voice almost desperate.

"It is a forest more than a garden," she said.

He stared at her.

She shrugged and looked at Gray, who shook his head and pulled a similar face to the one she was sure she wore. "Garden," he muttered. "Trees, flowers, leaves, only all made of metal."

"Is it solid?" Michaels asked, stepping forward. Isla was tempted to put herself in the middle of them.

Gray nodded.

"You touched it," Michaels said in awe.

"Accidently," Gray said, looking at Isla as though not sure what to say.

Michaels leapt forward and grabbed at his hands, turning them over as though looking for damage or signs of Rohen. "Amazing," he whispered.

"Has anyone else gone into the garden?" Isla asked.

"We have had some volunteers," Michaels said, looking towards the soldiers. "They didn't survive the experience."

"Hummer." The soldier almost spat the word, as though she were tainted. But his eyes moved between the two of them, and Gray slowly raised his hands.

"I'm no hummer," he said, as though he agreed the word was dirty. "You just need manners." He was using that sweet tone he used when mocking Isla. The soldier raised his duster. The hum of the gears shifted something in Isla, and she was between them before he could do anything stupid. She had been tempted often enough to shoot him herself.

"And I don't need you," Gray said as he placed his hands on her shoulders and moved her to the side.

"He wouldn't be dumb enough to shoot the Hendra's prize hummer, no matter what he thought of her," Michaels said.

"Oh, I wouldn't be too sure," Isla said.

"Don't try to claim you know me, Tarle. I know all about you. You might be touted as some war hero, but I know all you did was survive the day. Any fool could have done that. If you hadn't been distracted, you might not have been where you were in the first place."

"What do you know of where we were?" She managed to keep her voice calm. "The official record never mentioned it, and if it had, it would have been wrong." She was certain of that too, although she still couldn't remember where they had been or exactly what had put them there.

The man grinned. Isla wondered just how many men Calder had working with him and just what they might know, or at least think they knew. She doubted the man would tell those around him the truth, even if his life depended on it. He would tell them what they needed to know to get done whatever mad mission he or Hendra had concocted. What they would do with that information or power, she couldn't work out. The Elite always followed the lead, no matter who was in it or what they thought of them.

It was hot, too hot, and she was reminded of the time she had run from a racer to help a man she didn't know. But the sun had cut through their skin. She had been protected then, but Gray hadn't. She still remembered the blisters rising quickly on his exposed skin. She felt the heat radiating from the garden, but it wasn't the same, as though something had taken the edge off it. It was a comfort, and a worry.

The soldier continued to grin, and Isla felt more uncomfortable than she had in a while. She had been in some different places and met some unexpected people, including those who glimmered in the dark. Yet this man unleashed something that made her want to take the duster from his hands and turn it on him.

She could, she realised, taking a deep breath. She was more capable than all the soldiers they had come across. It might have been some years since she had seriously used her skills, but she could use them. The soldier still had his weapon raised, but he wasn't really clear on which one of them he was pointing it at.

"Where is Calder?" she asked.

His focus moved to her, the duster with it, his grin not so manic.

"I was there when the Hendra tasked him with this. It is odd that he would go against her direct order."

The man glared, and Gray cleared his throat. "Not something I would do," he murmured.

"No matter what you think you know," Isla said, "the Hendra has sent us here. Your only task is to keep us safe."

He worked his jaw.

"Are we safe?" Isla asked Gray, then looked to Michaels.

"I don't feel safe," Gray said.

Michaels, to his credit, laughed. The soldier moved the weapon towards him. Although he was odd, he might be the best mind working on the Rohen. He would therefore be another important part of Hendra's plans. For Isla, it still wasn't clear what those plans were or what the Hendra thought they would be doing for her out here in the sun.

Twelve

---

endra stood surprisingly steady with her hands holding the back of the chair. She was tempted to grip it to ensure she didn't fall. She had managed to walk here under her own power, but it had drained her. She might not be well, but she could give the illusion of health and strength.

Her brother looked the most surprised when he came in and sat down at the table, then stood again as she had yet to sit down. She gave him a shake of her head.

"Thank you all for coming," she said, surprised that her voice didn't betray her. Taking the time to catch her breath had helped her energy levels as well.

"There are rumours," Ebberah was quick to say, watching closely. Hendra wondered exactly what the woman had heard.

She sat down carefully, but the pain didn't flare across her torso as she feared it would. She waved her hand for Ebberah to continue as the older woman glanced around the table at the others. Her gaze only landed on Solon momentarily. Maybe he wouldn't share what he knew or didn't want to give away that he had said anything to the other council members.

Silence surrounded her, and she suddenly longed for the chatter and questions she usually had at such meetings.

"Well, then." Brown cleared his throat. "We heard you were ill, dangerously so. It has put the Complex on edge."

"Wherever you heard such stories, they have been extremely exaggerated, I can assure you. I have been under the care of my doctors as I had contracted an infection." She glanced at her brother. "They wanted to be sure it was nothing serious, and at this stage they have no reason to think it will have any ill effect on the child."

"I am pleased to hear it," Brown said, looking at the others as though there might be something else and he didn't want to be the one to say it.

"I assure you, no one else is at risk," she added.

"That wasn't my concern, but I am glad you raised it."

Hendra wondered what his concern was, but it didn't look like he was going to share it with her.

"Where did you pick up the infection?" Chief Sem asked, "I mean, how? I mean..."

"I am not sure," she said. "The doctors are still working on the cause."

"Then how do they know not to be concerned?" Ebberah blurted.

"They have a number of ways of monitoring such things," Hendra said with a wave of her hand, hoping they did know what they were doing.

"Were you injured? Or could someone have infected you?" Sem asked, appearing to be filled with concern.

"That I don't know either."

"There seems to be much that you don't know," Solon murmured, but it was loud enough to be heard by the whole table.

"And more that I do know. Such as your attempt to sway the council—perhaps you were involved?"

The focus of the table shifted to her brother. For the first time, he sat back and smiled. "If only life were so simple, sister. But as you are well aware, I only want to watch over my small part of the Complex, not all of it ."

She raised her eyebrows, but it was some time before people turned from him and back to her.

"I have decided to pardon the war hero. She is a hero, after all, and I think there was a misunderstanding."

"Misunderstanding?" Chief X'ang of Urgway asked, his voice raising uncharacteristically. "She killed half a race full of racers."

"There was no real proof that she was behind the attack."

"There was footage," he snarled.

"We know what the woman has done as an Elite for the Complex. I'm sure there were some who were jealous of her skill and framed her."

Murmuring started around the table.

"It is also rumoured that she was not the only one of the unit to survive the day," Solon said. "Is that worth following up?"

"Calder was on that rumour after the attack, and there is nothing to it," she said, wishing there was water at the table. There was nothing. She looked it over, not sure what they usually did for council meetings, but she was confident it was far more than the bare table displayed now. The room itself didn't even appear as it usually did. The windows to the view across the city were tinted, and all of them were there in person. It must have taken some time for that to happen.

Then Alice was standing in the doorway with a cup of juice. Something made her feel uneasy, as though the thought of having to drink it would be the end of her. Hendra shook her head, but Alice stepped forward. She was too casually dressed and appeared too tired, as though she had been sitting by Hendra's bed for days. Hendra didn't think she had seen that much of her.

She bowed to the group as though offering her respect, a movement in itself that surprised Hendra. As she sat the glass down with a plop, Hendra was certain that the viscous liquid within didn't move. She stared at it, wondering at the sound.

"No, thank you," she said, sliding the glass back towards Alice. She wasn't drinking this, and she wasn't drinking it in front of the council. The doctors had also warned her against drinking or eating anything they hadn't prepared to be sure no poison or other substances were being introduced to her system.

Alice's face crumpled, a tear welling in the corner of her eye as she nodded slowly.

"Don't be harsh. The woman cares," her brother was quick to say.

"Water," Hendra said, turning back to the council. "Would you mind?" she asked, looking back to Alice.

Alice stared at the tall glass already on the table.

"Alice," Hendra prompted. "I need water."

Alice bowed her head and backed out of the room without removing the vile liquid. Solon growled something.

"If you would prefer, brother," Hendra said sweetly, "you can drink the juice. She does go to such lengths to make it, only my stomach can't handle much yet."

Hendra pushed the glass across the table. He glared at it but didn't reach for it, nor did he indicate he would accept it. Maybe he knew more than she did—maybe Calder was right. Ebberah smiled at her across the table, and Hendra tried to refocus. Why had she wanted them here? Why did she want to talk to them?

A servant appeared, bowed low despite the bulky tray and unloaded a large crystal jug of water. He then unloaded glasses, poured and sat one before Hendra with a bow. Without waiting, he did the same for the other members of the council, working around the table and pausing by her brother. He nodded, and a glass was left. The man disappeared without taking the green drink with him.

Hendra cleared her throat. "There is unrest, and I will not have it. See to it that each planet of the Complex is behaving as it should."

"And the hummer?" Ebberah asked.

"I did not think you believed in such things," Hendra said. "Either way, the Island girl is secure and not a threat to the Complex."

"I thought you said she was pardoned?" X'ang murmured, a small smile pulling at the corner of his mouth.

Could it be a smile? Hendra didn't think the man had it in him. She gave him a genuine one in return and bowed her head.

They bowed their heads in turn as a show of agreement, although she was sure they didn't believe a word of it. Hendra wasn't so sure herself that she had made the right decision. She needed someone in there, and Island Tarle was the best option. If they struggled to do as she needed them to, Michaels knew to kill the enforcer.

Whether Calder would allow that, she wasn't sure.

"Is there a particular reason we were called to an unusual meeting?" Victor asked. "I have things to be doing."

Hendra nodded slowly and stood. She glanced at the water as Brown took a sip of his own. "I just wanted to reassure you that we were on track, that all is as it should be."

"Truly?" Ebberah asked, also standing. "There are rumours everywhere, not only that you are using a hummer—and we still don't know why. Now you tell us you have pardoned her."

"It must be hard for you to keep up," Hendra said, trying to smirk. She was losing her edge.

"You wanted to prove you weren't dying," Brown said, standing slowly and coming around the table. He laid his hand on her arm. "And I am pleased." He gave her a genuine smile, and she wondered if this man would be truly loyal if she needed him to choose. Not that she would. She was making the best decision for the Complex. This would save them all, only she hadn't been able to tell them that.

Hendra walked along the corridor and then paused as a servant stopped and bowed. "When you clear the table," she said, "I left my drink behind, the juice. Bring it to my room."

The servant bowed his head again and disappeared down the hall. She should head back to the medical room, but she couldn't face them. She headed for the office instead. Perhaps the doctor could review the juice. Not that she doubted Alice; she just wasn't sure who else might have reached her.

By the time she reached her office door, she was struggling. Struggling to stand and walk, and in part regretting the decision to move so far from where her doctors were sure she needed to be. The door was closed, but the desk that was usually occupied outside her doors was empty. The variety of secretaries gone, the desk clear. She wondered then if someone else was redirecting the workings of the Complex.

She pushed on the door and headed into the dark. She could have come the other way, through their own private path, but she wanted to be seen despite her struggles, to reassure the people that she wasn't dead. And she was far from it. Although right at this point, she was tempted to lie down and allow whatever was working through her body to take her.

There was no one in the office when she entered. It seemed larger than she remembered, darker, colder. But it was her own. She moved forward and leaned against the desk. The monitor flashed to life. Several documents were open, and she wondered if she had been reading them before or if they were new.

She used the desk as support as she worked around it and sank into her chair. Michaels' name jumped from the screen, and she wondered what he had managed to find. He was useful, but when it came down to it, he would do what he thought best in the interest of science rather than the Rohendra Complex. Except the document itself didn't make any sense. It wasn't a report, more a reporting of him. She wondered who was watching him.

She glanced through the document and thought it must be a mistake. It was a claim of treason. That he was working against the Hendra with his research. That the rohen had been banned for good reason and he was a risk to them all.

She searched the document for an idea of who had authored the report, but it wasn't detailed. The document began to blur before her. She rubbed at her eyes, flinching as a wave of pain rushed across her abdomen. She reached for the intercom, but the button wasn't working. She wasn't even wearing her usual Rohendra star pin, which contained a security alarm. Why hadn't she thought to put it on when she'd dressed? She wore it every day.

She longed for Calder for the first time in too long. He would know what to do. He would keep her safe. She rose from the chair and staggered out to the private lounge. If nothing else, it was all under surveillance—someone would find her soon enough. Hendra lay down on the long sofa, curled in around the pain filling her whole body and squeezed her eyes closed.

Isla sat slowly at the desk in the small room adjacent to the large open space beside the garden, and stretched. She was exhausted, but she wasn't sure why. She was also losing track of time and convinced they had been somewhere else.

"Explain to me again about the heat?"

"What heat?" she asked the man across the table. She needed to sleep.

"The surface temperature of Urgway is unbearable away from the cities. The planet isn't designed to support life."

"And yet it does," she said.

He gave her a quizzical look. She glanced at Gray sitting silently beside her, his head down, and wondered if he had managed to find a way to sleep.

"There are a lot of people living on this planet, despite the heat," she said. "And we went out there in protective gear to shield us from the sun."

He nodded, a pensive expression forming on his face as though that hadn't occurred to him. She thought of Reilly then, and his family out in the desert far from the habitats of the cities. Or maybe there were heat sinks and only some places were inhabitable. How long had Isla lived on this planet? How had she not known anything about it?

"You came back in without it," Michaels said, his voice low.

Isla looked at Gray slumped beside her. She nudged him, hoping he could help this conversation in some way. She wasn't sure when they had removed the heavy suits, why the sun hadn't burnt them as they'd walked through the silver forest. Maybe the temperature wasn't as intense here as they thought. Gray looked up at her as though he hadn't been listening.

"What does she want me to do?" Isla asked, attempting to draw the conversation back to why they were there.

"Get it to do as we want," he said simply.

"The Rohen?"

He nodded.

"I can't do that. No one could do that." Did they really have so little understanding of how the metal worked? Had they not been paying attention?

"It is just a metal, but it is odd. It has been so useful to our universe, and now..."

"How long have the experiments been going on?" Isla asked.

"I think you have misunderstood the meaning of this meeting," the soldier announced at the door. "It is for you to answer our questions, hummer, not for us to answer yours."

"You don't have any information I need," Isla said without turning around to face him. She was still surprised that he was even present for the conversation, or meeting, or whatever it was they were doing.

"Can we sleep?" Gray asked. "The sun got to me, I think."

"You touched it," the soldier spat. "Likely infected. You still haven't explained where the suits went."

"Hendra wants us here to learn about this," Isla said.

Michaels looked at her closely, as though he wasn't quite sure that was true. But then, Isla wasn't sure he was fully cognisant of what the Hendra did want, what she planned. It had far more to do with the glimmering humanoid forms of Rohen, or Rohendra as they called themselves, than simply controlling the metal.

Did she want some form of negotiation with them? Did she even know they existed?

"Maybe if we could sleep," Isla said, "we would have the chance to think a bit more clearly about this. And something to eat might be nice."

"There are the scientist quarters across the..." Michaels waved in a vague manner across the room.

"They should be locked up," the soldier insisted.

"The Hendra said they are not prisoners."

"I'm sure the colonel thinks differently."

"Where is he?" Isla asked.

"Missing him?" The soldier had a smirk on his ugly face.

Isla smiled and nodded. "We've grown close," she said sweetly.

The smirk fell from the soldier's face, and he growled something as he stomped from the room.

"Just go over again what it felt like," Michaels said to Gray.

Gray shook his head, and Isla looked at him properly. Was he ill? Had something happened with his exposure to the Rohen and the intense heat of the surface?

"Sleep," she said.

"Fine," Michaels conceded, pushing his chair back and then waiting as though it was a hassle to help them. "This way."

Gray moved slowly to his feet, and Isla was sure he leant too heavily into the desk. She was exhausted but otherwise felt fine. They followed Michaels out of the small room and across the expanse of the building. The soldier had moved back to the door, and he did not to look up as they moved across the room.

"Do you need a hand?" Isla asked Gray as he staggered a little, but he shook his head. "How far?"

"Just here," Michaels said, holding his hand to a panel by the door. It slid open. "Beds there," he said, waving his hand to the right. "Kitchen there." He waved it to the left.

Isla stared at the blank, white walls and then put her hand to one. It disappeared, opening the space into a large dining hall. "Kitchen?" she asked. He looked a little confused again, as though it wasn't what he thought it was. Then he stepped in and headed to the end of the room. A large number of panels opened up to display replicators Isla hadn't seen since her time in the Elite. It would feed them, but it wouldn't be the same as real food.

She turned at the sound of a chair scraping across the floor. Gray had sat down and rested his head against the table.

"There is no one else here," Michaels said. "She wanted you to have full access."

Isla nodded and turned back to the replicator. She didn't know what they would be better doing, eating or sleeping.

She put her hand to the panel and thought of the tea she used to make Master when he was feeling unwell, but she was unsure how to describe the ingredients. The machine beeped, and a cup appeared. She pulled it out, sniffed at the contents and then walked over to Gray and sat it beside him.

"I don't need it," he murmured.

"You need something."

She returned to the replicator and, with the same thought, put her hand back on the panel. Another cup appeared. When she turned back, Michaels was smiling.

"Great, isn't it?" he said.

She nodded.

"Only the best for us. When we arrived, you had to ask, but it is like it knows your thoughts."

Isla nodded again as she took a slow sip of the hot tea. The effect was calming and revitalising. "Rohen," she said.

"Pardon," he asked, his face falling.

"The Rohen reads the request."

"Rohen?"

"It is everywhere," Gray murmured, and she noted he hadn't picked up the cup.

"But it can't read people. It can't determine how a replicator works."

She sipped again at her tea, and Michaels looked it over. His face paled somewhat. "It is in the tea?"

"I don't think so," she said.

Something glittered on the end of Gray's fingertips. Isla moved around the table to sit beside him. "Gray," she called softly, but he just murmured. For the first time, she wondered if instead of the Rohen being used by the people, it had moved through their world on its own. Perhaps it flowed through everything because that was how it could get close to them, work with them. She felt a strange nervousness, the cutting sharp blades flashing through her mind again.

"Gray, drink the tea," she said softly.

"Poisoned," the sikduer said, appearing in the doorway. Isla wondered if he was going to follow them around for their entire stay. She still wasn't sure exactly why they were there or if she would be able to help in the way she wanted. She wasn't even sure she wanted to help right now.

She took Gray's hand, closed her eyes and focused on the Rohen. Only she couldn't. She tried to remember her time in the caverns beneath the planet and the plants and animals she missed in the forests of Rennet. A groan from Gray and a growl from the soldier made her open her eyes. Her fingers were silver. The Rohen had moved from somewhere to coat her skin. Gray looked at her with wide eyes. As he reached for her, she stood and stepped back from the table. The bright fluid metal ran over her hands and then stilled as the hum of the soldier's weapon echoed through the too quiet room. She stepped back and put her hand to the wall, and the metal instantly disappeared into the hard white surface.

"Did that go into you or the wall?" Michaels asked, stepping forward and taking her hands. Pinned against the wall, she had little choice. He turned them over as he had with Gray when they had first come in from the garden.

"What happened?" Gray asked, standing more steadily by the table.

Isla shook her head. She wasn't quite sure. She hoped the Rohen didn't mean any harm. They had taken Gray in before, and yet it had clung to him and drained him—poisoned him? She had no idea.

Michaels guided her back to the table and sat her down, but his fingers had snaked around her wrist. He appeared to be taking her pulse.

"I'm not for experimenting on," she said, trying to keep her voice low and level. There had been enough of that.

"What did you tell it to do?" he asked, the excitement palpable.

"Nothing."

"You pulled it from his skin."

"I..." She had only asked, but she didn't want to share what she might be able to do with this man. She was certain the Hendra didn't want her to work with the metal, but rather to find a way to remove it. The Rohen, on the other hand, had different ideas. "Can we sleep now?" she asked.

Michaels nodded slowly as Gray stood back from the table.

"Drink your tea," she directed. He stepped forward, drank it down and then headed for the door. The soldier stood back, and they crossed the hallway into a large room filled with narrow metal beds. It reminded her of her Elite days. Too much of this was reminding her of training with the Elite. Surely scientists would have been given more comfortable quarters. She walked to the nearest bed and sat down. When the door closed, she half expected the soldier to be standing there watching them sleep.

She let out a long breath and lay back, looking up at Gray.

"What?" she asked as he leant over the bed.

"I kind of got used to sleeping with you." When she glared at him, he continued, "I would feel more comfortable sleeping closer to you."

She rolled out of the bed on the opposite side, indicated he move, and pushed the light bed up against the next one.

"Not quite what I had in mind," he said.

"Just go to sleep," she said, lying back down on the blanket.

"I don't think this is for scientists," he murmured.

"No," she agreed. "I don't think so either."

Thirteen

Isla couldn't sleep. The day's events—the whole lot of events that had led to this point—turned around in her head. She couldn't rest as the images rotated around and around in her mind, the fear building in her chest. As Gray's hand rested on her arm, she jumped.

"You aren't sleeping," he murmured.

"I'm trying."

"Not hard enough."

"Sorry," she said.

"I'm not having a go."

"Really?"

The narrow bed shifted as he raised himself up, and the dim light slowly increased. "Is it morning?"

"Sensor," she answered. It had been the same in the Elite—a reason they couldn't sneak in or out, and a way for the sergeant to wake them up by turning on the lights just by walking into the room.

Isla rolled over. Gray had an arm across his face to block the extra light, although his attention was focused on her.

"I'm sorry," she said again.

"Are you worried about the Rohen?"

"More than I was," she admitted. "I thought you were a friend of theirs, and yet they infected you."

"I'm not sure that was what it was, nor that it was deliberate."

"They accidently tried to kill you? I think the Rohen knows exactly what it is doing. What they are doing."

"Should we call them Rohendra?"

She wanted to shrug, but rolled back and looked at the ceiling. She knew she had no idea what was going on, but it all seemed to make less and less sense the more she discovered. Everyone wanted her to talk to the Rohen or hum, or whatever it was she did, although they all wanted something different, as did the Rohen themselves. She wasn't sure what it was. She closed her eyes against the increasing light to find the sharp blades flashing in the darkness. She drew in a deep breath as she sat up.

"I need the dark," Gray murmured, but he was wide awake and focused on her. "Are you going to tell me?"

"No," she said simply. She had to get her head around it before she shared. But then maybe if she talked it through, the whole situation would make more sense. She looked across at his pale blue eyes looking only at her, and the intense stare scared her more than the knives in the dark.

"You want a rifle? Or an old duster?"

"It might help," she said, smiling at the idea and the comfort it had given her. Not that it would save her from the Rohen. "Have you had dreams?"

"I'm not really getting enough sleep to have them. And I thought you weren't sleeping."

"Thoughts, memories."

He shuffled closer. "Memories of the attack, what happened, why you were there?"

She shook her head. "I had wanted to leave all that," she said. "The Elite, I didn't want to remember, even when I was given a story to remember."

"The racing." He nodded as though he fully understood why she had run to Urgway, hidden amongst the racing and obscurity, to a degree. It had seemed like a good idea at the time. She might have been seen, but not as the war hero any longer. Just a racer—just a face at the start line and statistics for enthusiasts.

"I don't want to talk," she said, rolling over with her back to him, hoping they were still enough that the lights would dim back down. Surely, they were set so people could move in their sleep. If they came on at every little movement, they wouldn't get any sleep no matter the time of day.

It was daytime, after all, although her ability to measure it was skewed.

"How long were we down there?" she asked.

"I don't know. I can't work it out. Hours, days."

"Could the Rohen..." She wasn't sure what she was going to ask or what she hoped he could answer. Neither of them knew what they were really dealing with. And even when she did, it surprised her, or scared her. She shivered at the idea. Then strong arms closed around her as Gray shuffled closer, his body on the narrow cot with hers. Although she wanted to elbow him sharply enough to send him several beds over, she appreciated the security he offered and stayed silent. Her fear ebbed away with the strength of his hold. He remained silent, and she offered a silent thank you as she closed her eyes.

"Do you think they have infected the Hendra?" she asked, remembering the odd look in the woman's eyes.

"Didn't they call her the queen? Maybe they have a relationship we don't understand," Gray offered in return, his breath too close to her neck. Despite the need to talk through the options, she needed sleep more. She wasn't herself, couldn't grasp what she or her crazy thoughts were doing. She had no idea if she was of use or being used.

It was dark when she opened her eyes again, unsure if it was day or night or if she was awake or dreaming. Gray's chest moved slowly beneath her head, a soft, regular sound indicating his sleep. The surety of his firm body beneath her was comforting and calming. But in the distance across the room, a soft light shone. She raised her head slowly, missing the warmth of

Gray against her cheek. The light disappeared and then reappeared beside the bed. She held tighter to Gray to stop herself from flinching away. Glancing around, she half expected the lights to come on.

She waited, desperate to ask what this being wanted, but although she tried to think of it as an individual, she knew without asking that they were one. That all the Rohen was connected. No matter where in the universe it was.

It bowed its featureless face, and she sat up slowly. The lights remained dark.

"Will you speak?" she asked.

It was odd that she knew it didn't need to, that they didn't need to. She could feel it like a hum moving through her body.

The feel of the metal beneath her fingers, the understanding she got when she was in the forest, working with the fungi and patting the cats. The universe suddenly made sense, and yet she felt as though she had less understanding than she did before.

The Rohen reached for her. She reached back as though it called to her, as though she needed to touch the hand more than she had ever needed to do anything in her life. The world changed around her as their fingertips touched, and she was lost and found in the same instant.

Gray stretched. The weight of the woman on his shoulder was surprisingly comforting, and he wondered if this closeness would continue. He was finding it harder to be away from her. Despite his fears at times both for and of her, he needed her, although he wasn't sure he could articulate why.

She blinked at him slowly, her silvery eyes catching the morning light illuminating the room. Something in him stopped, as though his heart failed to pump the blood he needed through his body. The door opened, and the soldier stepped in, his hand too tight on his gun. Gray moved slowly, whispering something he wasn't even sure of as he rolled them out to stand beside the bed. The cold eyes of the soldier were on him, and the woman was clutching at his arm as though afraid. Isla would never be afraid. Gray looked down as large silver eyes blinked back at him.

"Who are you?" he whispered.

He had done all he could to help the Rohen, and yet it had made him ill, poisoned his system. As he looked at the hand wrapped too tightly around his arm, he wondered if it would do so again, or worse.

"It's me," she said with Isla's voice, but it wasn't. He was certain. He shook his head once, and the eyes blinked before settling in a green he found even more unsettling than the silver.

"The scientist wants you to see something," the soldier said, stepping nearer.

Gray nodded and headed towards him as the being not-Isla walked too close behind, her hand too tight around his arm.

"Will you back off a little?" he murmured through gritted teeth.

The hold instantly loosened. She nodded once, her soft red ringlets, too neat, bobbing with the motion. Michaels sat at a table in the dining room, a portable screen before him.

"What is it?" Gray asked, wondering how long until they realised this Isla was too quiet to be the real thing.

"The garden," he murmured, still looking at the screen.

Gray moved around behind him to look at the screen, but he couldn't see anything. "What is it?"

Michaels held out the screen for him. He looked more closely, but all he could see was sand.

Isla made a hissing noise beside him.

"Exactly," Michaels said.

"I'm missing it," he said.

"Look at the garden," Michaels said louder, tapping the screen, and Isla's hand took his. Gray wanted desperately to pull away, but he allowed the movement as he studied the screen again.

"Has it moved?" he asked, looking at the sand again.

"It's gone!"

"Gone," Gray said slowly, locking eyes with the creature beside him. Then he looked down at his hand.

"What do you know?" the soldier asked unkindly, watching Isla too closely.

"Nothing," Gray said quickly.

"Ms Tarle," Michaels said. "Could I ask you to go out there again? I know it is a lot to ask. We can offer you..." He was pleading, looking out towards the wall and the garden that had grown beyond it.

Isla was studying the man as though he wasn't making sense. Then she turned, her hand still in Gray's, and tugged him with her towards the wall. It opened before them. The soldier shouted abuse as the scientist threw his arms up over his face. Gray tried to tug her to a stop.

"Stop!" he cried. "You have to stop."

She turned then, looking him over, and the wall closed to provide them protection from the sun again. "Stop," she whispered.

He nodded slowly, and she let go of his hand. "She would not wish you harm," she said, the voice not quite Isla's and yet hers at the same time.

Michaels nearly pushed him out of the way as a strange noise emanated from the back of her throat, like a growl but not. Gray wanted desperately to step back, but he didn't. She reached for his hand again.

"Isla," Michaels said, looking her over closely. She stepped in behind Gray again. "You will need something to protect you if you go outside." He said it as though talking to a child.

She shook her head and leaned against Gray.

"Give us a minute," Gray said. "Yesterday was a big day."

Michaels nodded, but he looked doubtful as he stared at Isla.

"Please."

Michaels bowed his head and dragged the unwilling soldier from the room.

"Who are you?" Gray asked as they left the room.

"Island Tarle," she said.

He shook his head and tried to pull from her hold. But the hand was firm.

"Island Tarle would like you watched over," she said.

"She left you here?"

"Not exactly. She was taken rather than opted to leave. I am to help you. I am to watch over you."

"You aren't doing a very good job, and I worry you will make me sick."

Her head turned a little to the side, her eyes flashing as she looked him over. "No, I am to keep you safe."

"Did you make me sick?" He pulled his hand from hers and then crossed his arms so she couldn't take it again.

She sighed, and he almost thought it was Isla. "No, Gray E'anah, we did not."

She looked down at the ground. He walked back to the table Michaels had been sitting at, pulled out a chair and sat down, then stood and pulled another out to offer her a seat. She took it with a nod, and then he sat back opposite her. "What made me sick?"

"Likely the heat. It has not affected Isla as much, but we forget you are not the same. Your kind is not made for the surface of Urgway, or at least some parts of it. Would you like to visit with your friend's family?"

"Reilly?" he asked. Then, as she nodded, he shook his head. He couldn't face them, not yet.

"They live in a special place. The land is sheltered; they can be comfortable in the sun."

"Why are you here?"

"We thought there would be risk to you if she was discovered missing."

"There is greater risk to you. They will think you something other than a hummer and cut you open to find the metal."

"We are all Rohen. Hummers are Rohen," she said as though he should understand that.

"What is a hummer?" he asked as the door slid open. The soldier stood there, his hold too tight on the rifle. Gray put himself between them, although he wasn't sure what good that would do.

"We need her to go out, and soon. The colonel is coming to check on things himself."

"Calder?"

The woman who wasn't Isla made a noise that Isla would have made if she were there. Something between anger and annoyance and fear.

Fourteen

H endra stretched and rubbed at her eyes. She wasn't sure how long she had slept, but she felt all the better for it. She focused on the dimly lit room around her and Alice resting in the chair opposite. She wondered how long Alice had been there. Had she offered any assistance for the pain she had felt earlier, or was she was simply watching her sleep?

Hendra searched the room for the familiar green liquid, but there was nothing. She sighed with the relief. She wasn't going to drink any more of it, no matter what that meant or what offence it might bring to her wife. She was done doing what was best for others; she had to look after herself. And it was clear from whatever had been happening to her over the last few weeks that no one else was looking out for her.

Not even Calder, she thought as she sat up slowly and leaned back into the soft cushions. She had slept well, and she felt more rested than she had in a long time. He might have watched over her, but then he had gone. All to do her bidding. She remembered the reports and strange claims from the previous evening. Was he trying to win her over for his own purposes?

"Hen?" Alice murmured, and she refocused on the slight blonde woman. What was it she had wanted from all this?

"Mmm," Hendra murmured as she swung her legs out of the bed. She stood slowly, feeling steadier on her feet than she had for some time, and headed for the door.

"I was worried." Alice's soft voice followed her out into the corridor, although the woman herself did not.

Hendra stopped. "Is my brother still here?"

"I don't know," Alice said, appearing in the doorway. "I could find out."

Hendra shook her head. She didn't need to see him. It had been odd to see them talking when she had woken in the hospital bed, and she wasn't sure she had seen them interact before. It was unsettling.

"Where are you going?" Alice asked.

"I thought I should see the doctors. They are so particular in monitoring me, I wouldn't want them to be worried."

"I let them know."

Hendra noted that Alice hadn't given any indication of whether they were concerned or not. She felt a different woman this morning, as though whatever had been sapping her strength had gone. She was sure their scans would show something very different today than the ones they had been running.

The room was empty when she reached it, as though they knew they didn't need to be ready for her again. She wondered then if they were more aware of what was going on, or of something she hadn't considered. Unsure where to go next, she paused at the door when a hand on her shoulder made her jump. Victor smiled a friendly smile, but it was one she couldn't trust.

They had all looked at her as though she might drop at any moment, as though there was a chance the world would be a different place—and they might like the idea.

"How do you feel?" he asked, appearing concerned.

"Better," she said. "Not that I was that ill."

"Of course not," he said quickly, but he looked at her like her father had when she was a child, indulging her as she worked through ideas and problems as though her solutions would save the universe. They would now. Now she had the answers to fix it all. "You did look tired last evening," he went on, walking into the room and looking out the windows. "But you carry so much responsibility, and now pregnant... You must look after yourself."

"I was just thinking the same thing," she said, coming to join him at the window.

"Your father would be proud," he murmured, still looking out over the view.

"I would like to hope so," she replied, turning to take in his old, brown features. How long had she known this man? All her life or just most of it?

"Have you done this for everyone or for yourself?" he asked, his focus still beyond the glass before them.

She stared, unable to read how he intended the question to be taken. He turned and smiled at her, although it was sad and perhaps a little disappointed. Did he not understand what she was doing?

"It isn't that I doubt you," he continued, taking her hand, his smile still sad, "but I wonder if you do the right thing for the right reasons. Your father would never have considered closing the mines, would never have limited the access to the rohen. And there are too many rumours."

"Rumours?" she asked, dreading what the universe said about her.

"That you are studying the rohen, seeing what it can do for you, how you might use it against the Complex to ensure your rule is absolute."

"My rule is absolute," she said with a laugh, as though they were all in on the joke.

He gave her a more disappointed and less sad glare.

She looked down at the floor as though her own father was disappointed in her.

"You need to be careful."

"I am. And all I do, I do for the Rohendra Complex—that I can promise you."

"You say that, but do you truly think so?"

"Of course," she said, more hurt by his words than she expected.

She shook the feeling off and looked back out over the city that spread as far as she could see. The centre of the universe, of the Complex, and the only planet she had lived on. Her child would also remain mostly within this building, guiding the people behind the scenes, keeping the world alive.

She remembered her surprise when they had found rohen on Rennet. She shouldn't have been surprised, but they had only ever mined it on Urgway. The metal flowed through the universe, and she wanted to be in control of that flow. She needed to be in control of the flow, to prevent it from taking control of them.

There was a subtle cough at the door, and she looked to see the doctor before he disappeared again. She took a deep breath and smiled for the man next to her. "I have work to do, Victor. We shall talk again."

"Of course," he said, bowing his head. "I'm glad you are well."

She bowed her head in return and headed out to follow the man in the too-white coat through another door. She silently sat on the narrow bench, lay back and closed her eyes as he moved the wand over her body. She could hear the gentle buzz of the monitor coming to life above her, but she didn't want to look.

At the continued silence from the doctor, she looked up and stared in wonder at the small blob moving around inside her. The fuzziness of past scans was gone.

"How do you feel?" He tried to keep his voice level, but the wonder was there. All she could do was nod. Whatever it was had cleared from her system. He stepped back and pressed a panel on the wall but didn't say a word. Hendra stared at the movement above her. She was healed. The child was well, and their futures were assured.

Hendra studied the scan as the doctor stood to the side and chewed nervously on his cheek. She was pleased that Victor hadn't stayed. She didn't need him here for this, but she couldn't see the issue.

"It is moving?"

The doctor nodded slowly, as though she might react badly.

"Heartbeat strong? Growing normally?"

He nodded again.

"I'm not sure I see the problem?"

"The infection, the odd…" He pointed vaguely to the scan.

"It is gone," she said. And she was sure it was. She didn't feel ill. In fact, she had never felt stronger, and she was sure that was in part due to the hideous green juice being banned. No matter what good her wife thought it did. Maybe Alice needed a holiday; maybe it had all been too much of late. She could return home to her forests.

"It might have infected the child," he said.

Hendra looked again at the scan. If it had, then they wouldn't be seeing this level of detail. "I am satisfied with my care," she said curtly, and the man appeared to relax somewhat. "You were more worried about yourself than my health," she snapped as she stood from the table. He backed up, shaking his head. "I am content," she continued, "enough that I won't take your head."

He bowed awkwardly as she strode from the room. She headed straight to her office. She could talk to Alice later about her health and the idea for a break. The office appeared much as it had before. She settled at the desk and looked over the document still open when she activated the monitors.

"Who wrote that?" she wondered aloud as she enlarged the report and leaned back in her chair. There was no author. Usually that wouldn't worry her—both she and Calder used a range of informants who did not wish to be named and received anonymous reports from various officials. But this worried her. She put it to the side and started rereading the various reports that had come into the office over the last few months. Many of which she hadn't paid proper attention to. None of them suggested anything of Calder.

She needed to see him. It had been too long. She just needed to be sure, and if he stood before her, she would know if he was lying. Or at least, she hoped she would. Alice had alluded to the idea that the man was not what she thought, that he would do what was best for him, yet Hendra was more certain of him than she was of her wife. She had created him, after all. And if he hadn't been willing to step up when required, he wouldn't be in the position he was now.

Her hand hovered over the communication panel. But she thought better of it. He had work to do, work she had sent him out to oversee. She didn't want to interrupt that. Although, that work involved the hero and her enforcer friend. Both of whom had far too much history with Calder and had escaped him in the past.

"Michaels," she said, placing her hand on the panel.

"Hendra?" a shaky voice returned.

She waited, but when he didn't continue, she cleared her throat. "How is my garden?"

There was another long pause, and she looked down at the green glow beneath her hand as though she might have lost the connection.

"Gone," he whispered.

She stood slowly, leaning on the desk, her hand pressing deeper into the panel. Then she moved her fingers across it and crossed her arms. "Find a monitor," she growled.

She heard mutterings and movement, and then his face appeared before her.

"Your Grace," he said, bowing awkwardly as his Adam's apple bobbed.

"Where is it?" she asked, trying to keep her voice level.

He shrugged and then collected himself. "We woke this morning to find it gone."

"Has the hummer been in it?"

He bowed his head and glanced over his shoulder. "And the man."

Really? she thought. *What are these two to each other?* "Have they explained it?" she asked.

"Not really," he said, disappointment evident in his voice. "The colonel will be here soon. He will get the information from them."

"I don't want her hurt," Hendra said quickly.

"I'm sure he can ask politely," Michaels said, glancing over his shoulder again. Then he stumbled, and Calder came into view.

"Tell me," she demanded.

"Are you feeling better?" he asked, his voice too kind.

"My garden, Colonel," she growled.

He cleared his throat and then shook his head, his face serious.

"Did she do this?" Hendra asked.

"I will find out. They spent some time out in the garden yesterday. She opened the wall of the building. Lucky the contaminates didn't kill us all."

"Keep them there and…" She wasn't sure what she needed to ask him or how to phrase it. She shouldn't be worried about offending this man.

"Hendra?" he prompted.

"Just find my garden," she snapped and disconnected. She thumped her hand on the desk and the monitor disappeared. A secretary stood in the doorway, looking more nervous than the doctor had earlier. Hendra wondered if she looked as well as she felt. "What?" she snapped at him.

"I have a message from your wife," he said, his whole body shaking. She wondered what Alice was doing now. Trying not to sigh, she waved the man forward and held out her hand for the message. But he shook his head. "She has gone home," he stuttered.

"Draroh or our rooms?" Hendra asked. Had she not just been thinking of sending Alice away for a while? Was this all because of the green juice?

"She did not say, but she is not on Rennet," he continued.

"She has her bracelet," Hendra said, a gift that ensured she knew where Alice was, mostly to ensure she could protect her.

"She was wearing it, but..."

"Are you sure she left willingly?" Hendra asked, coming around the desk as the man backed up.

"Yes. She stopped by my desk, her bag in her hand. But when I scanned to check, as I do often..." Hendra bowed her head. "There was nothing."

"Nothing?"

"Not even a blip," he murmured.

"She couldn't have destroyed it. She..." Hendra had no idea what she might be playing at with this sudden flee home. Alice hadn't returned to Draroh in a very long time.

"The ship?" she asked.

He looked at her blankly.

"Could the ship have been destroyed?" Panic started to close her throat. "Send a unit after her."

"I don't know which ship she took," he said.

"She didn't go alone. There must have been a pilot." Hendra stopped, an odd thought filling her mind. "Is my brother still on the planet?"

"No, he returned to Arnin after the meeting."

"Immediately after? Do we have a record of the ship leaving?"

"The Planet Chiefs are closely monitored for their protection, Your Grace."

"Check it," she growled. He bowed nervously and left the room. Hendra returned to her desk. If there was no indication what Alice had done or how she had done it, it must have been with someone else.

She pressed her hand back to the communication panel, the old man's gentle smile coming to mind. "Dekka," she called sweetly. "Did you take something of mine?"

"Your Grace?" a confused voice asked. "I can come to your office if you need me to. But I don't think so."

"You are still on Rennet?"

"I am."

She wondered why, but she wasn't going to probe. He clearly hadn't helped Alice disappear, unless she had taken his ship while he remained. But then, why would Alice need to disappear?

A doctor appeared in the doorway of her office, his face serious. She tried not to sigh. "I don't need you, Chief Brown."

He didn't get the chance to reply before she cut the connection.

She had not taken her eyes from the doctor. He looked serious, but not as scared as the other had, despite the health of her child and their future ruler. "It was in the juice," she muttered.

He nodded slowly. That explained why Alice had disappeared, and so completely. Was she trying to kill them both, or just the child? She might have tried to be supportive, but it wasn't her child. That might have been harder for her to accept than Hendra realised. She wouldn't have accepted anyone else's child growing in Alice. But Alice was something very different—it was why she had been drawn to her in the first place. Only it now appeared she had been very wrong on that front.

"What was it?" she asked, sitting down and waving the man forward.

"It appeared to be a pure form of rohen. Trace amounts, but it was enough to make you very sick, and the metal interfered with the scanners."

"Rohen?"

He nodded.

"How did she get her hands on rohen? Pure rohen?"

He remained non-committal. Hendra waved her hand over the communication panel, and the secretary reappeared in the doorway. "Send for Calder," she demanded, "and the top Elite soldier in the building. Any news on the ships?"

She waved the doctor from the room as the man stepped forward, more confident than he had been. "Your brother is not traveling directly back to his planet."

"Thank you." She waved him out to do as he had been requested and glanced back at the doorway, but the doctor appeared to be gone.

A soldier appeared in the doorway not long after, saluted and bowed low.

"Send word to Draroh that my wife is to be arrested the moment she lands, for treason."

He nodded once in understanding of the order. If he was surprised, he didn't show it. Then he was gone, and her communication panel was buzzing. She placed her hand on it, and Calder filled the monitor.

"I am needed here," he said, as though he would not consider a call from her as more important than what he was already doing.

"You were right about Alice," she said. He nodded. "Where would she get pure rohen?"

"A lab? A mine?"

"She hasn't travelled."

"I will ask for it to be reviewed. She shops—perhaps she met a contact somewhere on the way."

Hendra's stomach tightened. Who else might work with her to help kill her? That was what it appeared to be. Someone—Alice—trying to kill her. Hendra wondered what the woman thought she would achieve. She nodded once and cut the connection. Right now, she needed to discover just what harm had been done to her and her child, and who had lured Alice into such a plot. She certainly hoped it wasn't her brother.

No Hendra had been dethroned during their time in office. It was an office for life, and she planned for it to be a long one.

Fifteen

Suited up and standing in the space that had been the garden, Gray wanted to be as far away from here as possible. Perhaps the Rohen could take him to be with Isla, wherever that was. They had taken her, the other Isla had said—she hadn't gone willingly. He wondered if she was scared or worried.

He glanced across at the woman not-a-woman standing in the sun, smiling at the dirt.

"When did this disappear?" he asked.

"It hasn't."

"You aren't making sense," he murmured.

"It moved to somewhere safer," she said, as though it were simple.

"Safer?"

"These people..." She indicated the building, and Gray turned to see a face at the window he had really hoped never to see again. Calder. "They would cut it, study it. Why not just enjoy the beauty of what it is?"

"It is like the forests we found beneath the ground," Gray said.

She nodded, then turned her head to the side again as though trying to read him. He was reminded of the Readers for a moment.

"You would not betray the trees," she said.

He shook his head. Not that he had grown amongst them. But whatever the Readers had done to him, he felt the same understanding, the same protectiveness that Isla did of the forests. Even if it was not the forest she had grown in, they were all connected. The entire Complex was far more connected than he had realised.

"There is a relationship with that man," she said, her focus on the building again, but Gray didn't turn around.

"It is complicated."

"No, it is simple. He betrayed her. He hurt you both, but he will help her. I will protect you."

"Me?" he asked, almost laughing. Not that the real Isla couldn't protect him.

"She would be hurt if you were hurt."

"It isn't like that between us," he said quickly.

Her silver eyes flashed behind the tinted visor, and yet she remained silent. He wondered what the Rohen thought they were. Did he even care what they thought, or what Isla might think of him? Ever since the moment he'd thought he had killed her—too still beside him, too much blood on her clothing—a fear he had never known had filled him. They were in this together; that was all it was. They were doing what they had to for the Complex.

She smiled then, and an odd sensation filled his chest. She looked so like Isla and not at the same time. Whether he meant her harm or not, Calder knew her—he would see the Rohen for what it was before they made it two steps inside.

"Maybe we should leave," he said, trying to not look at her and not think about Isla.

"You are needed here. We are needed here."

"Are we? What for? The garden is gone."

"A distraction," she said.

"If he sees you, it certainly will be a distraction, but maybe not one we want. Couldn't you take me to Isla? I'm not sure I like being separated from her."

"You will find your way back to each other. You have, so far, even when you were going to leave her behind."

He opened his mouth but then closed it without voicing his protest. Maybe the Rohen was right. Maybe he hadn't been as good to her as he could have been. The same sick feeling covered his skin as when he'd thought she had lied to him on Oric.

"He will know," he tried again.

"Perhaps," she said, striding towards the window. In a rush, the anger on the face of the colonel scared Gray almost as much as the wall opening and her striding inside as though it were nothing.

The wall was still closing after him, and she was already removing her helmet.

"Hi Kalli," she said casually, as though they had only been chatting this morning. Gray tried to bite his lip as he removed his own helmet, to prevent his surprise giving her away.

"Decontamination," Calder said as his eyes narrowed and the too-perfect version of Isla grinned at him.

She managed to maintain it as they stepped out of the suits and the air nearly removed the top layer of Gray's skin. Without a word, Isla moved through to the dining hall. By the time Gray had followed her in—Calder, he was sure, hot on his heels—she was standing with a cup outstretched.

"It will be good for you after the time in the heat. You did not fare so well last time," she said politely. He looked, unsure what to do. Calder stopped behind him, and with a grin she added, "Weakling."

Gray snatched the cup and drank it down, feeling surprisingly refreshed. It appeared to be the same tea Isla had forced on him only the day before.

Michaels entered the room at a run, spotted Calder and skidded to a stop.

Calder looked between them and grunted something Gray didn't quite pick up, but the new Isla sat down immediately. Michaels was quick to follow. Calder glared at Gray, and he ran a hand through his hair before he pulled out a chair and sat down. Isla rested her hand on Gray's arm, then removed it almost as quickly.

"Where is the metal?" Calder demanded, staring at Isla.

She opened her mouth and, as Gray turned to face her, she closed it and nodded to him.

"The garden has moved," he said, as though it was the only explanation. The Rohen nodded beside him.

"Garden?" Calder asked.

"That is what we called it," Michaels mumbled, clearly disappointed. "Where?"

Gray shrugged, and the Rohen pressed Isla's lips closed. Sure he could see more silver than green in her eyes, Gray looked away to see if Calder saw it as well.

"Then how do you know it moved?" Calder asked, his tone indicating there was no patience there now or ever.

"Well, it isn't where it was," Gray said. "It might have melted into the surface. It can move through sand easily enough."

"Why would it do that now? It has been here for years." Michael sounded even more desperate and upset than Gray had expected.

"Hummer." It wasn't a question.

The Rohen glanced around, then focused on Calder. "Oh, you mean me."

Gray was sure Isla wouldn't have been this patient.

"Where is the garden?" Calder asked, leaning forward. His voice made the hairs on the back of Gray's neck stand up.

"It is not here," she said.

"Have you seen others?" Michaels asked.

She shook her head. He wondered if that was a lie and the Rohen could conceal the truth; but then, they had kept a lot hidden for a long time.

"No," she said, "I was just as much in awe when I arrived here as the scientist continues to be."

"Why was he out there with you?" Calder asked, turning his icy glare on Gray.

"He is important," the Rohen said. Gray looked at her and wondered whether that was another lie or a truth he didn't understand.

"I don't know what you think you are planning, but you are here to do as the Hendra needs you to do."

Gray was tempted to ask how she was. Isla had given him the idea that there was something more to the Hendra, and the Rohen had said something about her being their queen. He wondered just what she was up to and whether she realised she was doing what they needed her to do. If that was, in fact, the case. He wasn't really sure what was going on. So far, he was running after a pretty girl he just couldn't leave on her own, despite the fact that she could look after him much better than he had managed to hold on to her.

Calder's hard gaze continued to bore into him, but Gray couldn't answer his questions any better than his own.

Isla stretched and looked around the garden, at first wondering why the heat of the sun wasn't burning through her exposed skin. Her singlet top left her arms and neck exposed to the harsh light. But when she looked up, she realised they were not under the harsh sun. The silvery molten trees and shrubs glinted like they had in the sun, and yet it wasn't the sun she could se e.

At first it scared her. But the trees moved slowly, as though blown by the breeze, and she felt at home. She stood slowly. Her bare feet dug into the soft, cool sand. It was like the surface, only it wasn't. She couldn't see the walls she half expected that would tell her she was in the caverns beneath the surface of Urgway.

She walked between the trees, her fingers running over the bark-like texture of the trunks. She closed her eyes and continued, the feeling taking her far away to forests she knew. And then she was standing on the edge of the silver garden. The blue sky stretched out before her, the soft sand continuing into nothing.

She turned back, looking for a sign of someone, the figure she had seen in the room. How long ago had that been? How far had she been taken, and how was Gray to explain it when he had missed the whole encounter?

"Don't fear," a soft voice whispered behind her like the wind in the trees. She turned, and the gentle movement of the leaves continued. From behind a tree she had just passed, a silver figure emerged. "It is time for you to learn just what you can do."

She watched as the figure stepped closer. With every step, it became more solid and more human. When it stopped within a step of her, Isla froze to the spot and tried with everything she had to focus on the sand between her toes—anything other than the figure before her. The master appeared as he had in her memory of when she had left the colony, undamaged by the attack and familiar.

"I thought this would help," the master's voice said.

As she tried to form the right words to address the man she knew wasn't there, he changed back to the smooth, metal form, then dissolved or disappeared into the ground at his feet just as quickly. "Who else can you be?" she called after him.

"Anyone," the Hendra said, appearing with her self-certain smile. She curtsied before Isla, who laughed. The figure turned into Gray, and her smile slipped. The figure returned to its featureless form, its head tilting a little to the side. "He misses you too."

"Why have you separated us, again?"

"It was necessary. The garden had to be moved, and you need to know what you are. It seemed the best time."

"You had that opportunity when you took us from the garden the first time."

"They would have torn it apart to find you. He will always try to find you."

"Gray wouldn't do that to the garden," she insisted.

"Not Gray."

Isla shivered at the idea of Calder, and of Kalli, although she knew he would never be that man again. Just what he was up to, she might never know, and she wasn't sure she wanted to know. She might have started this to learn what the Hendra was doing, but the Rohen were in control. They knew what was happening and they, she was sure, were behind everything.

The Rohen held out a limb towards her, and she stepped back. Something tightened in her chest. He looked at the end of his slender arm, where a hand should be, and then back to Isla. Would she always fear?

"Why?" she asked.

"Come," he whispered. Something in the voice pulled at her like when she could feel the cats in the trees, when she knew the fungi and what she could make with the leaves. It pulled at the centre of her soul, her fear dissipating as she reached out and a hand formed. They linked fingers, the breath left her body as she stepped in closer and the Rohen closed around her.

Isla breathed out slowly as the darkness closed around her, and then she was standing in a white hall. Her hand still held tight to the silver fingers, far more solid than she imagined. As she glanced at the figure beside her, she wondered if it was solid all over or if her fingers would disappear into the liquid like the rest of her just had.

A cloaked figure appeared before her as though from nowhere. She looked around the odd, bright space for some indication of where she was, but there was nothing. The hooded figure bowed low, hands held before it, but she couldn't see any skin. Something gnawed at the edge of her stomach. Something like fear. As she started to pull from the hold of the Rohen, the being before her stood tall—taller than she'd thought—and raised covered hands. She stepped back despite the pull of the Rohen trying to hold her in place.

The arms kept rising, her heart rate increasing to something far higher than she had experienced recently, and then the hood fell back. A gentle face with silver eyes smiled, and she felt the tension lift from her shoulders.

"Welcome back," the deep voice rumbled through her, deeper than she expected. The silver eyes were a little unsettling. She couldn't be sure whether he was looking at her or the Rohen.

"Reader," she whispered, and his smile grew.

"I was not sure you would remember us."

"If only you had helped me to remember," she returned.

"But you did," he said slowly, the voice echoing oddly from the walls.

She looked down then. The Rohen withdrew from her hand, and as she turned it was gone.

"You know the Rohen," she said instead.

"We are all Rohendra," he replied, turning slowly. She looked beyond him to the room and the hooded figures that filled the space. They hadn't been there before—or had they been silent and she hadn't seen them somehow? They had dragged her from a ship once. Or had she gone willingly? Oddly enough for memory collectors, she couldn't quite remember.

"Am I on the moon of Oric?" she asked.

"I thought you were on Urgway."

"I was," she murmured, looking around again, but she couldn't remember. She had no idea where they could be. "I thought…" She wasn't actually sure what she thought.

"He is safe. He is watched over," the deep voice continued as though she had asked. "Gray E'anah."

"Did I think of Gray?" she asked.

"He is always on your mind. He is always close. They do not know you are missing."

She opened her mouth to ask how, but she closed it again. That wasn't the reason she was here. They wanted to see her and what she could do, although she was fairly certain these beings had a much better idea of what she could do than she did.

"I don't know what you want from me," she said, trying not to look into the silver eyes. "I don't know what you think I can do for you."

"You are a way for us to be heard."

"I'm certain you don't need me for that." The Rohen were powerful, but as yet the peoples of the Complex didn't know the metal they mined was a being that populated more of the universe than they did. "You outnumber us all."

"Your memories are not accurate," he rumbled, and a consensus went up from the group behind him. "Your memories are tainted with fear."

Isla shook her head. She remembered most of it clearly. The flash of the metal in the dim light, the pain.

"It could have been worse."

"You mean I could have died. Most days I think that would have been a better option," she admitted. "You could have killed me—you may have.

They needed a hero, and I was dragged back. It was only luck they dragged my body off that field."

"It was not luck."

Isla's heart stilled and her mouth dried. Why was it that so many knew so much more than she did about that day when she had been there? "Tell me the truth," she demanded, her voice low and calm. The being before her blinked and turned with a sweep of his arm, his hands still covered. Isla couldn't help but wonder what lay beneath the thick, rough cloth. The room was empty, white walls seeming to glow with a light of their own, and she was tempted to shield her eyes. They walked deeper into the space where a chair sat in the middle of nothing.

It was hard and metal, and she paused. It was everywhere, she could feel it; but then, these people were metal. Although she couldn't quite grasp if they were just as the featureless creatures, choosing a face for her, or if the Rohen ran through their veins.

He bowed his head, his hand outstretched towards the chair. She reluctantly sat down and was surprised at the soft comfort as it seemed to mould around her. She leaned back, closing her eyes against the surrounding bright light.

"You know exactly why your unit was there that day," his deep voice whispered over her.

"I heard them talking."

"No. She told you."

Isla shook her head, but an image of the Hendra filled her mind. She glanced at Kalli standing at the front of the group. He looked more serious than Isla had ever seen him. Isla's own heart beat fast. She'd been prepared to go into whatever situation they deemed necessary, but there was something about this—a hesitation, a fear. The Hendra had never addressed them previously, let alone lined up ready to deploy on whatever mission she had for them. This was frightening. And when she glanced at Kalli, he gave nothing away, his gaze fully focused on the Hendra.

"We are under threat. The Rohendra Complex has been compromised by a race we have not seen before."

Isla had thought she meant visitors from another world or galaxy. She had not expected the threat to already be here, to have been in the universe longer than they had. Although the Hendra explained the threat, she didn't explain the extent of it.

"There is a group on the surface of Urgway. We will go in after dark as they have the advantage in the sun."

It seemed odd, now that she was reliving this, that she would willingly remain on Urgway after all she had survived.

The image before her shifted to her standing in the dim light of the garden. The metal was bright around her, reflecting the setting sun as the world cooled. Heat radiated from the sand and the odd metal before her. It was a sculpture, something that someone had created, she had tried to tell herself, and yet she could feel the forest even then. The creatures came from the dark, the world dissolving into fear, blades, screams and weapon fire.

Why hadn't she remembered them when she had seen them in the lab, and then again in the trees? Why was her fear not overwhelming?

"You know the truth of what and who we are," he rumbled as though reading her mind. She focused on his face then, his odd eyes. They were Readers.

"She sent us in to destroy you."

"She did not understand what we were. What we are to the universe."

"Why hasn't she tried again?"

"She has, in different ways."

"Have her ways included the Elite? Or just Calder?"

The Reader before her stood straight, looking away from her, and she wondered just what threat he truly was. She feared Calder despite knowing who he had been before, or what she'd thought she had known of him.

It was suddenly too hard, as though she didn't want to know. Not that long ago, she had wanted to know it all, had wanted to really understand.

"Why does she want you gone?"

He turned back to her with a smile, and she realised he was waiting for her to come to an understanding on her own. Not that she thought she had the understanding—there was still too much that didn't make sense. The Rohen were everywhere. Whether or not she fully understood just what they were, it would be impossible to win an advantage over that.

"She knows that she is not in control," his deep voice rumbled through her.

"I assume the Hendra before her had a similar understanding."

"To some extent, they understood the need for us. The reason the universe cannot survive without us. And yet they may not have fully realised why."

"You are everywhere," Isla said aloud. "Will you tell me?"

"You know in your way. We do not need to say it aloud."

"Don't we?" Isla said too quickly. She wasn't sure that she understood as much as they thought she did.

"We are the universe," he whispered. "We are the reason for life. We are the Rohendra."

She did understand then, the feeling of the metal throughout every surface and being within the universe. "Where do I fit?"

"You are Rohen," he said as she shook her head. "You are Rohen," he said more firmly, leaning forward. His strange, solid metal eyes saw into her very soul without focusing on her. It scared her as much as the memories of the blades.

"You would have known what I was as they cut into my skin." She was certain. They seemed to know her, and yet they didn't. Would they endanger her if she was one of them, or part of them?

"Gifted, your master had said."

She nodded. She had always hated the term, and yet she had called for a gifted one herself at the colony. "How many?" she asked. He smiled and then slowly raised the hood over his face. "You wanted to see what I can do."

"No, Island—we want you to see what you can do."

She stood slowly from the chair and followed him from the empty room, the bright light not as harsh as it had been.

She stopped as the hooded figure continued into the hot, bright sunlight. He turned then, waiting, and she hesitated, unable to step into what she knew would kill her. "I am reassured," he said, walking back towards her, "that you do not want to die."

"If I am Rohen, would it matter?"

"You are Rohen," he said firmly, as though he had to reinforce his earlier words. "And yet you are not as we are."

She blew out a long breath. He wasn't going to tell her without making this hard.

"We are connected, all Rohen, and thus you are connected. In many ways we are one, and yet we are different. The liquid metal you feel around you, the solid beings and plants are the same and yet not quite, and then there is us."

"Am I like you?"

"I may be more Rohen than you, but you contain it. It flows in your veins. Others may not detect it, but it is the reason you can connect to the land, the forests and the animals. The reason the master called you gifted. There are many like you, although some may be more connected to the

Rohen than others; it depends on whether they appreciate the connection or run from it."

Isla held his gaze. She might have run from much, but not her skills. She still practiced despite not understanding the connection to the land until more recently.

"Why hummer?" she asked.

"You feel the hum of the heart of the universe. You hear the Rohen."

"Is Gray connected?"

The soft face smiled beneath the hood, and she wondered if they chose when they were completely hidden. But he didn't answer.

"You didn't answer my other question either," she murmured.

"Which was that?" he asked, turning away again.

"That you knew what I was when you cut into my skin."

"That is not a question."

Isla stepped out into the sun after him, ready to scruff him by the back of the hooded cloak. And then, as the hot sun touched her skin, she sucked in a scared breath and longed for her military-issue cloak. It was around her shoulders then. She pulled the hood up and raced after the Reader moving quickly across the sand.

"How?" she asked.

"How do you change the fungi to cream? How do you remove what would kill others?"

Isla opened her mouth and then closed it. She wasn't really sure. It was just the way it went as she worked through the process. "What did I change?"

"The sand at your feet," he said as though it were nothing. Just what was he trying to do?

She stopped, squatted down and collected a handful of hot sand. It burned against her skin, but she held it tight, thinking of gloves. Then the sand was gone, and she was protected from the sun. She stood slowly, looking after the man who walked into the distance. Had she wished for protection and the sand provided? She could feel the Rohen around her, in the sand, in the gloves and in the fibres of her clothing.

"I can direct it?"

"In a way," he called back.

"Can I direct you?"

His laugh travelled across the sand, but he didn't look back. She raced to catch him up.

"Why did you try to kill me?"

"Did we?" he asked. Her fingers moved absently to the dip in her collarbone, annoyed to find it gone. He stopped then and looked back. "We had a message to send the Hendra. It was an acceptable loss. We did not kill you."

"Are you sure?"

He nodded slowly and motioned for her to follow.

Sixteen

Isla ran her fingers over the material of the cape around her shoulders. It felt the same, and yet she was highly aware of the Rohen within it. She had become more and more aware of it surrounding them of late. She stopped, the hooded figure moving away from her, and squatted to run her hands through the hot sand. Despite the gloves, she could feel the heat, the texture of the grains, the Rohen. She closed her eyes and felt the sun blocked against her skin. She opened her eyes and stood as the hooded figure stood over her.

"I need to understand."

"You do understand."

Isla shook her head. She felt it, she understood it, and yet she didn't know what it was. If she had always been this way, always connected to the Rohen like only a few others, why had she only recently felt the connection? "Some are more connected," she thought aloud, thinking of Ebberah's child.

"She has allowed herself to feel."

Isla blinked at him. But instead of continuing, he turned and walked away across the sand. She hurried her steps to keep up. There was nothing around them, and she wasn't sure what they might be headed towards.

"She has more skill?" she called out, but he continued in silence. "What about Gray?"

Isla bit back her frustrations as she followed the silent Reader across the sand. They were different forms of the same. Did that mean they were the same species, or something different like the other species of the Complex? There were more kinds of people than she had seen. Some kept to themselves while others mingled and worked, adapting to different languages and ways of life. The Hendra was always human, she noted and then bumped into the back of the Reader, startled that she had been that lost in her thoughts. They were standing in the middle of the desert, the sun just as hot above them.

She came around to stand before the man who stared at her. "Gray?"

"He asked, and we could not let you die. You are needed, Island."

"What for?"

"Close your eyes and tell me what you feel."

"Scared, frustrated…" She stopped at his glare. She sighed, closed her eyes and allowed herself to focus on the air around her, the warm sun, the grains of sand beneath her feet. The hum of Rohen in the Reader. The hum far beneath her feet. She opened her eyes and mouth, but he slowly shook his head.

She closed her eyes again, listening to the world around her, imagining the cool forest of her childhood, and then they were slipping through the sand as though the world had opened beneath her feet. Soft, warm metal closed around her.

Isla opened her eyes to the science facility. Her cape and gloves gone, she only wore her white singlet, her sandy-coloured combat trousers and no shoes. Had she been walking barefoot through the hot sands of Urgway? Panic closed her throat. In the dim light, moving silver shone. Her heart rate increased, her hand reaching for a duster that wasn't there—and then it was, as though she had conjured it from nothing.

She looked at the weapon in her hand, the solidness of it, and felt the hum of the mechanism within it. In the silence that surrounded her, it disappeared. Isla looked around, and the garden came into focus as though it hadn't been there before. "Did I do this?" she asked.

"What are you asking?"

She stared at him. He knew more of what went on in her head than she did herself. He knew what she was asking. "The garden?"

"No, we did this."

"The weapon, the people, the Rohen," she corrected quickly.

"We are what we are," his voice rumbled around the cavern. "We are no threat to you."

"But you think I might be a threat to you." The realisation surprised her. "You needed me alive."

"We do. We would foster all those who are Rohen."

"And those who are not?"

"We protect him." There was almost a hint of hurt in his voice, as though she should not have doubted him. But who was the "him" they protected? Gray? Was it that important to her that he survive? She had lost many before.

The Reader lowered his hood, silver eyes crinkling around the edges as he smiled warmly.

"I needed to find out what Hendra planned. Ebberah is worried. The risk to hummers is very real."

"Only to those who do not understand."

"I don't understand," she insisted, her voice too loud and echoing from the cavern. The garden shifted. She was sure she heard movement, but as she looked at the trees and shrubs and silver flowers, there was nothing but the slightest movement to indicate the wind moving through them.

She stepped forward and ran her hand over the bark of a tree, then stepped back. It didn't feel the same as it had before. It didn't feel like the forest. The memory of another being stepping out from behind the trees startled her backwards, and a soft hand rested on her shoulder.

"We will not harm you," the deep voice of the Reader vibrated through her.

"You have before," Isla said before she thought of the words. She wasn't sure she could trust them. They weren't giving her enough to trust yet.

"We need you." He said it as though it were an admission of weakness.

"There are enough of you that you could destroy all life in the Complex before anyone knew where the threat came from."

He raised his eyebrows and tilted his head to the side with his solid silver eyes unfocused. She shivered at the movement. "That is not of benefit to us or the Complex."

"You need us as we need you," she said.

He bowed his head.

"What do you want me to do?"

He smiled but said nothing. She waited. He picked a silver flower and presented it to her. She took it, sensing the heaviness of the metal and the feel of the forest in the narrow stem. The flower wilted in her hold as though it needed the connection to survive. She placed it back on the plant it had been picked from, and the metal flowed seamlessly together. The flower tilted back upwards, petals opening wide.

"You need to be connected," she said. "All of you."

"We are. Although the Hendra would attempt to break that connection."

"How?"

He shook his head. Isla wondered just what experiments were happening in the laboratories around the solar system, how many other hummers they might have collected along the way to use. Not that she had done very much in her short time in captivity. She had watched the Rohen, tried to talk with it. That wasn't quite it either.

And it had drained her so much, the effort. "Why don't I get tired now when I talk with the Rohen or use it?" She indicated the cape that she no longer wore.

"Because you aren't trying anymore. You have allowed it in."

"I'm trying," she said.

"Your understanding has grown, and your connection is stronger."

She wasn't sure that was true, but she was more aware of the Rohen all around her.

"I..." She wasn't sure what she needed or what she wanted to know, but she was still struggling to trust the Rohen. Any of it. "Is there a number?"

He cocked his head to the side again. "No."

"I understand that you outnumber the rest of us, that there is more Rohen in the Complex than all the other species combined. What is the number? How many of you are there?"

"We are more," he said, his voice low.

"More than us?"

"Just more. We do not define ourselves as a number. We cannot define ourselves as such, for we are one and yet we are many."

"Your different forms are connected." She knew that; it made sense. She had thought it was all one, but it wasn't. She refocused on the flower growing at her feet. In many ways, it was like the carbon in every cell that connected the life of the planets and their people. But the Rohen was an element that flowed through everything as well. It formed various peoples but then connected them in a much more physical sense than carbon did the rest of the population. "You know what other forms know."

He smiled. It worried her more than she could understand. They were connected, as she had said. But it was more than that. They were one. Every particle of Rohen, no matter the form, was connected to every other. They understood it all because they saw and knew it all. Even if they were the threat the Hendra feared them to be, there was no way to defeat them—no way to remove them from the universe. It would be like trying to remove carbon from the universe. It just wasn't possible.

"You don't need me," she said, taking a step back.

"We do." His voice was softer, kinder, but his unseeing eyes seemed to stare beyond her. "You are the way to stop the Hendra."

"Stop her? She can't destroy you. What is the harm?"

"She might hurt herself and her people by trying to win against something you understand she cannot."

Isla nodded. She did understand that. "What if there was another Hendra?"

"There will always be another, one who follows. One has always followed the next, but she is different. This Hendra is not like those who have gone before. She might end the Complex and all of us with her."

"End the Complex? You mean destroy it."

"She is not as focused as she should be."

"Alice?"

"It is more than one element, more than one person. It is many steps that have brought us to this point. She must find her way."

"You want the mining to continue?"

"It is a sacrifice, or at least it appears that way. We give and the Complex uses, and in turn it strengthens us. She is searching for something that cannot be given, and she cannot be allowed to find it."

Isla wondered what they weren't telling her, what other aspect there was to these people that would bring about the destruction of the whole universe.

"She doesn't trust me," she said.

"He does." His voice was firm, his stare hard.

"You don't mean Gray," she murmured.

"He could be your greatest ally."

"Calder is my greatest enemy at the moment. If he could see me dead, he would ensure it happened."

The Reader reached forward and brushed at her wayward hair, his fingers cool against her skin. He closed his eyes. His face looked sadder when she wasn't focused on the solid metal eyes. "He is still Kalli."

She pulled out of his reach, the anger building in her chest threatening to overwhelm her. "He was never Kalli," she spat, surprised at the hate that laced her words, the sharp stab of pain that sliced through her chest as she said them. For so much of her life, she hadn't known who she truly was or the people around her. Her mistrust of Gray had been one of those moments of regret, and she hoped he was what she hoped he was.

"He will help." Then the Reader was gone, and Isla was alone in the garden.

"Which one?" she screamed into the empty space, her voice echoing through the cavern. Nothing responded. Now she was even more uncertain of the encounter. Maybe she hadn't really met with them... But she could still feel the icy touch of his fingers against her skin. She moved into the garden, looking for the comfort of the forest.

The conversations with Calder couldn't really be called conversations. They were him trying to determine information, and not in a friendly way—and then not listening to the response because he clearly didn't believe it. The longer the interaction went on, the more frustrated Gray became and the more he wanted to take the woman beside him by the hand and leave. Although she wasn't a woman, and he didn't know where to go. Nor whether he should leave at all, because Isla could come back.

He sighed and pushed the chair back, making a loud scrape across the floor. The room dropped to silence. All eyes were on him, including the Rohen disguised as Isla. He wanted to scream, and then Calder was pushing to his feet and Isla appeared across the room. She looked tired, her face flushed as though she had been running, her hair fuzzy. Gray stepped forward and took her in his arms before he thought about whether it was a good idea or not. She actually leaned into him before she pushed out of his hold, swatting him off as though he were an over-attentive grandmother. Her eyes focused on the woman at the table.

Calder had stood in the meantime, his chair squealing across the floor, open mouthed until he realised Gray was looking at him. Then he snapped it shut and narrowed his eyes. "I knew there was more to this."

"Anything you want to share?" Isla asked. She sounded as tired as she looked. "You have known far more than anyone else involved in this. Other than you, perhaps," she said, turning to the woman still sitting at the table.

She bowed her head and stood slowly, the movement far more graceful than Gray imagined the real Isla could manage. The difference was so stark, to him at least. Calder still looked from one to the other in confusion.

"You may leave," Isla said.

"May I?" the Rohen said in Isla's voice, and Calder leaned forward across the table. "Or should I?"

Isla crossed her arms, and Gray wondered how Calder had ever confused the overly polite version as the woman herself. "You are not needed."

"I am always needed. We are always needed."

"And you are always close. I appreciate that you will come when I really need you. I don't need you for this."

She bowed her head as though in agreement, or acquiescence, and then dissolved into a puddle of Rohen and disappeared into the floor.

Calder sat heavily in the chair. It made a noise as his weight shifted it across the floor, and his body made a strange *oof* sound as he landed. Isla only glanced at him and then back to Gray. Despite her pushing out of his hold only moments before, he rested his hands on her shoulders to reassure himself that she was real. He gave her a gentle squeeze. She nodded, a small smile pulling up one corner of her mouth, and then her hard focus shifted to Calder.

"What did I miss?" she asked.

"Not much," Gray admitted. "He's trying to prove he is the top dog."

Calder's cold gaze zeroed in on him, and Gray smiled in return.

"He couldn't even tell that wasn't you."

"Good likeness," Isla admitted. "It didn't fool you?"

"Wrong colour eyes, and the hair was too neat."

She let out a laugh that was almost a snort and then gave him a genuine smile.

"Are you ok?" he asked. As much as he wanted to know where she had gone, what had happened and what it meant, he didn't want Calder knowing any of it.

"She called me Kalli," Calder stammered.

Gray looked at him, wondering why that was the key takeaway from the experience.

"They know who you are," Isla said. But her eyes only rested on him for a moment, as though it was hard for her to accept. Again, Gray wondered what had happened, what she had been told and what she might tell him. "We need to go," she said, her eyes on Gray—her perfect green eyes.

He almost shook his head to remove the odd thought, but he had missed her far more than he realised he could, far more than he wanted to admit to anyone, including himself. "Where?" was all he could manage, and then he wasn't sure it was loud enough for her to hear.

"Ebberah. I have questions."

"So will she," Gray said without thinking, then glanced at the man still sitting at the table, staring at the woman across from him.

"What Hendra needs me to find here has gone."

He nodded slowly.

"I must return to Oric."

"What did you do?" Calder whispered.

Isla leant over the table as though interrogating him. "What did you do, Kalli? What did you become, and what is the Hendra trying to do?"

He looked up at her, confusion flickering across his features before they settled into the usual angry hatred he always seemed to wear around her. "She is in danger," he growled.

"She has put herself there, if that is the case. They want to protect her," Isla said, turning back to Gray, "but if she continues as she is, she will destroy everything."

"You don't know what you are talking about," Calder growled.

"I know the Rohen is worried." Isla's voice dropped to a low whisper. "And if they are worried, it is clearly a problem bigger than the Hendra can fix."

"She is *the* Hendra." He crossed his arms as though to end the conversation, as though that were enough to solve all the problems of the universe.

Gray studied her set expression. She was back, the woman he had met in the desert. He wrapped his arms around her, pulling her reluctantly against his chest. She surprised him by wrapping her arms around him in return, and Calder growled something as he stomped from the room.

"We're leaving him behind, right?"

She sighed and clung tighter.

"Seriously?" He looked towards the door the large man had stomped through. He wasn't the man Gray remembered from so long ago, and he still seemed to want them dead.

"He'll help," Isla said as though understanding what he was thinking. "Or so the Rohen think."

Seventeen

Hendra waited too long for Calder to connect. It hadn't been so long ago that they had been talking, and she needed him here. Alice had not disappeared to Draroh with Chief Brown, or at least it didn't appear that she had. Hendra had tried to gather more information, but very little was coming. There was no indication of Alice's location—or Solon's, for that matter, and her fuzzy memories resurfaced of their conversation while they thought she'd been sleeping.

She couldn't trust if they were her memories or just what she thought she had heard. She hadn't been well at the time. The infection, which appeared to have disappeared, had ravaged her body, or at least hidden it from the scanners. Rohen. Where had Alice found Rohen, and why would she think feeding it to her was…what? Hendra had no idea what Alice might have been thinking, or even if she understood what she had done. Had someone else contaminated her supplies? Had the Rohen already been in the produce when Alice had used it to prepare the drinks?

"I am dealing with something here," Calder snapped.

"I'm sure it can't be more important than my missing wife."

He paused, as though he thought it might be.

"Alice?" another voice asked, and he looked off the screen.

"Is that the hummer?" Hendra demanded. Had the whole world been turned on its head?

"There has been a... development."

"Calder, the rohen can wait. I need you to find Alice."

"The hummer wants to go to Oric."

"I don't care if she... Why?" Hendra caught herself. She wasn't thinking as clearly as she should. Wasn't paying attention to all she should. And now her wife had not only been trying to poison her—to what end, she didn't know—but she had disappeared.

"They need to..." He waved his hand, and Hendra disconnected. Neither of them were making any sense, and she didn't know if it was something she should allow. Calder would know what to do. If the hummer was to run back to Ebberah, he would be there. Although she really wanted him searching for Alice.

A secretary raced into the room and bowed stiffly. He was followed by the Elite general who would do as she asked, but he wasn't Calder. The secretary retreated and closed the door.

"Is there any news?" she asked, sitting forward and wondering who else might be involved. "Is there any connection to Oric?"

The man looked confused for a moment, then shook his head. "There is no sign of the First Wife on the planet."

"I knew that much," she snapped, standing and striding around the desk. He kept his stance the same. "She can't have disappeared. There is a tracker in her bracelet, and someone must have seen something. Where is her manservant?"

"Also missing."

"Is he responsible in any way for the Rohen finding its way into my hideous green drinks?"

"Thankfully, it appears to have left your system without lasting damage."

She nodded slowly, remembering the scans and the odd writing that had moved along the screen. The doctors had thought it a glitch—she had thought it a message. An unknown language. A sick feeling filled her, chilling her to the bone. She refocused on the man before her when he put a hand on her arm.

"Are you well, Hendra? Call the doctor," he cried. She shook her head. "I don't think you are as well as I heard; you have lost all colour. Please, Hendra, sit down." He guided her to the long table in the room and the nearest chair.

She sat down, thankful that her legs had managed to carry her there. "I've just had a sickening thought," she admitted as a doctor burst into the room. She waved him away, but he squatted down before her and, without asking for permission first, took her wrist and measured her pulse. He raised a wand, scanned over her body and then stepped back to look at a tablet.

"Your heart rate is elevated," he announced after a short time. "But the infection does not appear to have returned."

She waved him away again, and he disappeared.

"What do you need me to do?" the general asked.

Hendra wasn't focused, not like she should be. She hadn't been for too long. This child was important, more important than even Alice had understood, yet she hadn't been herself since the moment it had been conceived.

"I need you to find the First Wife. I need you to determine, through any means necessary, who else she was working with or for. And I want you to lock her away somewhere safe and secure where no one will be able to reach her but me."

He stood, bowed low at the waist, saluted and headed out of the room.

Why was she having to explain to these people what their jobs were? They shouldn't have to be told. She couldn't do everything.

The comm at her desk beeped softly. She stood, steady on her feet, and walked toward the desk. Would Alice be working with the rohen? Did she know what they were, and did they—it—think it could use the woman against her? She would find a way to isolate them. The glass went a long way, or at least it had appeared to. She had watched the footage of the hummer disappearing in the lab. In the tube one moment and then not. Hendra was almost certain she had caught sight of something else in there with her, but she couldn't quite see it.

The comm beeped again. She put her hand to the panel, hoping it was someone with news, and her brother appeared. "Solon," she whispered, trying to keep her voice level. "Has something happened that you would not be heading home?"

"Are you tracking me, sister?"

"It is my solar system, and I have lost something."

"I haven't taken anything of yours," he said, smiling. "It isn't like when I was a child. I would have liked to have said when we were children, but we never were children together."

"No," she muttered, "we weren't." She wondered then, if they were closer, might he have been more supportive? But she didn't need his support. She just had to be sure he wasn't working against her. "Where are you going?"

"Home," he said. "That wasn't why I called."

Hendra looked towards the door. She had been told he wasn't headed back to Arnin. "What?" she snapped.

"Felice would like to meet with you. She thought she could offer some support or advice, but I didn't think you would take that about the baby."

"What baby?"

He stared into the monitor.

"Who is Felice?" she asked, shaking her head. She was too scattered to deal with her brother.

"My wife," he said, a small smile lighting his face. It surprised her more than the offer. "We have three of our own. It can be challenging with the first. She thought you could use the family support."

"I haven't met her."

"She would like to meet you."

Hendra shook her head. "I have more important things to consider at the moment."

"What have you lost?" he asked, concern creasing his brow. Then he looked off to the side and nodded once.

"Is Alice with you?"

"No," he said, his focus intense. He didn't even shake his head. "Has something happened?"

"Goodbye Solon." She pressed the comm and sat back in her chair. Something was off with him. She might only see him for meetings, and then he rarely came to Rennet. He was too often linking in, as many of them did. But it was never the same as having them all in the room together. They had been together recently, and she was sure it had been just to see her fall over.

"Draroh has acknowledged your request," a secretary said, poking his head through the door.

She nodded once, and he left, closing the door loudly on his way out. She leaned forward and rubbed at her temples. Now she was developing a headache. But she was sure that was the stress.

She pressed her hand to the comm once more.

"Are you feeling unwell?" came a serious voice.

"The scans you took that you couldn't quite read," she said. "I would like you to forward them to me."

"Yes, Great One."

It appeared instantly on her screen. The same grainy image, which told her nothing. The same fear filled her chest as when she had first looked at it. But there was nothing along the bottom of the screen. She scrolled back through other scans the doctor had sent from before the infection. Her name appeared on the bottom of the monitor along with what they were looking at. The date, the time.

She went back to the latest one. Only a blank black line marked the bottom of the scan. Was it a glitch? Was it that the computer couldn't read what it was trying to send due to the Rohen in her system?

"Hendra" flashed in the black band, as though it would have been there already. She rewound the short clip and started it again.

"You will not find what you seek here" scrolled across the bottom of the screen.

She rewound and started one more time. The blank black line was present, but not the text.

She lifted her hands from the desk, and everything closed. The lights on her comm panel winked out.

The secretary popped his head back in the door. "Umm, excuse me."

"I appear to have lost power," she said, still looking at the desk.

"Communications and screens are out. Lights are still on."

She looked up at the man and scowled. "I can see that, thank you."

He bowed his head and disappeared. The entire building, it appeared, had been affected. She wondered if it was the virus or infection or whatever it was that had screwed with the scan that had impacted the rest of the building. If it could have done so, then surely it would have when the scans had been taken.

She couldn't reach anyone to ask the question. Michaels or even Warren would have been useful at this stage. What was Michaels doing with the hummer? Was he fine for her to leave, or was he going with her? What was on Oric that she would find of use?

"What did the rohen want to keep hidden?" she wondered aloud. Their very existence, perhaps. She wondered what the hummer had found at the garden. Hendra had hoped she would find a way to talk with them, a way to keep them from her Complex, or maybe a way to remove them.

Isla watched the tall man as he led the way to the ship. It was one she knew well, one she had travelled in, and yet the shiny metal of the hull made her pause. Gray gave her a friendly nudge from behind, but her feet weren't working with rest of her.

"You wanted to do this," he said. "You were the one insistent on travelling to Oric. What do you think you can find there?"

"More answers," she murmured, but she wasn't really sure that was the reason. She had been on the moon of Oric herself just the day before, in the strange cavern of the Readers, if that was what it had been. They could move—she could move. She stared at the ship parked in the hot sun. She could find her way to anywhere she wanted. With just a thought, she had done that very thing.

Ahead of them, Calder stopped, and she wondered if the Rohen were right about him. If he was really the help that they said he would be, if deep down he was still Kalli, if he still cared. But when he turned his severe glare back on her, she wasn't sure they were right. Kalli was long gone, and Calder wouldn't give up the power he had to help him return.

"The Hendra is annoyed about this," he murmured, walking back towards them. "Have you changed your mind?"

"Isn't she more concerned for Alice?"

Isla looked back at Gray, who raised his shoulders as though he had no idea what the Hendra should be focused on. Calder groaned and looked at a small panel in his hand.

"Do you know what has happened to Alice?" Isla asked, unsure how she felt about the woman. She had thought they were on the same side, that Alice had been helping them, and she had still delivered them directly into the arms of the Hendra.

"Not missing," he murmured.

"Found?" Gray asked, but Isla had the sense that he meant something very different.

"She has run," Calder growled, and Isla remembered just how dangerous he was. The hatred was evident in his voice. "I said she couldn't be trusted."

"When?" Isla asked, and he turned his focus on her. "When did you say that?"

"Before all of this, before the Hendra became ill."

"I don't think she is ill," Isla said, squinting into the light beyond the forcefield above them.

"She was poisoned, infected with something."

"I don't think that was the case," Isla said again, although she wondered what the Hendra thought had happened to her and who might have been responsible. She looked at the gruff features of the man before her, his shoulders set. "You think Alice was responsible."

"She wouldn't have run if she weren't. I told Hendra that the woman was not what she thought."

"Who did you think she was working with?" Isla asked. Gray gave her a quizzical look, as though she might know. But Isla could only guess at who might have swayed the First Wife to take such a risk. The Rohen might be involved somehow, but Isla doubted they would put themselves at risk of discovery. "She is gifted," Isla said aloud, surprising herself.

Was Alice also a hummer? Was she someone the Rohen would talk to, share with? Not that they had shared much with Isla—but they were wanting something from her. Everyone wanted something from her.

"What is Hendra planning?"

"When she catches her?" Calder asked.

"No, with the Rohen."

He glared at her. "Why am I helping you? Why am I flying you about the solar system?"

"You don't have to," Isla said, trying to smile. But the cold eyes staring at her prevented any smile from forming. "I could take us to where we need to go," she murmured. But she wasn't sure she could. Maybe she could drag Gray with her, but she couldn't take them both. Although, looking at him now, she wanted to be as far away from Calder as she could get.

"Where would Alice go?" Gray asked.

"Draroh," Calder mused. "But surely she would know we would be waiting."

"We aren't."

"Elite are," he said with a grin that made Isla shiver.

"They know she is coming?" Gray asked.

"They are waiting, in case she arrives."

"How would she get there?" Gray asked. "Surely every ship leaving Rennet would be checked or scanned."

"We were disappeared from the surface often enough at the hands of the Elite," Isla said. "But then, the Elite would be monitoring their own—or would they?" she asked, turning to Calder.

"I didn't get the woman out," he snarled.

"Someone did," Isla said, wondering again if she had worked with the Rohen, if they had helped her run like they had helped Isla find the connection to move between planets. "They could have used her to prevent all this if that was the case," she murmured.

"Isla," Gray prompted. When she looked up, he looked towards Calder.

"Used her to do what?" Calder asked.

"Watch the Hendra, learn what she was trying to do to the Rohen."

"She isn't doing anything."

"I remember," Isla said, crossing her arms. His face creased into confusion, and then she could see that he understood. "And they have talked to me," she added.

He shook his head. "They tried to kill you." The hatred was clear in his voice.

"You tried," she corrected. "They were just defending themselves."

"We couldn't kill them, not like we would want," Calder muttered, turning back for the ship.

"We should go after Alice," Isla said quickly. That was where they needed to be, working out what she was doing and for whom.

"Where is she?" Calder swung back around, the angry hatred set on his face, and she wondered if he had any other facial expressions. He was so angry all the time. When had that happened?

"When did things change for you?" she asked. "When did you become Calder? I know it was before we met. Only you were able to hide it then, but you can't now. You've allowed it to build and grow and take over, like a cancer."

He stomped back to the ship, not saying anything further, and Gray grabbed her arm. "Don't provoke him. It would only take a split second for him to decide we are better off dead."

She watched as the large soldier climbed into the ship, Gray maintaining his tight hold on her arm. "He wouldn't betray the Hendra. I'm not exactly sure what they have, but he wouldn't." Isla was sure of that.

"You might have thought he wouldn't betray you at one point. And look what happened. He handed you over to an unknown enemy to be slaughtered."

"I thought you could win," Calder called from the cockpit.

Isla climbed up in the ship, Gray following close behind. "No, you didn't," she said. "You used us as a test, to see just what they could do if cornered. It was unlucky that I survived."

"I thought you felt you hadn't." Calder grinned.

"Maybe remembering has allowed a better understanding of the day. I was wrong."

He looked at her as though he didn't really know her, and for the first time, Isla realised he didn't. He hadn't listened to her stories. There were many things she had kept from him, and she didn't know him either. The two years she had spent with him were not what she remembered them to be, nor what she had thought she'd experienced at the time. She looked at him now as though he were a stranger. Not Calder, not Kalli—just another soldier doing as he was directed.

Eighteen

The silence on the ship was palpable. Despite wanting to ask so many questions, Gray kept quiet. Calder had spent a lot of time talking to a lot of people, but he didn't seem to be getting the information he wanted. At one stage, he got up from the controls, came back into the narrow cabin and sat opposite them on the small, hard plastic seats.

His focus was on Isla, and Gray desperately wanted to put himself between them. Only he was strapped in, with very low gravity. And Calder would likely snap his neck before he had the chance to stop him doing anything.

"What do you know?" Calder asked Isla, who shrugged.

He sighed and sat back.

"I expected more of a fight," Gray said, looking at Isla. "I'd like to know what you know as well."

She reached out and put her hand on his. "Did you find Alice?" she asked, looking back to Calder.

"There is no sign of her anywhere in the Complex." Calder sounded defeated, looking at Isla as though trying to work her out. Gray wondered then if she was more to Calder than he had indicated, despite his trying to kill her. Something tightened in Gray's chest. He couldn't compete with that history, even if he didn't think there was a competition. She squeezed his hand gently. He looked into her focused gaze, having forgotten she was holding on to him.

"There must be tracking devices. What if she was kidnapped?" Gray suggested. "Could that have happened?"

"She might claim it, but she left a message in person before she left. She was wearing a tracking device, although it doesn't appear to be submitting a signal."

"Oh," Gray said.

"There are rumours spreading quickly through the Complex. That there is something else happening, something bigger."

"What sort of bigger?" Isla asked.

"Do you have an idea of what it might be?" Calder asked with the hint of the snarl. He didn't trust her, then. Part of Gray was relieved.

"No," she said simply. "I couldn't even begin to guess." But her fingers tightened again around Gray's.

Calder's gaze shifted to him. Gray shook his head once, but maybe he did have an idea. Maybe there were more working against the Hendra, or at least questioning her, than he could imagine.

"Revolution," Calder muttered.

"Pardon?" Isla asked.

"Urgway—there has been a demonstration calling for the mining to be reinstated."

"And you fear others will think it is an opportunity to call for change," Gray said.

"I'm sure Hendra could handle any situation," Isla murmured, looking down into her lap. Gray wondered what she was thinking about.

"There is no doubt of that. My concern is if this spreads across the Complex, it will get in the way of what we are trying to do."

"Hard to move secretly when the whole Complex is watching," Isla murmured with a nod.

"What do you know?" Calder asked, but it wasn't the usual harsh demand. He appeared to really want to know, or at least understand.

"Not enough," she said softly. "What issues might make people call for change?"

He shook his head as though they weren't important, or he didn't care enough to ask. He was focused on the Rohen, and he might be right that it was where the focus should be. Gray wondered if perhaps the plans for an uprising could be inserted into the current unrest. Or was it already underway?

Calder returned to the cockpit, and Gray wondered if there was any chance his old friend was still somewhere deep inside the cruel man. The boy he had known, the scared boy who had made him promise to look out for him even though he was far across the solar system. What had happened to him?

Gray was surprised to find Hari standing on the landing pad, a rifle in his hands. It wasn't pointed at any of them, but he had the look of a man eager to shoot something. "This is a surprise," the older man said, although his voice gave no indication that it was.

Isla walked closely beside him. Although Calder walked behind, it almost seemed that they were travelling together rather than under his watchful eye. Gray wondered if Isla could convince the chief of Oric to allow her to do whatever it was she needed to. As they got closer, Hari remained unmoving. Gray feared this wouldn't be as easy as he had hoped.

"She will see you," he said, his focus on Isla, who nodded and walked past him. But the soldier surprised Gray by grabbing his arm. "Only her," he said. Isla had stopped just inside the door, and she turned back. "She is in her quarters." Hari's focus was on Gray.

"Both of them?" Isla asked, and Gray wondered who she could mean.

Hari, his hand still tight on Gray's arm, turned slowly and took her in, but he said nothing.

"We'll wait here," Gray offered as she gave Hari a small nod and disappeared into the building.

"I would rather be involved in whatever conversations she is having," Calder said, but he made no move to follow and was looking back towards the ship.

"No, you wouldn't," Hari returned.

Calder appeared somewhat lost, but Gray feared it was a ploy, that he thought Isla would trust him with whatever information Hendra needed. Gray could only hope she wasn't sucked in by the act.

Isla had half expected Calder to follow her into the building and into Ebberah's suite. She knew the girl would be there waiting, and she was surprised Hari hadn't tried harder to hide the fact. Perhaps he thought it might be misunderstood if he didn't fully acknowledge what she had said.

Isla raised her hand to knock, but the door opened before she reached it. She knew it was the Rohen, or at least the child—or was it young woman? Ebberah was sitting on a long, lush settee as the door opened. Isla glanced around the room without looking like she was searching. Ebberah never took her eyes from her, maybe hoping she wouldn't remember the girl who had allowed her to be taken by Calder.

"What would you like that you don't already know?" Ebberah asked. She stood, the movement graceful. She placed her hands across her midsection, but Isla could read the tension in her arms and the way her fingers gripped.

"Is she going to come out?" Isla asked, openly looking around the room.

Ebberah shook her head slowly.

"I'm sure she knows more than you."

Ebberah's jaw dropped open as she sat back on the settee. "She is a child."

"Of Rohen," Isla said, perching on the edge of a seat uninvited. The child stepped forward from the wall and bowed, the motion smooth like the flow of metal despite her dishevelled appearance. Isla wondered just how much time she spent in the walls.

"Do you see what she is doing?" the child asked.

"Not how she is doing it, although I wonder at the glass," Isla said, thinking of the lab. It—they—would not have remained within the glass if it didn't have to.

"I heard the screams," the child said, as though understanding what she was thinking.

"Could you not have helped, like you did Gray?"

Ebberah sat forward, her focus on the child. The girl didn't even turn to her as she shook her head once.

"The screams," she whispered, as though that were explanation enough. Isla thought that it was.

"May I?" Isla asked, holding out her hand. The child held out her own, then stepped awkwardly forward and put her hand in Isla's. Her eyes contained silver flecks, and her skin felt like warm fluid metal. She smiled at Isla. She was older than Isla had first thought, but Isla wasn't sure how long she had been kept hidden away.

"Something is coming," she said, leaning in towards Isla. "The world is changing."

"Have you heard the rumours of unrest?" her mother asked with a wave of her hand. "We would be lucky if that becomes as I hoped."

The girl grinned at Isla and held her hand somewhat tighter. "You know what is coming."

"What do they want?"

"They want to right things. They want things as they should be."

"Who?" Ebberah asked. "Tevia, what have you done?"

The child turned to the woman then, smiling, her hold still tight on Isla. But she didn't say anything. Isla stood slowly, as though the movement might scare the child. She reached for her with her free hand and gently touched her face. The girl leaned into her as though she hadn't experienced enough contact.

"They want us to help this change," Isla said.

"They need you to stop Hendra—stop the containment."

"I don't understand how it works. What is in the glass?" Isla asked.

"Something from somewhere else."

"Not from Urgway?" Is that what Michaels had said? Did he have a clear idea, or was he guessing? Or had he been led to a different idea? "Only Hendra knows."

The girl bowed her head. "Will you help us?" she whispered as she stepped in closer to Isla, wrapping her arms around her, holding her close. Isla was sure she would disappear inside this girl as she had with the Rohen, the silvery being she had met in the caverns beneath Urgway.

"I will try."

"You must do more than try," the girl said, releasing her hold and standing back. "You will do as you have been asked."

"Or what?" Isla asked quickly, seeing the girl's words for the threat they were. They, the Rohen, had tried to kill her before. Would they try again? She knew what they were, after all. She knew the secrets of the Rohen.

"Not all of them," the girl said, the silver shining in her eyes. Isla wondered how much Rohen this girl contained. She smiled as Isla had the idea.

"We are different," she whispered. The girl barely nodded her head. She was part of the connection. She was part of the *they*.

Isla was also part Rohen, or so she had been told, but she knew she didn't hold the same connection this child did. She looked at the woman sitting back on the settee watching them.

"She doesn't leave the room," Isla said, looking back to the child, "yet you know it all."

Tevia grinned.

"You knew that when you allowed Calder to take me."

"You needed to be with him. You needed to see what they are doing."

"What are they doing?" Ebberah asked, paying attention now, looking at the child as though seeing her for the first time. The girl waved her off as unimportant. Ebberah had thought she was doing what the people wanted, and all the while the child had been doing as directed by the Rohen. Ebberah still didn't understand that, and Isla wasn't going to be the one to explain it to her. She was still trying to get her head around it herself.

"You are here with Calder?" Ebberah asked.

Isla nodded. "Hendra thinks I work for her."

"And my mother thinks you work for her."

Isla smiled at the child, but her eyes were cold. It appeared every time Isla looked at her that her eyes were more silver. Was this how the Readers were created? "Do you go to them?" Isla asked.

Tevia bowed her head. "I understand what you have been tasked with," she said, "but I cannot help you in the way you hope. You must find the answers—you must find the way." She stepped back and, before Isla could even raise her hand, she had disappeared into the wall.

Isla studied the space for too long, wondering if she could follow, if she could do as the child did. Was it the Rohen allowing her to do that? Or were they doing it for her, as they had when they had moved her from Calder earlier? Isla turned back to the door. Was that just for Ebberah's benefit, to appear as though they were helping her and would support whatever idea she had against the Hendra?

A pale face appeared in the wall, smiling.

Isla sat heavily in the chair she had perched on the edge of not so long ago. Too many needed something from her, and their needs were all conflicting. The more she learnt, the less sense any of it made.

"How do you know my daughter?" Ebberah asked. Isla looked away from the wall to the woman sitting back on the settee. "The child doesn't leave the room."

Isla laughed, a small cackle that escaped before she could stop it. "That child roams the universe."

"She doesn't leave the room," Ebberah insisted.

"She isn't really here," Isla said, standing and brushing herself off. "I don't know that I can discover what you need me to. Hendra is doing something with the Rohen, but why I can't guess." She could guess—fear, mostly—but she wasn't sharing that with Ebberah because she wasn't sure it was founded. "Hendra thinks I will help with that. Although I'm not sure I can. You want more; you want change. And I think Tevia is right. Change is coming, but it's not anything either of us is aware of or will understand when we see it."

"You don't think we will understand it?" Cool anger laced her words. "I am more than the Hendra thinks I am. I have always been, and I knew what I must become the moment I became Chief. She will not continue to destroy the solar system in the name of her family, to maintain the power she thinks she has. The people deserve better."

"And it might be that there is something else out there, someone else who agrees with you and has a plan of their own. A plan we will have no choice but to follow." Isla turned for the door and the men she'd left on the landing pad, although she had no idea what they were to do next.

"It might have already started," Ebberah said.

Isla wondered which she meant, the Rohen or the other plans and the idea of the demonstration. She stopped and turned back.

"More will follow. The people will not take it any longer," Ebberah insisted.

Isla headed out of the room, unsure whether she wanted to know what Ebberah was planning or what it would mean for her if she were somehow connected to the middle of an uprising against the Hendra.

"You can't run from this," Ebberah said, following her from the room. "You know more than you are saying. You are making false claims in my home."

Isla stopped and turned back.

Ebberah looked firm, but her eyes darted back to the door she had just left. "She is hiding."

"She is gone," Isla said, turning and walking away. "She was never here," she said again, wondering just how the child had been created in the first place. Was the Rohen involved? Or was it just luck, like eye colour or hair, that some contained more Rohen than others? She looked over her own hand and then focused again on where she was going. She couldn't see or feel the Rohen in her own veins, and she doubted she contained as much as she had thought. But as she ran her fingers over the wall, the flow of metal within it paused and followed her fingers. She pulled away from the wall, half expecting it to reach out after her, but it didn't.

She thought of the gloves and the cloak, and the ease with which she had formed what she'd needed from nothing. She wasn't what she had thought; the child wasn't what her mother had thought. Isla stopped. There was suddenly too much of the world she didn't understand. The colony, the child who knew that she knew, another gifted one, another filled with Rohen. She wondered then... When the colony's gifted child had been amongst those killed, had the world found another way? Had the Rohen found another way?

She did know more than she had remembered. She understood the fear behind the Hendra's decision, and her own fear that night. And yet she understood the Rohen and their need for freedom, to be what they needed to be for the good of the Complex.

She marched back out onto the landing. Calder stood by the ship looking out over the city, his arms crossed. Gray remained by Hari—waiting, it appeared, for he looked quite relieved when she returned.

"Is there a lab on Oric?" she asked, walking past him and directly to Calder.

"Of course," Calder murmured. She wondered what he was thinking, what he should be doing.

"Have they found Alice?"

He shook his head. "What do you want?"

"What lab?" Ebberah asked, and Isla turned to find her too close behind. Had the chief really followed her straight out onto the pad? She glanced back at Hari, who stood where she had left him.

"I need to understand the Rohen," she said.

"I thought you understood," Ebberah said, confusion creasing her brow. Then Calder turned and took her in. She would need to be careful; she might need Calder, but she didn't trust him.

"I need to know about the containment."

"What containment?" Ebberah asked.

"Just take me to the lab," Isla said, climbing into the ship and strapping herself in. She waited too long before Calder climbed aboard and Gray sat beside her.

"What makes you think it isn't here?" Gray asked.

"Ebberah would not allow it, and Hendra doesn't want the Complex knowing what she is doing."

"Someone knows," Gray said softly, and Isla nodded as the ship lifted from the ground.

"I think there are fewer secrets out there than the Hendra hoped. Only I don't know what will be done once they are learned."

Nineteen

Isla could sense the Rohen before they entered the building. It could have been any other government building they had landed on the top of, and she wondered whether Ebberah really knew what was happening on her planet. Calder was saluted as he headed inside, the guards not questioning or even really looking at the rest of them as they followed.

Calder put his hand to the panel beside a door flanked by two well-armed guards, and Isla heard the screaming. She tried not to wince. Did the Rohen know he was coming, or had it been screaming all along?

The doors opened to reveal a lab that looked very much like the previous one, with many stations surrounding a glass cylinder containing liquid metal. Several scientists were positioned at each station. Isla wondered what was different here. Just what did Hendra hope to learn that she hadn't already?

Gray looked angry as they made their way into the lab, but Isla doubted he could hear the Rohen's noise. And then it stopped. Everyone in the room was looking at her. Every scientist had stopped. All the Rohen stood tall, leaning against the glass as though pleading with her to save it.

"Don't do anything stupid," Calder growled under his breath.

Isla raised her hands, and the strange silence continued. She wondered if her face was on a database somewhere as someone to watch or someone they needed. She stepped forward to the closest station and bowed her head to the Rohen. It relaxed somewhat, becoming more of a puddle in the lower part of the cylinder than reaching out towards her. But it bubbled and swirled as though in a storm. Isla looked over the screens, but nothing made sense. Then the image flickered. As she stepped closer, one of the scientists slammed his fist into the panel beneath it.

"They have been glitching all day," he grumbled.

"Glitching?" Isla asked as the image on the monitor flickered again. A strange symbol appeared and was gone before she could really be sure it was there.

"Glitching," the man repeated, holding his hand toward the monitor as though that explained it all. "We haven't been getting accurate readings for days."

"What are you reading?" Isla asked.

"Temperature, movement, electrical pulse, radiation. Anything we can measure. Occasionally we even measure something that appears to be a heartbeat, but it isn't really there."

Isla nodded and looked around at the other stations.

"You don't seem surprised by that," Calder said, his voice surprisingly soft and far too close behind her.

"It is the heart of the universe. Should I be surprised?" She turned and took him in, the serious man still trying to work her out. "You know it is more than it appears to be, don't you?"

He looked away, glancing at the other cylinders. "Do you want to go back inside?"

"I don't think you could keep me there..." she said slowly, thinking of being removed last time she'd been trapped inside the thick glass cylinder. Rohen of one form had been able to get in and get her out, but the liquid metal familiar to so many couldn't. Hendra had only worked out how to contain part of the Rohen, and that was enough to disrupt the balance.

Another malformed character appeared on the monitor before her and, as she looked around, it appeared on all of them.

"I don't think that is a glitch," Gray murmured.

"I've seen that before," Calder said, so softly Isla wasn't sure she had heard him.

"It has been doing it for days," the scientist said. "A week or more."

"A week or more," Calder repeated.

The man gave him a frustrated look and went back to the controls.

"Is it the same on all of them?"

"Not always," the man admitted. "We are monitoring individual specimens, but the system is networked, and therefore we assumed whatever is impacting it is in the whole system."

Calder looked around the room. When his gaze returned to Isla, he looked almost panicked, if Isla believed the man could ever be. "It is in the system," he breathed, leaning forward.

Isla smiled. It was always in the system. The Rohen was everywhere; it ran through every surface, every circuit. She just wasn't sure if it was unable to help or if it needed her as the Readers had claimed.

The Rohen began to move more violently around each cylinder. Gray stepped up, pushed the scientist out of the way and leaned across the panels towards the glass. "Why can't it get out?" he asked.

Isla shook her head.

"You know why," Calder said through gritted teeth.

"The glass," Isla said.

He nodded once, as though confirming it.

"Something in the sand," the scientist said. "It took us some time to find it. Initially it was as though the metal just flowed through it. But this is different. Although I can't see how. It is made the same—the ingredients are just what any craftsman would use—but the sand is different."

"Where does it come from?"

He shrugged and went back to tapping on the keyboard before him, banging the console as different glitches appeared on the monitor.

"Calder?" Isla asked, turning to him as he watched the glitched symbols or characters flash occasionally on the screen. She reached towards him to get his attention, but she didn't want to touch him. And she never wanted those hands to touch her. "Kalli," she whispered, and he looked at her through slitted eyes, the anger palpable. "Where does the sand come from?" He shrugged and turned back to the screen. She watched him for too long before she asked, "Where have you seen that before?"

"The glitching?" he asked, turning to her.

"No, that language?"

The conversation in the room dropped to nothing, and again all eyes were on her.

"There are different languages within the Complex," she said, wondering why these people hadn't worked that out. "Or at least there used to be." Most people spoke the same common language no matter where they went. Even in the colony, they had spoken common. There were occasional words they used that described something the common language couldn't. Isla had always thought that more from necessity than the hangover from an older or different language. How odd that it was only making sense now.

"Can you read it?" Gray asked, but she shook her head and looked to Calder.

"What does it matter where the sand comes from?" he asked.

"This can't continue," Isla said. "I know she wants to understand it, but she never will—not unless it wants to be understood," she added, trying to hide that she understood more than she was sharing with these people.

Calder appeared even more frustrated.

"What did you expect me to do? Why did you think I wanted to come?" Isla asked.

He sighed and then looked towards the door as two guards came in, one remaining by the door and the other running towards them, weaving his way through the scientists. "Get out of the way!" he hissed as one man, not looking up from the panel before him, stepped out in front of him.

"What is it?" Calder asked, an icy calm settling over him. Isla did her best not to shiver. This was when this man shone, in difficult situations, and this was the reason Hendra allowed him the freedom he had.

"The outer doors have been breached."

"By whom?" Calder asked, heading towards the door.

"We heard there were protests in the area, but this is something else."

Isla looked at Gray, but he shook his head. Either he didn't know what was going on or he wasn't going to share that information here.

With Calder gone from sight, Isla turned back to the station and ran her hand over the screen. The image cleared, and a molecular structure appeared.

"They could have hacked into that," Gray said.

"I don't think they can," Isla returned as the scientist watched. "They are trying, but something is blocking them; it may be the same material."

"That was why they needed your help before."

"I don't know," she murmured.

"You are going to let it out," the scientist said too loudly, then stepped back.

"I am trying to understand what you are doing," Isla said, holding up her hands and finding that Gray was too close. She took a deep breath and put her hand on the screen as it shone above the panel. The image went blank. There was a sigh amongst the scientists in the room as every other panel went dark. The man closest to Isla made to grab her.

"Wait," Gray called, his bulk blocking the man. "Look." He was calm, and the man looked around the room.

"What is this?" someone else asked.

Isla watched the symbols flash across the screen, one after the other, their smooth curved edges not appearing to be any sort of network glitch. She couldn't grasp what they meant. She knew they were trying to tell her something, but it was as though it was just beyond her.

"Can you...?" Gray murmured.

"No," she said, watching the string of characters flash on the screen.

"What is most important here?" Gray asked.

"Other than freeing the Rohen? Learning how they are contained."

"Would you like to be contained?" the scientist asked, his voice harsh. "I've heard you were a specimen yourself not so long ago."

"And did you hear that she was out of the cylinder in a flash? You are men of science—are you not interested in this? What if the metal is giving you this message?" Gray sounded as frustrated as Isla felt.

Isla looked around the lab. Most of the scientists' attention had returned to the images on their monitors, each one the same, each trying again and again to tell her something. She looked back at the monitor and the metal bubbling away in the cylinder. "Do you know what it is?"

The screen went blank. She knew they didn't. If they had any idea, they would find a way to prevent it rather than sending her in.

An alarm sounded throughout the space. The scientists' attention was on the panels again as they worked at something at each station. The monitors disappeared, the lights went out and a hum that Isla had assumed surrounded her wherever she went disappeared.

"You are shutting it down?" she asked.

"We are breached—time to go," he said, directing her towards the back of the lab where the staff were now racing towards a back door.

"But the Rohen," she said, looking back as she was shoved forward. The metal was reaching up to her. "We can't leave it."

The man growled something under his breath and raced forward. Someone else banged into her as they tried to rush past. Then someone was dragging her by the arm behind a panel—Gray. He watched the front door as he moved her carefully around behind him, putting himself between her and the staff. No one else paid them any attention, and within moments they were alone in the silent room.

"You can do something, can't you?" he said.

"Should we be worried about what might come through that door?"

"Likely Calder," Gray said, but he didn't take his gaze from the door. "Do what you can."

Isla rested her hand on the cool panel. Odd that the Rohen felt so distant when, moments ago, she had been sure she was surrounded by it. She needed the power, and then she could do whatever she had done last time. Although she wasn't really clear what that had been.

"Isla, I think you should hurry it up." There was a loud bang at the door, and Isla closed her eyes. Nothing happened. She reached forward and touched her fingers to the glass. The same feeling of cold seemed to wash over her, as though she were empty.

"Don't you have some skill? Come on hummer—hum."

She looked at him and took in his worried features. He glanced around, and then his face softened. "Reilly always thought you were magic."

Isla sucked in a deep breath, closed her eyes and pulled the Rohen from the surface before her. The long silver tendrils grew like a plant around her fingers and along her arms. She breathed out slowly. "Where have you been?" she asked. The monitor at the station they were standing at flashed to life as a string of characters typed across the screen. Not the large individual characters she had seen before, but smaller letters. If she had been looking from a distance, she might have thought it any other text.

"Is that instructions?" Gray asked.

"Not sure; I can't read it."

"Open the cylinders."

"I'm trying," she muttered. "There is something else here, like the glass. I don't know what it is—I can't see it. I just can't feel beyond it."

"Magic," he murmured as the door was forced open and a rabble ran in. They could have been anyone. They looked like everyday people from the street.

"Is this your revolution?" she asked.

"Something is going on," he murmured, looking around. "Why don't we have dusters?"

One formed in Isla's hand, but as she looked up at the people moving into the room, their progress had slowed. They were looking around as though they weren't quite sure what they had broken into. Isla handed it to Gray, about to suggest he fire over their heads when Calder appeared at the back of the group.

She wasn't sure if he could see her or not. The Rohen in the cylinders stilled.

"Old and abandoned," Calder snapped. "A hangover from the mining days."

Several of the men nodded while others pressed at the silent, blank consoles. An orange light flashed under Isla's finger as she rested her hand back on the panel.

"Where?" Gray stammered, looking at the weapon in his hand.

Isla moved her finger slowly towards the top of the console, the light following beneath her finger. When she stopped, it changed from bright orange to green. The movement in the room stopped as an audible click sounded throughout the space.

"Highly unstable," Calder said. A cylinder across the room creaked.

Shouts sounded. The men who had breached the facility raced back out past Calder, who turned and glared towards Isla. She wondered how he knew where she was. As the last of the men left the room, the cylinders all rose up from the centre of each station and the Rohen ran out. At the station Isla was at, the Rohen flowed across the panel, up and around her shoulders, and then it was gone.

"You promised," Calder snarled, marching across the space towards her.

"No," she said. "My promise is to another."

Gray fired the duster across the room directly at Calder, but he managed to miss. The shot hit one of the panels, causing a hole to form in the station. Distant shouts sounded from those who had left. Calder kept coming.

"Do you think your little diversion is going to help you?"

"Diversion?" Isla asked, looking at Gray as though he might know more than he had told her. But he'd told her everything now—there were no secrets.

"Where did you get a duster?"

"This has nothing to do with us," Gray shouted across the room. "We only came for answers, for a way to help."

"But not to help those you should," Calder said. He looked back over his shoulder, but there was no one else entering the space.

Gray looked to Isla, wondering where the metal had gone and if she was herself. But her green eyes sparkled as she futilely tried to push the messy curls out of her face just to have them spring back. His hand closed around the duster. They needed Calder, as much as he hated the idea. They needed him so that Isla could learn what she needed to know to help the Rohen. And that was so they could help everyone.

"Hendra will be disappointed," Calder said, moving swiftly across the room with his own duster in hand. Although it was down by his side, Gray didn't doubt he would use it. Particularly if he thought Hendra was at risk.

"She is playing with something she doesn't understand," Isla said. "I don't know what she thinks she is doing, but she is putting the whole Complex at risk."

"She is the Complex. It would be nothing without her."

"Nothing without its queen," Gray murmured. He jumped as Isla's hand rested on his arm.

"What in the name of all the stars do you two think you are? The Hendra is not your enemy. She is singularly focused on the running of the Rohendra Complex, for all that live here."

"Not all," Isla said.

Calder shook his head. "What do you think you know?" He sounded bored, as though he didn't believe Isla could know anything.

"I know of the Rohendra," she whispered. "That is all I need to know."

"And you think you work for them, that you are helping them. You are only being used, you stupid girl. They meant to kill you with the others that day."

"No." Isla sounded so sure as she stepped between Gray and Calder. He put his hand to her shoulder, but she didn't move. "I was never meant to die. I was meant to help."

Calder laughed then, as though she were a silly child, but there was something in the sound that took Gray back to a distant place. He kept his hand on Isla's shoulder. As Calder's cold blue eyes failed to reflect the laugh, Gray was reminded that this man was the reason Reilly was gone. His fingers tightened around the duster as Isla reached back. He lifted it to hand it to her, but as her fingers touched it, it was gone.

"Was it real?" Gray asked, unsure whether the words were loud enough for her to hear.

"Yes," she returned, but her focus was still on Calder. "She will see what they are—I just hope it is before it is too late."

Calder shook his head. Two soldiers appeared behind him, glancing around the empty space and the blackened hole in one of the control panels. Gray realised the weapon had been real, but the woman before him might be something very different. What had she learnt while she was away from him that she hadn't told him? They hadn't had any time alone since she had returned.

"Tell me about the sand." Isla's voice was soft, but the command was there.

"They've gone," one of the soldiers said to Calder. "Not quite sure what they thought they were doing. You want us to follow up?"

"Get the enforcers on it. Something is brewing, and now is not the time for civil unrest."

"Is this the first demonstration here?" Gray asked. Both men looked at him, but neither answered.

Calder flicked his head towards the door, and the other soldier disappeared. "Come out," he said.

Isla walked forward, slipping out of Gray's hold, but she waited for him to stand beside her before they walked towards Calder.

"Show me the sand," Isla said.

He shook his head. "I think you have seen enough."

"Is that why you allowed us to come—why you defied whatever other task Hendra set for you?"

"Her wife has run away," Calder said with a shrug.

"And you don't think that is important."

"She is what I said she was. She is not worthy of the position she was put in."

Isla smiled, and Gray was distracted by how it lit up the room. "If you want me to hum, I need to understand the containment."

Calder turned and left the room. They followed behind him, Gray wondering whether he would assist them and why he had brought them here in the first place.

Twenty

Hendra looked at the monitor and tried not to show the flood of emotions that were coursing through her. The general stood before the desk, his face unreadable, yet she was almost sure she could see a smirk. He wouldn't dare. Calder would have, but he was still with the dragonfly and sparrow claiming to be doing what he could for her benefit. If he had found Alice when asked, this would not have happened.

"Play it again," she murmured.

Alice's face appeared on the screen, her hair dishevelled, her eyes red—and was that a bruise forming on her cheek? Little of the background could be distinguished; she could have been in any room anywhere in the Complex.

"My name is Alice, and you may recognise me as the First Wife." At least she sounded in control. "I am currently being held against my will for daring to speak out about the wrong being done in our solar system. As First Wife, I am... I was..." She cleared her throat, and Hendra tried not to grimace. "I was privy to more information than I ever expected, and much of that information I felt should be shared with the people. You should know that what Hendra does on your behalf—what it claims to do on your behalf—is only for the benefit of those in power." She wiped at the corner of her eye. "The Hendra is not what you think she is. To maintain her control of the Rohendra Complex, she has put us all at risk. And to ensure that she maintains her power, she has..." A large tear rolled down Alice's cheek as she slowly shook her head. "The child is not mine," she whispered, and the screen went black.

"Who has seen it?" Hendra asked.

"It only appears to have been sent to your personal account. But we are unsure whether someone has manipulated an image or forced her to say these things. Are you sure it is her?"

Hendra nodded. It was. But did she think Alice was being held against her will—or was it all an act?

"You have tried to trace where it was sent from," she said. They must have.

"Here."

Hendra looked up sharply. "Here?"

"It originates from Hendra Central. If anyone else were to receive it, they could trace it easily enough."

"Are we sure it wasn't sent to anyone else?"

"No." The general bowed quickly, as though that would lessen the threat of his words.

"Where is Calder?"

"Oric."

"Bring him home."

"He is occupied with another task," the general said, bowing again.

She opened her mouth and then closed it. Could she really claim that Calder was the only one who could help her here?

"We are turning the building over, and we have suspended all communications."

"That is good thinking, unless they are able to access the network separately. Or unless they are playing with us. And do we know who *they* are?"

He shook his head.

"She was angry, but she wouldn't do this to me."

"We will find her."

"Put out a message that she has disappeared, is lost or something." Hendra waved her hand, unsure what would be the best option.

He nodded, then opened his mouth and closed it again.

"What?" she asked.

"You directed that she be arrested if she were to arrive on Draroh."

"Say it was a plan to flush out the plotters..." She waved her hand again, then pulled it into her lap. She wasn't appearing as in control as she wanted. "You should be able to come up with a story of your own."

He bowed, too low, and left the office quickly as Hendra sat back at her desk. She waved her hand over the control to start the video again, but she paused it before Alice spoke. Had she been mistaken about the woman? Was she no threat at all, or a bigger threat than Hendra had ever given her credit for?

A message blinked across the screen. Hendra closed down the image of Alice and opened it up. It was a blank screen. The same strange symbols that had appeared on her scans flickered occasionally across it. She wondered if there was a system error or if someone was truly trying to tell her something.

"You got my message," whispered a disjointed electronic voice.

"What could you want?" she murmured.

"Everything," the voice replied, and Hendra glanced around the office. This was a recorded message. She looked at the communication button, but it was off. When she put her hand over it, the voice continued.

"I wouldn't do that. We hold far more than your wife."

"She has gone on a holiday; she told my secretary herself."

"And yet you were prepared to arrest her. Did you think she was working against you?"

Hendra shook her head. She wasn't sure what to think anymore. "This is because of the rohen," she said.

"We do not care if you mine the metal or not."

"You are a group, then," she said. "What do you want?"

"Everything," the voice said, and then the connection was gone. She pressed her hand down over the communication button.

It took too long before the disembodied voice of her secretary returned. "Your Grace?"

"Get Calder here now, and take no excuses."

Hendra waited too long with no response from either the secretary or Calder. He had taken the hummer as she had wanted, but he was too focused on her—on what the hummer needed. And Hendra needed him to do as she required first and foremost.

She moved the image of Alice to the fore on the screen above her desk and started it again. There was something about it... Whether it was just wrong, familiar or something else entirely, she wasn't sure, but she knew there was something.

When Alice wiped her eye, her bracelet caught the light. She still wore it. So that wasn't missing, but they hadn't been able to trace her. Maybe whoever had her had managed to block the signal, but Hendra couldn't guess how—or who would have such technology. She had been so focused on the Rohen of late that she hadn't been paying enough attention to everything else that had been going on.

Calder had thought Alice was acting against her; he had put the idea in her head. Did he know about the Rohen in her drinks? He was the one who had suggested she was being poisoned. The reports came to mind that had arrived when she was unwell. She looked back through them, the anonymous ones, the random reports of events going on. There was nothing. Michaels' name had also been raised, yet she couldn't see that either now as she scrolled back through them. She had to get better at marking things she wanted to go back to. Now there was nothing, and she had been so sure there had been something. Had she been deceived?

Was there something more going on within Hendra Central than she was aware? How could that be? How could that happen?

The secretary appeared at the doorway, and she waved him in.

"I can't reach Colonel Calder, Your Grace," he said. "There have been some odd reports of unrest."

"On Urgway, the mines." She waved a hand. "I know."

He shook his head. "On Oric, at a facility."

"Which facility?"

"Reports are varied. Do you want to send in the Elite?"

She nodded once, and he disappeared from the doorway. This needed to be shut down before it became something people might think was significant.

Or worse, they might start questioning her authority, her ability to rule the Complex as her family had done for so long. The idea of her father came to mind, the quiet words he had spoken of the Rohendra as he had lain dying.

It was knowledge she had struggled to come to terms with, and the Rohendra were more than what he'd known them to be. No matter how she had searched, there was no indication that they existed. She had found them once. Maybe they had wanted to test her—she would never know. But no matter her hunting skills, those she sent out to find them and those she pressured to tell their secrets, she couldn't find anything to indicate where they were or what they were doing.

Sending in the Elite that day had been luck, and then not very good luck. They hadn't even made a dent on the Rohendra, and she'd had to come up with some story to cover it up. There had been nothing left of any of them other than Sergeant Tarle. She had wondered if he had found a way to keep her safe or out of the way. Hendra should have realised then that there was more to the girl than she'd thought. No matter what story they told her, she hadn't remembered the truth of it anyway—only she might learn it now.

And what was Calder doing that he wasn't running back to her side when she needed him? He had instructions, but he was to do her bidding first.

"Hendra," a hesitant voice called over the comm. One Elite man she could count on at the moment.

"Yes, general?"

"It appears that Calder was at the facility infiltrated on Oric."

"He's not there now?"

"No, Your Grace. They had shut it down, and the people believed it was decommissioned. But the Elite and soldiers on site have given rise to talk. We can explain it away, watching over old facilities to ensure they aren't misused and so on, but we can't determine where the chatter is coming from."

"Try to keep an eye on other facilities without it looking like we are."

"Yes, Your Grace."

It might be time to work on her back-up plan. The Elite at least were on her side, no matter what anyone else was doing. But she didn't know who else might have gotten close and couldn't be trusted. Hendra walked out to the secretary, who looked up. Then he stood to attention quickly.

"I want this building thoroughly searched for anything unusual," she said, and the man nodded nervously. "Get the general on it." She pointed at one of the soldiers standing by her office door. "You are to come with me," she said as she walked towards the lift. She wasn't going to take him through her personal quarters, but she needed to check other areas that Alice had previously thought private.

"I would think that Colonel Calder would have checked this area already, Your Grace," the man said after a time of walking through dimly lit connecting corridors. There was a range of private offices and spaces hidden behind the public world of Hendra Central.

"He may well have," she murmured when she reached the door. "I want to do it again."

She tapped the door and then stood back, allowing the soldier to move through first.

"Nothing," he murmured as Hendra ran her hand over a panel and the light increased. The soft green walls had never reminded her of the forest. Was that truly the reason Alice had hidden down here?

"Where are you?" she whispered.

"Your Grace?"

She shook her head as she moved through the space, pulling open doors and then standing in the narrow doorway to the bedroom. The bed was pulled about, and she tried to remember the last time she had been here. Had Alice returned after it had been discovered?

"Is that blood?" the soldier asked, moving past her and pulling the sheets back.

Hendra felt her own blood run cold. What might have Alice become involved in? Or had it already been underway when she'd met Hendra and won her over? The blood on the sheets was brown and dried. She remembered that the enforcer and Tarle had been injured, or was it only one of them? He'd been shot, she thought.

"That doesn't belong to Alice," she said, hoping she was right. It had been there some time, and Alice had disappeared just recently.

She needed advice. She needed to know what to do. Should she put out a statement—a plea for the woman's safe return—and possibly bring an enemy back into her home? Or had she been mistaken and the rohen in the juice had been planted?

Although, she had to admit, she felt far better since she had stopped drinking it.

Twenty-One

I sla walked slowly towards the ship. She wanted to run, but she had to move at the pace Calder set if she was going to find a way to work with him and get what she needed. Although she wasn't exactly sure what that was or whether he would give it. She was aware, though, that in the time they had been on Oric, the Hendra had tried repeatedly to reach him, and he wasn't answering.

She wasn't sure if that was because he wanted to help or because he knew of something else and didn't support the Hendra as closely as she'd thought.

"Do you know where Alice is?" Isla asked as she watched the tall man before her. He stopped and looked back.

"Do you think I would have taken her? Or helped her hide?"

"It is hard to guess," Isla admitted. "You do know what she is?"

"A pain in the..." Calder studied Isla as though guessing there was something else. Something he didn't know about her. Isla was honestly surprised he didn't know the power she had.

"Ah hem," Gray coughed, and they both looked at him. He gave her a wide-eyed look as though just working it out himself. She wasn't sure she had said nearly enough to the man who had risked so much for her and lost so much.

"What do you think you know?" Calder asked, his tone cold and sharp.

"More than you," Gray said, then gave Isla an apologetic look.

"It doesn't matter what you think you know of the First Wife; she will never be considered as that again. She made Hendra sick." Something softened in his voice, and Isla was surprised by the stab of pain that crossed her chest at the idea of him loving someone else. He wasn't the man she remembered, and he had never really loved her. "I don't know whom she is working for or with, but she will be found."

He continued towards the ship. Isla doubted he understood Alice's skills. Whether that was because she was gifted or a hummer or they were the same thing, Isla wasn't sure. Could she be working on another issue for the Rohendra? Could Alice be trying to find a way to end Hendra?

"Queen," she murmured.

"Which means they wouldn't harm her," Gray whispered as they climbed into the ship and strapped in.

"Or are they creating something else?"

Gray shook his head. "What do they really want?"

"I don't think we'll ever know," Isla replied as the ship lifted from the ground. "Where are we going?"

"Michaels sent me something about the sand. We'll see what we can find out, but I'm not sure it is going to help you."

"There has to be a better way, a different way to work with the Rohen."

Calder shook his head without turning back or saying anything else.

"I'm not sure he really wants to help us," Gray said.

"No, but he needs to know what I can do and what I know to share that information with Hendra."

"But he hasn't raced back when she asked him to. If Alice is missing, taken rather than run, this could be his chance."

"What did you think of the writing?" she asked quickly, aware suddenly that they had some quiet time to talk.

"What writing?" Gray asked as the ship lurched sideways.

"What is it?" Isla asked, raising her voice above the hum of the engines. Then she unbuckled and pulled from Gray's grip as she moved through to the cockpit. "What has happened?"

Calder looked at her as though just remembering she was on the ship.

"And in Area 3," a voice said over the comm.

"How are they learning where they are?" Calder asked whoever was on the other end of the comm.

"We don't know. What would you have me do?"

"Shut them down, hide the staff, make them look abandoned. Although they might not believe that for long. Check out every other facility on every planet in the solar system.

"Arnin 4 has just alarmed."

"Sit down," Calder growled. Isla sat down in the co-pilot's seat and belted in. "Back there," he said, looking over his shoulder.

"You have to tell me what's happening," she said.

"I don't, and you likely already know."

"The facilities are under attack. But I only just guessed that from listening to the report. Do you have hummers trapped in other facilities?"

"Some," he murmured.

Strange that the Rohen hadn't asked for them to be freed along with their other requests. But maybe if Isla could prevent the containment, they could help themselves. She hadn't noticed anything while she was trapped that had prevented her humming, if that was what it was, other than the difficulty in fully reaching the Rohen in the glass. But she didn't fully understand what she was.

"Where are we going?" she asked.

"One of the facilities didn't get emptied in time. I need to get in there to prevent it turning into something bigger."

"How will you do that? Once they know, word will spread. And someone knows something if they are all being targeted at the same time."

"Hey E'anah!" Calder called, and Gray appeared behind them, gripping her seat. "These your people?"

"I don't have anyone left," Gray said, his voice giving nothing away. Again Isla thought of Reilly—that if they hadn't come after her, he might still be alive and with his family.

"You're across everything," she said to Calder.

"Not always," he replied.

"This is something very big to miss. How many are involved across the Complex?" She turned and looked at Gray, not expecting him to answer. But he might have an idea of how big this was. "This could just be the beginning," she whispered.

"The beginning of what?" Gray asked. Isla let out a slow breath. "A revolution," he said before she could even pull together an answer.

"You were trouble from the start," Calder said, but he looked beyond her at Gray. "We knew that the moment you went off the rails on the Sparrow."

"You caused that. You started that trouble and sowed the distrust in the Hendra. Doing what you wanted through the Complex, not caring for laws or people. I'm surprised it has taken this long," Gray said. "Unfortunately, I'm not involved."

"Too busy chasing after a girl," Calder murmured, looking back to the controls. The comm light flashed again.

"Are you sure we should be landing in the middle of this?" Isla asked.

"Never thought you would be scared of some action," Calder said, his eyes still on the controls.

"Not when I know the odds. We don't know anything about this."

Gray's hand rested on her shoulder. Then they banked, and he skidded across the cockpit. Isla only just managed to grab him. "Sit down," she said. "And belt in."

He nodded, then wove his way back into the main seating area as she watched Calder at the controls. "You know this is bigger than a possible revolution," she said. "Trouble has been brewing for a while. We were putting out flames years ago. Only now there is more to consider."

"You think the Rohen is a threat?" He turned and looked at her. "I wasn't there." As though that explained so much.

"You knew what we were going into, didn't you?"

He nodded once, his eyes on the controls rather than her.

"And you didn't try to help us or stop what we were doing. You just blindly sent us in. Did you have any idea what Hendra was starting?"

"She did what she did for the Complex," he murmured.

"No. She might tell herself that—and you, late at night to make you feel better." He looked up sharply then, surprise on his face. "We both know that she does what she does to ensure she stays where she is. Did Alice ask too many questions?"

"Alice?"

"Is that why you disappeared her?"

"She ran," Calder growled, and Isla believed that he believed what he was saying, even if it wasn't true.

"To where?" Isla asked, knowing she was pushing someone she shouldn't. And maybe he didn't know. But he needed to think about it and the implications of what they were flying into. "She is known throughout the Complex. Her face is as recognisable as Hendra's."

He sighed. "She must have had help—friends, someone working with her."

Isla wondered at the servant who had admitted them to the room that night, when she'd been sure Gray was going to die in her arms as she'd tried to carry him through the corridor. But then, Hendra had known just where they were. Nothing had been as safe or secret as Alice had thought. Again, Isla wondered if anyone else was aware of Alice's skills and possible Rohen connection.

A loud explosion drew her attention. She pushed her hand into the control panel and triggered a monitor to appear before her. Calder grumbled something beside her but didn't look at what she was doing. A fiery building appeared before her on the monitor. People ran from the scene and, as the services began to arrive, sirens wailing, others ran towards the building.

"What is going on?" Isla asked the monitor.

"Calder, don't land," a concerned voice said over the comms.

"Nowhere to land, looking at that mess."

"We've lost nearly everyone."

"Who survived?" Isla asked, and there was a silence.

"Who?" Calder repeated.

"A couple of scientists. We had a girl in the cage, but we can't get into the building to get her out."

"Try harder," Calder growled back. "We don't want services finding her in there—she'll spill it all."

"Can it get any worse?" the man snapped.

"Flint?"

"There's a newsflash, with the First Wife. I'll fix this—you have to go."

"Damn it all to the hells," Calder murmured, and Isla wondered at the notion he had never used before, at least not in her hearing. "Can you bring up the news on that?"

Isla moved her hand, and Alice appeared on the monitor. She moved her fingers, and Alice's strained voice filled the cockpit. "The child is not mine."

"What is she playing at?" Calder asked, then glanced at the monitor. "She looks rough."

"Perhaps she was forced to make a statement."

Hendra appeared on the monitor next, looking even more distressed than her wife had moments before, although Isla was certain it was a plot rather than a reaction to what she had seen. "I have received this communication of my wife being forced to announce falsehoods, and it was followed by further threats to me and the Complex along with a ransom request, or it would be released to the world." She took a breath, trying to slow her words. "I knew that no matter how much I paid, this would be used to harm the Complex, and I couldn't allow that. This is the reason I have shared it. With nothing to use against me, I hope that those who have taken my loving wife, mother of my child, will return her." She wiped a hand across her cheek and took a deep breath.

"I think this could put Alice at more risk," Isla whispered.

"We are looking for you," the Hendra finished, her voice too calm. Isla wondered if that was aimed at Alice or whoever had taken her.

"You don't think Alice was taken," she said to Calder.

"I'd be surprised. Do you really think if someone had made her say those things and then demanded a ransom that Hendra would put it out for the whole Complex? She is calling a bluff."

"But whose?"

Calder shook his head.

"She looked more hurt than coerced."

Calder sighed. "Tell me what you think is going on."

"I don't know," Isla said. Looking back at the newsflash of Alice playing over and over again and the Hendra promising to find whoever was responsible in that cold, calculating way... Isla was pleased that Hendra's focus was no longer on them and the Rohen. Although there might be more to connect them than Isla had first thought, and the Hendra might already have considered it.

Gray felt an insistent uncertainty when they landed amongst the trees and headed out across the quiet landscape of Oric. He had half expected them to return to Rennet and the Hendra as the news of the trouble and Alice had emerged. Calder and Isla had been talking and sharing, and he was frustrated that she hadn't returned to him during the flight.

"How does Ebberah not know you have so many facilities on her planet?" Isla asked. "Or do you just assume she doesn't know?"

"She isn't very bright," Calder murmured, shouldering a Barilla and holding out a duster for Isla. She shook her head, and he held it out to Gray.

Surprised by the action, Gray had to stop himself snatching it from Calder's hand. He bowed his head as he took it and checked the settings. He wondered at Isla not taking a weapon—she didn't seem settled without one—but then he remembered her handing him a duster at the facility. Did she have one secreted away, or was it something else?

He shook his head to try and clear his thoughts and holstered the duster. "Do we expect trouble?"

"Always," Calder said. "There has been no sign of a breach here, but if they found the others, chances are they know where every facility in the Complex is located."

Isla shivered. Gray wondered if it was due to the number of facilities or the fact that they weren't safe. Except he wasn't sure who these people were. There were others he had worked with, or for, at different times; one of the reasons they had been at the races was because the word had been out something wasn't right.

How many others were prepared to go into a fight when they weren't sure what the Hendra was up to or doubted that she was doing good for the Complex?

"Where is it?" Isla asked.

Calder pointed to the ground beneath his feet, and Gray looked around at the trees and grass. It almost looked familiar, or at least similar to somewhere else he had been. Could they be in the grove the Rohen had pulled them to, and had they done that for a reason?

"Isla?" he asked. She shook her head without looking at him. He wasn't sure whether she had the same thought or wanted them to be quiet.

"Here," Calder said, walking towards a tree that wasn't. In fact, it was very clearly false. It was a similar colour, and the surround had been textured, but it looked and felt nothing like a tree. The trunk opened, and he moved inside. Isla paused only momentarily at the dark entrance. Gray looked around the clearing for any other signs of people before he followed them inside, and the door closed behind him.

"Keep up," Calder's quiet words floated back to him. He wondered how far the tunnel went and if their voices would carry to a possibly empty facility at the end of it. In the dim light, he held tight to the duster and tried not to jump when Isla brushed against his arm. He reached out and took her hand, and they continued along the corridor towards he wasn't sure what.

"Shouldn't there be someone else down here?" he whispered, leaning in towards her.

"This feels different," she returned quietly.

He glanced at her, wishing he could see her better in the dim light as her fingers ran over the rough wall. "Not a cavern?" he asked.

"It might have been, but I can't feel it."

Gray gulped down the uncomfortable feeling growing in his chest. They were too trusting of Calder, that he was taking them to where they needed to go. He was taking them to where *he* needed to go. And something else was happening—something Gray wasn't sure of.

"Here," Calder said. They hadn't been walking very long, but there was no hint that there was anyone else around. Something clicked, and a door opened into a brightly lit space. They followed him in, Isla relaxing somewhat in the light. But she maintained her hold on his hand, which he didn't think too much of until Calder was staring at them.

Isla didn't seem to notice as she looked around the space, her forehead crinkled. "Where is it?"

Calder turned to sweep an arm across the space and stopped. Like the previous facility, it appeared to be abandoned. There was no hint of scientists at the work benches, and it was different than the setup of the previous one with technology and large glass tubes. Many of the surfaces were clear. Gray stepped forward to the first one as Isla released her hold. He ran his fingers over the white surface. It was dusty, but not like it had been abandoned forever—more like something had fallen across it.

"What were they doing here?" Gray asked.

"The same as all the others. Trying to find out what it is, what it can do."

"You could just ask," Isla murmured, looking up at the ceiling. Gray followed her gaze. "Where is the Rohen?" She sounded calm enough, but Gray sensed something else—an anger or a fear for the metal, he wasn't sure.

"They keep it over here," Calder said, moving across the large space towards the back wall. Finally, Gray could see the glass. As they drew closer, it was empty.

"Were they expecting you?" he asked.

"No," Calder said, walking through the array of glass containers and searching for something they all knew was gone. "But they are always ready."

"Ready to run if they come under attack like the others?" Isla asked.

He nodded, still looking over the glass as though disbelieving that it could be empty.

"You don't think they took it," Isla said, stepping forward. He shook his head slowly.

"Why?" Gray asked.

Calder looked up as though no one had thought to ask that question before. "It is dangerous."

Isla looked at Gray. "Someone is helping."

"A hummer?"

"It is in the walls," she said. "Whatever stops it getting out of the glass is in the walls. It is throughout the space. There is no tech here," she said, looking around. Gray had noticed that it was different than the previous facility; but now, as she said it, he realised there wasn't any tech at all. No control panels, no monitors.

"They didn't bring it in. They didn't want to bring it in other than what they were researching or studying." Gray moved around the space and was surprised by a stack of papers that had been brushed to the floor, fanning out. He squatted down and scooped them together. Again, they appeared to be covered in dust, and as he stood, he was sure something creaked above him. A fine layer of dust fell down over him. "I really think it is time to go," he said, heading back to Isla and pushing the pages into her hands. "No tech," he said quietly.

She held them out, flipped through the six or so loose pages and then brought one closer to her nose as she squinted. Gray hadn't taken the time to read through them; he had just picked them up.

She handed him one, and he realised then that he couldn't read the writing. This wasn't the language he knew, but he had seen it before. "The glitching."

"I am starting to think the Hendra is not employing her scientists for their skill or knowledge."

"What is it?" Calder asked, and Gray was tempted to hold the sheet against his chest so he couldn't read it.

"There was tech here at some point," Isla said, looking around again as another creak caused more dust to fall down on them.

"Who took it out?" Calder asked.

"The tech or the Rohen?"

"There hasn't been anything here for a while," Gray said. "When were you last in contact with them?"

Calder shrugged. "Last week."

Gray looked around again. "Are you certain?"

"Yes," Calder said, standing taller as his cold eyes focused on Gray. "It might have been some time since I was in here, but I contact them all regularly."

"Did you see the person you spoke with?"

"Of course."

"Could they have lied to you?"

Another creak shook the world around them as a large crack ran down the wall Isla was standing beside. She leapt to the side, and Gray spun her around and pointed her back towards the entrance. As he started to run, Calder grabbed her arm and pulled her back.

"This whole place is going to collapse," Gray growled.

"There is a faster exit this way." Calder pulled Isla in the opposite direction, and then the lights dipped and flickered. Gray worked his way around the benches, trying to keep up as the noise increased to a roar and the world went dark.

Twenty-Two

"Gray!" Isla screamed into the dark as the noise filled her senses. She continued forward, stumbling over her feet and hitting furniture, Calder's hand too tight around her wrist. She longed for the feel of the Rohen. She had never thought she would miss it so much, and its absence was painful. Now that she understood the feeling of the Rohen, she better understood the containment and why it had to be stopped.

"He'll catch up," Calder groaned as he stopped.

"Gray!" she called again.

There was no response other than the sound of the world collapsing around them. The dark was unnerving, but Isla wasn't afraid anymore. She had been. Even in Ebberah's dark cell trying to sound like she wasn't afraid of this man, she had been sure there was something else in the dark.

There was always something else in the dark. Always something else nearby. She wasn't sure now that it was there, and in some ways that scared her more. She needed Gray—she needed to be sure he was ok. She had dragged him into this, into all of this.

A door opened, and there was light, but as she looked back, it was still dark behind her. The ceiling above them was gone, the path ahead caved in. Calder still held her arm too tight, as though she might run. Something rumbled beneath her feet and, with one last loud crash, the room behind her crumbled.

"We'll have to climb," Calder said, pushing her towards the rubble in front of her. She wanted to argue, but he was right. The space was filling with dust. Isla coughed as she scrambled up the rubble and out into the bright sunshine beneath the trees. She stepped forward and placed her arms around the nearest one, breathing in the scent of it, feeling the Rohen flow around her once again. Then she turned, holding out the duster she had pulled from the Rohen, and pointed it at Calder's chest.

He raised his arms, but he smirked. "That isn't going to help you right now."

"It might help Gray. We have to go back. We have to find him."

"He would have found a way out. He's hard to kill."

Isla hoped he was right as she lowered the weapon. "Where might he come out?"

"He'll find us," Calder said, looking around the trees. "Right now, we have to find the Rohen and those who worked here."

"You want to find the Rohen?" she asked. Surely it had run away when given the chance. "Who could take it?"

"Your friend might be right; it might be a hummer. Maybe someone has infiltrated the staff and stolen the metal."

"To release it or for some other reason?" Isla asked. She wasn't sure who was pulling what strings anymore. "Is this happening around the Complex?"

He nodded. She wondered then if Ebberah was involved, if she had more information than they thought and was using it to make trouble for Hendra. But the child had more; she was planning something else or involved in very different plans. Isla doubted they supported her mother's ideals. Could the Rohen have found another way?

"We need to find it," she said, wondering if there was any sign there had been others here. If the Rohen were involved, could they have hidden from her?

Isla took a deep breath and looked around the quiet grove. The trees didn't look any different from when they had first arrived. Other than a slight dip in the ground between them, there was no indication that the world beneath had collapsed. Someone else must have known this was here. Was the Rohen working with others?

Calder worked his way through the trees ahead of her, moving slowly, testing the ground, clearly thinking he could disappear down a hole like the one they had climbed out of. When she turned back, she couldn't find it, and she wondered if others would work their way down there to see what had happened. As long as Gray was able to find his way out. She watched Calder get further ahead. If he got lost or assumed she was following, she could double back and find him.

And then Calder was gone, and she was alone. Isla stopped, wondering if it was worth trying to find Gray and get lost herself, as Calder was likely right. As she looked back through the trees, a hand took hers. She flinched at the unnaturalness of it and then looked up at Calder.

"What are you?" she asked as he pulled her closer, fear closing around her. "You won't go back for him."

"I told you he was hard to kill." His hand was still tight around hers. It wasn't that he was holding her hand—he was holding her *by* the hand. "He will find you. He always does."

She wanted to be comforted by that idea, but the way he said it made her uncomfortable. She found herself searching his face for signs of Rohen. There was nothing, unlike the Readers and Ebberah's child who hummed with it. There was nothing. And there was nothing in the ground and in the tree nearest them. She reached forward, but his hold prevented her from touching it. It was as though the Rohen pulled away from him.

"What are you?" she asked again, and his brows creased.

"I'm Elite," he said, as though that was all he needed to be. But she knew there was more to it. If he was the father of Hendra's child, that might have been why they called her the queen. Had he done something to Hendra to allow him the power he wanted?

"You keep staring," he muttered, looking away. Isla thought there was a tinge of colour to his cheeks. "You found me handsome before. Is that what this is?"

"No," she said, looking away. "I'm wondering what made you."

"I'm a man."

"I don't think so," she said, trying not to stare but finding it hard to look away. "What do we do next?" she asked as they remained standing in the trees, neither of them moving.

"I'm not sure. Alice perhaps."

"You want to find Alice?" Isla asked, wondering what he was after now.

"She ran away, remember? We can't find what you want here."

"Containment," Isla murmured. "I'm seeing signs of it, and no matter what you say, you know what it is, what is involved. I think you are part of that. Did you not fight that day, or did they not realise you were there?"

"I was not there," he said, looking around rather than at her. She wasn't sure if he was looking for their ship or something else. But the words struck her as odd.

"You were on the transport. You led us in."

He shook his head without looking at her.

"You knew we would die," she said.

He opened his mouth and then closed it. She shook her head. She didn't want his excuses. She didn't want to guess at what he might have been doing or with whom. She wondered then if he had been sleeping with the Hendra at the same time—or was that a privilege that had come later?

"This way," he said, his voice level and calm as he pointed between the trees. Isla glanced over her shoulder. "This way," he said more firmly.

She could only hope he was right about Gray. But she didn't think she would get what she needed from Calder.

Gray coughed and spluttered in the dust, the sound echoing strangely around him. It was dark, the movement had stopped and he was sure he was trapped. He had lost sight of Isla when the roof had collapsed, and he had no idea if she had made it out or not. He could only hope so. He tried to call out, but his throat was filled with dust and he only coughed more. He wasn't quite sure how he hadn't been crushed beneath the stone as he sat against a broken bench. Dirt and rock surrounded him when he ran his fingers across the floor beside him. Getting out of this was not going to be easy.

He pushed himself to his feet. His head ached, the world spinning around him. He had to get outside. Once he knew where he was, he could find the others—find Isla. The Rohen wouldn't let her perish down here. He wondered then if he could ask them as he had before. But Isla had indicated that there were no Rohen down here.

"Is that possible?" he croaked, the words scratching his throat. Could Hendra have found a way to keep out the Rohen? A soft blue light caught his attention, and he wondered if something was still operational down here. Using the benches and the large stones that had pushed through the ceiling, or that were once part of the ceiling, Gray worked towards the light. It was harder than he had expected, and it appeared to move further away. Just when he thought he was nearly there, it was just out of reach. Other than a blue haze, he couldn't make out what was making the light.

Something shifted. He moved faster, sure that what was left of the building would come crashing down on him. His hand caught on something as he tried to rush, and he wished he had a weapon in the near dark. Not that it would do him any good, but he was starting to understand why Isla felt safer with something in her hands. Although she had found what had scared her in the dark, and she didn't seem so afraid anymore.

The blue light stopped moving. Gray rested his hand on the soft rippled fungus, certain that it wasn't poisonous, and felt instant relief in his hand. The Rohen was here. He had never in his life been so relieved to see a mushroom. Not that it was—but he didn't care about what he didn't know of plants. He just knew the Rohen was here, and somehow that would help.

"Or will it?" he murmured, realising the entrance was covered with stone, debris and dirt. He looked over his shoulder into the dark. He was going to have to dig his way out. "Don't suppose you could send help?" he asked, his voice rough. The dust he inhaled as he spoke made him cough all the more.

Gray leaned back against the wall. Not quite giving up, he assured himself. Just catching his breath. He couldn't stay down here. He stood up, his eyes watering from the coughing, and pushed his fingers into the unstable surface before him. Curling them around the edge of something hard, he pulled. The rock came away in his fingers, but little else moved. He repeated the action, and then something creaked. He jumped back as several rocks and chunks of debris fell down onto the floor. He stepped out to try again when something larger shifted, and the dim blue light was engulfed in a dark cloud. The noise was overwhelming. He slid under the edge of a bench that was still standing, hoping it would go some way to help him when the ceiling came down on his head.

As the world quietened around him, he thought he could hear voices. And as the dust settled somewhat, the blue light illuminated an unnatural face in the entrance amidst the stone.

"Hari?" Gray croaked, leaning out from beneath the bench.

Hari stretched out a hand, and Gray scrabbled over the debris that had spread across the floor to take it. "How?" he asked, his voice raw, as he was pulled not very carefully through the wall of rock and into the bright light on the other side. But it wasn't sunlight. The world was dark around him other than the bright lights of the ship. "Did you find her?"

Hari ushered him towards the ship as the engines rumbled to life and echoed between the trees. The hatch was closed, and they were lifting from the ground before he was even fully inside. He stumbled forward. Hari grabbed his arm to prevent him falling over and directed him into a seat.

"Did you find Isla?" he asked again, his hand at his throat. Every word hurt.

"No," Hari said too calmly. "I think they are long gone."

"Calder?" he asked, fearful he would be separated from Isla again—that she might leave him, and leave with Calder. But she might not have had a choice. "How did you find me?" he asked more forcefully. He needed something from this man.

"Tevia," Hari said, not looking at Gray. Although he thought it explained a lot, the word meant nothing to Gray until a face appeared in the wall. A child stepped from the metal, handed him a cup and sat down on the seat opposite. It was only then that Gray realised there was no one else. Hari and the child had come for him—for them—and no one else.

"How would you have gotten us out?" he asked, but he looked at the child and not the soldier as he took one sip after another of the cool water.

"A way would have been found, and it was," the girl said, smiling oddly. She looked like she could use a bath, even more than Gray probably appeared to need one. This was the child from the wall who had helped in the other facility.

"You couldn't get in there," he said.

"I could have walked in as you did, but it hurts."

"Isla was sure there was something in the walls."

"She has been tasked with finding the containment."

"She keeps finding it—she just can't work out what it is or what it is made from. Do you understand?"

"I understand you," Tevia said, sounding like a child for the first time. "I understand that it is unexpected. I do not understand why it works. Or where it comes from," she added quickly as he opened his mouth to ask. "Calder does not understand either."

"But he was helping us find it."

"He only works to help himself." She twisted her head as though listening to someone or something else. "He would help her, although I do not understand that either."

"Isla?" Gray asked. "Where is he? Where did he take Isla?"

"They have gone where they are needed, or at least where he thinks they are needed. It may help. It may not."

Hari murmured something, and Gray looked at the man. He appeared just as lost as Gray felt. "We'll take you back to Ebberah," he said clearly. "We need to look at these facilities Hendra has planted over the solar system, and our planet, before the people tear apart the world we know to stop her."

"We have somewhere else to be," the child said, and Hari's jaw set.

"Your mother is to talk with him."

"She is not important in this. He has other work to do, others to talk with."

"There is a revolution coming," Hari snapped at the child. "You don't understand."

"You don't understand, Hari. I am not your child to direct."

Hari opened his mouth several times before he managed to croak out, "Whose child are you?"

Gray rested his hand on the man's arm. "She is a child of Rohendra," he said, fully understanding just what she was. This child was more than a hummer, different than Isla.

She smiled at him and bowed her head. "You have met with my family," she said. "You understand."

He understood some of it, but he wasn't sure he understood what good that would do in finding Isla.

Twenty-Three

"Where is she?" Calder grumbled as he looked over the controls before him. The sleek ship had lifted from the surface and moved far from the facility in the trees, but he had yet to leave the atmosphere. Isla wondered if he thought there was a chance Alice was here on Oric. Although, she doubted they would be able to find the woman if she didn't want to be found.

"Did you find something?" Isla asked.

He moved his hand, and a monitor appeared with Alice beaten and sad. Isla rewatched the footage with him, but it gave nothing away.

He shook his head. "That bracelet is a tracker," he said, pointing at the monitor, "but we aren't getting any readings. Either she has deactivated it—we didn't think she knew what it was—or something or someone else is involved. I don't trust her. I have never trusted her, but there is something about this that appears to be... real."

Isla looked at him and then back to the frozen image of the woman on the screen. She did look nervous. What would cause her to tell such stories? Isla was well aware that they were likely not stories; she had spilled the truth, and Hendra wouldn't like that. Not that the other parent of the child mattered, as long as it followed the line. If Alice carried someone else's child, that would be a different story again.

"She left the Hendra willingly," Isla said. Calder confirmed it with a nod. "That was why it was thought she ran. Did she talk to Hendra when she left?"

"No, she left a message."

"Maybe the messenger knows more than they have said. Perhaps the message wasn't so willingly given."

Calder's face grew cold. Isla double-checked her belts as the ship lifted up through the atmosphere. "It will take too long to reach her," he said, looking panicked.

"What are you thinking?"

"That she is on Rennet. Someone within the Hendra Central has taken her, and the enemy is closer to Hendra than I thought."

"There might be more watching over Hendra than you think."

"She isn't safe," he said, his voice losing the calm, detached sound it usually carried.

Isla looked back to the monitor. She didn't want to tell him of the Rohendra, that they thought she was their queen. But then, they might have a very different idea of what that was. Particularly when the woman was trying to kill them. Unless... she thought as she looked at the bruised face of the woman on the monitor. Unless it wasn't Hendra they had spoken of but the child within.

"She is pregnant," Isla whispered.

"Alice?" he asked.

She shook her head. But why now? Why had she needed to disappear now?

"The whole Complex knows that the Hendra is with child," Calder muttered.

"Not whose child."

"You can't believe this rant," he stammered, waving his hand towards the monitor.

"She is right. It is not her child. It is a child of the Rohendra."

"And now you are not making sense," he muttered, pressing something on the control panel. The monitor flickered and disappeared.

"It makes more sense than anything else," she said. The child was theirs, a way to ensure control of the Complex. Or maybe it was just balance they wanted.

Calder glanced at her and then back to the controls.

"I know you think it is yours," Isla said. "I've seen how you look at her. But this child is something else."

He shook his head. "They had told her she couldn't have a child, that Alice would have to carry any heirs. She didn't want that."

"Who told her?"

"The doctors. I've seen the reports, and they were certain it was not possible." He glanced at her then, the same worried expression returning. "What if they are working against her with whoever took Alice? What if Hendra Central isn't safe?"

"She is the safest woman in the universe," Isla said, even surer now that she was right and the Rohen—the Rohendra—had control.

They travelled in silence for a time, and then they were looping around and heading for the moon of Oric. She really thought he would try to make it back to Rennet, particularly if he thought Hendra was in danger, but he settled the ship on the dusty, empty surface of the moon.

"I think we should have warned Ebberah we were coming here." Isla said. "She is somewhat nervous of people on her moon."

"You came here."

Isla nodded, unbuckled her belts and stretched. She ached from the fall in and being dragged out of the building, and she was sure she had bruises up her arms. But she'd been more battered before; she didn't need to look. Gray would have insisted on checking her over, and she hoped he had made it out. He might be sitting somewhere in the sun under a tree, hoping she would find him. At least she wanted him to be doing that rather than crushed under the weight of the building. Would the Rohen help him? Would it help her?

"I need you to do whatever it is you do to talk to them," Calder said.

Isla shook her head, and his face hardened.

"They tell me what they need."

"You don't ask?"

She shook her head again. Maybe she had, but she wasn't sure they answered when she did. They tended to give what they thought she needed, or directly what they wanted.

"You have been here," he said. It wasn't a question. He knew where she had been. She wondered if he knew she had been there more recently.

"They don't do well with demands."

"I need to know she is safe."

"She is. My task is to understand the containment. You didn't get the sand from here to create the glass or the building we just left." Isla knew it wasn't the place she could feel the Rohen in every particle that surrounded her. "You have to show me how the containment works, and then they might be willing to help you, to talk to you." She doubted that anything he did would help, but they had said he would help, so perhaps it was possible.

"You promise she is safe?" he pleaded. Something Isla had never thought she would hear in his voice, even when she'd been sure he was Kalli. She gave a single nod, and he sighed, his hand hovering over the controls. The ship hummed to life around her as a map leapt to life, the holographic planets floating around a large sun. Isla put her hand into the image and dragged it into the middle of the space where she could walk through it. It was the entire Rohendra Complex, each planet orbiting the sun. The moon of Oric, where they were now, was so close they almost touched. Isla wondered then why it didn't have more impact on the planet below. Just how much power did the Rohen have? Even though the map had likely been created by a man with very little knowledge of the Rohen, she could see it as a silvery glow across each planet. Although it could have been the light. She walked between the planets, running her fingers through the gaps between them, and Calder stood on the edge watching her.

"There," she said, pointing to a space in the map. Something in the dark, not mapped and not marked, but she felt the absence of Rohen, even in the map that didn't contain it. She turned and looked through the fuzzy image at Calder, who stood with his arms crossed. "You have to take me there."

"How did you know?"

She shrugged, unsure if she should tell him when she hadn't felt she could before, even when he was her world. And then he had wanted her dead; now he wanted her for the benefit of someone else. Someone he cared for. She didn't know if it was real or a way for him to find the power he seemed to crave.

He was still watching her, his arms crossed, a curiosity she had never seen in him before. "How?" he asked again, but it wasn't harsh. He appeared to want to know.

"I can feel it." She was tempted to shrug again, but instead she held her ground. He watched her but said nothing. "Rohen is everywhere, and for whatever reason, I have a connection to it, to them. All of them. I can feel it even through this image, and I know that it is not here." She pointed to the spot again. "If I were to look more closely at each planet..." She stepped closer to Oric and pulled out with her hands to enlarge it. "I can show you every facility." Calder smirked. Isla closed her eyes and pointed to every place she felt a block. The number surprised her when she finally stopped and opened her eyes. "That many?"

He nodded, his face serious. "And nearly every one has been discovered."

"Maybe there is a hummer assisting."

"You are more than a hummer."

"There are others more than me."

He looked confused for a moment. But he nodded once, clicked his fingers and the map disappeared. "I'll take you, but I don't know how it will help."

"I don't either," she admitted. "But it is what I am to do."

"You aren't worried we are leaving him behind?"

"Gray?" she asked. He nodded. "He has his own tasks. And they will watch over him."

"You're sure? He hasn't done that well so far."

Isla smiled. He might not be a hummer, but he was one who could talk to Rohen. He would be just fine.

Hendra paced in her office. She wasn't sure she had done the right thing, and no one was willing to advise her around it. She missed Calder. He might not have been terribly useful, and likely would have reminded her that he had never trusted Alice, but he would have been keen to give advice. He would have ensured she was aware how her behaviour or actions might damage her image, what might influence the people.

A gentle cough at the door made her stop and look up. The general stood in the doorway with his hand on the handle. He appeared unsure whether he should enter. She waved her hand, and he stepped in and closed the door. He made no move to come any further.

"What is it?" she asked, looking at him properly as though for the first time. "You have news." She sat heavily against the desk, like Calder so often did, and he raced forward to put a hand to her arm. She was surprised, and more so when he helped her stand and directed her to a chair at the table, his hold firm on her arm.

"You found her," she muttered, feeling something hard and odd in her chest. Was it fear?

He nodded, then pulled out the chair beside her and sat down.

"She's gone," she whispered.

He sucked in a deep breath and nodded again.

Her stomach tightened. She stood, pushing the chair back, and he reached for her but waited. "I want to see her," she said.

"I don't recommend that, Your Grace."

"I don't care what you recommend. I need to see Alice."

He stood and bowed his head.

"She's here, isn't she?"

"Within the city, but not inside Central."

That was interesting. Despite her searching, she was sure Alice hadn't gone very far.

"Was she wearing her bracelet?"

"No," he said. Hendra stopped, unsure what to ask next. In the footage, she had been wearing the bracelet.

"What are you not telling me?" she asked.

The usually controlled man looked momentarily unsure of himself. He cleared his throat. "It appears she could not have been in the footage that was sent to you."

"That may have been taken days or weeks ago."

"It appears that Alice has been dead some time."

"How long?" Hendra asked. She had only been gone a matter of days. How did they know she couldn't have been in the footage she was shown?

"Months," he whispered.

"Excuse me," she stammered.

"Months," he repeated more clearly. "The team is working on the exact time."

"Someone has been pretending to be Alice?" Hendra asked, a strange sick feeling covering her whole body. That someone else had touched her, that someone who wasn't Alice had been that close to her. That someone else had been feeding her the green muck. Someone who knew that Alice could not have been the mother of her child—that it was all a lie—because she had told them that.

"Who else might not be who they seem?" she asked, her voice cracking and surprising her. She put her hand to her throat. "How? Was there a twin I was not aware of? Someone who had themselves altered to appear as her? But..." she stammered, looking at the man as he stepped back, "they behaved as she did. I knew this woman like no one else, and she was not an imposter."

"It appears that she was, and a very good one, as no one picked up that she wasn't the First Wife. She wore the bracelet. We have gone back over the recordings, the trace, the maps. She was here. She was, whoever she was, behaving as Alice did. And we cannot tell when the switch happened. There was nothing to link her with the place she was found, and there was no break in service."

Hendra sat back in the chair. She felt numb. All the conversations, all the times Alice had put her hand on her belly and it hadn't been Alice. She put her hand to her belly, and a soft ripple of movement tickled her palm.

"Oh Alice," she whispered, then leant across the table and let the tears flow unchecked.

"No one knows the truth of this," the general whispered after a while. Hendra wiped at her face and tried to calm her breathing. She sat up slowly and nodded. She had never felt so lost. Even when her father had died, she had been ready for the next stage of her life—it was what she had been raised for. But she wasn't ready for this. She sniffed, trying to stop another wave of tears, and wiped the back of her hand across her nose.

"It will start panic," she agreed, feeling the panic rising in her own chest. "Is there any sign of the new Alice?" she asked, lost at what to call her and whether that was even the case. "You still need to find her. If we announce her death and then she reappears, the people will never trust me again."

He nodded and put a hand to her shoulder. It was not a movement she had seen in this man before, and despite her anger at the situation, she was comforted by it.

"I want to be able to bury my wife," she said, taking a deep breath and clearing her mind. "This imposter is the one who was poisoning me. There is a threat out there somewhere, and I want it found and ended."

He bowed and walked towards the door.

"General," she called after him, and he stopped and turned back. "Ensure I am not disturbed, and find Calder. He also appears to have gone rogue, despite thinking he is doing my bidding. I want him here in my office."

"Yes, Your Grace."

She looked at the door for too long after he left. She wouldn't be able to say her goodbyes to her wife while the imposter still roamed, and no one could know the truth. But where would an imposter go? How did they know so much?

Twenty-Four

G ray looked over the man before him, then glanced at the girl as she moved around the room. She didn't look comfortable, as though she wasn't where she wanted to be. Gray wondered how much of her time was spent in the Rohen or with the Rohen. She glanced up at him as though understanding what he was thinking.

"What do you need?" he asked.

"Change is coming," she replied.

"And my part in this is what?"

She looked over her shoulder as though unsure what she should tell him. Gray wondered then if the Rohen was working for the good of the Complex or just themselves. They had asked for Isla to learn what Hendra was using to contain them because it was weakening them in a way. He pushed up off the seat as the idea formed that they wanted the Complex for themselves.

"It won't be as you think," Tevia said.

"Fighting on two sides, the people rising up, the Hendra trying to push them down and the Rohen sneaking in around the side and taking it all."

"I don't think they sneak." She crossed her arms, looking more like a child than the young woman she was.

"We don't want to fight them," he said. And he didn't. He had seen what had happened to Isla, and she had been lucky enough to survive. If the

Rohen wanted them gone from the Complex, there would be nothing they could do to stop it. "Hendra knows what they are," he said.

The child cleared her throat, looked back over her shoulder and nodded at the same time.

"This is more than containment. She is trying to remove them."

"Can you explain this to me?" Hari said, sounding impatient. He too appeared somewhat distracted, looking towards the door. Was he waiting for Ebberah? Whatever she thought she was manipulating, it was nothing compared to this.

"Hendra has learned the true extent of the Rohen, what they truly are," Gray said, although he wasn't sure he fully understood what they were. "She wants them out of her Complex."

"It was always theirs." The child's brow creased, as though it was known by all and he was stupid to think any different. Or was Hendra the one not fully cognisant of the ways of the world? How widely known was it? Did her father and his father before him understand what the Rohen was for the Complex?

"They called her the queen," he murmured.

"Did they?" Tevia asked with a small smile, as though she knew far more than he could ever understand.

He nodded. He was fairly sure they had. He had definitely heard the words used by Rohen in relation to the Hendra. Or was it something else? The child within? "She was poisoned," he said slowly, understanding that it wasn't right. That wasn't what had happened. The symbols that had appeared on the screens in the facility suddenly made more sense. "Can you read?" he asked the child.

She cocked her head to the side.

"Can you read Rohendra?" he asked, and she smiled again, that knowing smile. He wondered why it hadn't made more sense to him before. It was like he had been watching the events unfold while focused on something else. Someone else. Isla.

"She is important," the child said. "She has always been important. Perhaps not as you think, not as you expect."

"How did they learn where the facilities were?" Hari interrupted, looking between the two. "The people, the revolutionaries?"

"They have always known," Tevia said.

"I think he means those who broke in today, not the Rohen... I have been so stupid," Gray whispered, sitting back on the chair and putting his head in his hands. He raked his fingers through his hair, trying to understand why he had not seen this before. They had been everywhere all the time, not seen unless they wanted to be. There was a whole colony of Readers on the moon just above their heads, and the people of Oric had never seen it, never believed them there.

They were everywhere, hiding in plain sight amongst the people, disguised as people. Many would never see the difference. He thought of the copy of Isla, too perfect, and how despite how well he had known her, Calder could not identify that she was an imposter. How many more were out there, leading the people as they wanted them to be directed?

"They are planning the revolution," he said. "They are the people."

The girl smiled. "A change is coming."

"What have you done?" Hari asked as an alarm sounded. Ebberah was rushed through the door surrounded by soldiers.

As Gray looked from her to the girl, she was gone, disappeared into the wall or against it. He could just make out the white outline and her dark eyes, although he doubted the soldiers would be looking.

"We are under attack," a soldier said, directing Ebberah to the seated area like she was the child. Hari stood between her and the rest of the group.

"Who from?" he asked, but Gray had a good idea they already knew.

"The people of Oric are demanding change, understanding. They want to know what is going on in the universe and what Hendra has done to their worlds. They want control."

"They may not be asking for themselves," Gray muttered.

"And who might they be asking for?" Ebberah asked, reaching for Hari as he stepped towards the others.

"The Rohen," Gray said, looking back to the place her daughter had been against the wall.

Ebberah smiled then, a similar look to the one her child had worn. Condescending. She waved the soldiers back towards the door and, despite her trying to hold on to him, Hari left too. She sat down, looking over Gray and his dusty, torn clothing.

"The Rohen is on our side—if it took sides. My daughter is a hummer. She understands that the mining must continue. We need the Rohen."

"Your daughter is more than a hummer, and she understands far more than either of us. The Rohen wants more than to flow through our universe. They want it all for themselves."

"Themselves?" The woman laughed. "What do you think it is? Admittedly, it is far more than I understood. But it is only metal, after all. If clever, useful metal."

Gray shook his head. How did she not understand what it was? He glanced to the wall again, but there was no sign of the child. Perhaps they didn't want her to know. Maybe the child was using her mother to gain what they wanted. Using her position to work the people and distract the Hendra. That was all this was—a distraction.

He moved over to a window, looking out across the dark city, the lights almost pretty. And then he saw more. Flashes of energy. He stepped back as an explosion lit up a block not too far away. How had no one known this was happening? That this had been building? People didn't suddenly revolt overnight.

"What do you want from me?" he asked no one in particular. Ebberah was the only one he could see in the room, yet he knew there were others.

"I'm not even sure why you are here," Ebberah said, looking over his shoulder at the world outside. "Or how you came to be here. I had thought you left with your friends. Calder has some hidden agenda most likely, and Isla claims she knows more than she does."

"You don't seem to know enough," Gray said. "But that doesn't tell me why I am here."

"They will need someone who can talk to them, who is willing to talk to them as a conduit."

The child's voice filtered through the air as though she talked from the walls. Ebberah looked a little startled.

"You want me to stop this?"

"No one can stop it," her daughter said, stepping into the room from a wall. Gray wondered again just how much time she had spent hidden away in the Rohen. "It must run its course."

"And Hendra, Alice—where do they fit in this?" Gray asked.

"You have already been told of Hendra. Alice is what Alice is."

He stared at the child. She wasn't going to tell him any more than he'd already been told, which was little. He couldn't help anyone if he didn't know what was happening.

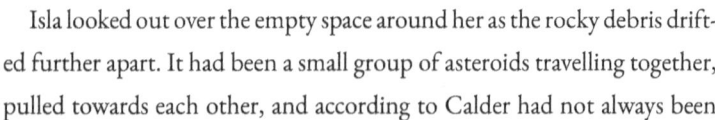

Isla looked out over the empty space around her as the rocky debris drifted further apart. It had been a small group of asteroids travelling together, pulled towards each other, and according to Calder had not always been there. Or maybe they had only been discovered more recently. They had been large when he'd brought up an image of them slowly rotating around each other, pulling together. It was unusual. They had wondered at the relationship between them and so taken samples. It was only by accident they had discovered the effect on the Rohen.

Isla thought of the underground vats and the large pools of Rohen. But it had never really been trapped—it had been waiting for her. It had wanted to be mined, wanted to be collected and shared, allowing the people to think they had used it.

"What is it?" Calder asked, his voice almost kind.

She shook her head, nervous of the Rohen and uncertain. Despite whom she had met and the conversations she'd had, she knew they were doing all they could to ensure they were where they wanted to be. "What happened?" she asked.

He enlarged an image of some of the floating debris, the scorch marks clear across a smooth patch on the edge. "Someone else wanted to see the area, it seems." He looked around at her as though trying to read her.

"I haven't had the chance to tell anyone. And who would I tell?" Isla thought of Gray then, hoping he'd made it out of the building when it had collapsed. The Rohen would know, she thought, putting her hand to the wall of the ship. It was everywhere—it felt, heard, saw everything. They were one.

She sighed. If that was all she had to do, surely it could have been done before. It could have been found before. Ships had come. Ships had taken it—ships with Rohen. She had no idea what they were using her for. Or was she a witness to what they had done, what they could do?

"Where did it come from?" she asked.

Calder shook his head. "Speculation, but it is likely part of the universe, or even our solar system, that just moved in closer for us to find."

"But there is not that much of it, and it was everywhere at the facility—at all of them."

"There was another," he said.

"You collected one of the asteroids?"

"When they were first found, there were four." Isla tried to imagine how they would have looked moving around each other. "It was long ago, and one was taken to look at. The other three moved into their own pattern; it didn't seem to affect them too greatly."

"How do you get an asteroid back to a planet to study?"

"Some work was done out here, I understand. Then it was broken down and taken to Rennet."

"Rennet?"

"I don't know the history," he said. "I just know it was used to keep the Rohen where we wanted so it could be studied."

"Tortured," she murmured. And now it was fighting back and using them to do it.

The comms buzzed again, and Calder ignored them.

"There is only so long you can ignore her," Isla said. "You are hers to command." She tried to sound light, but he nodded slowly and pressed the button.

"Screen," a terse voice said. Isla sat back in the co-pilot's seat, hoping she wouldn't be seen. Calder moved his hand through the controls, and the image of the remains of the asteroid was replaced with that of a stern older man.

"General," Calder said, but he made no move to salute.

"By the stars, Rick, what are you playing at?"

"Sir?"

"Rick?" Isla asked. He shot her a glare, then returned his attention to the screen.

"The Hendra has been trying to reach you for days. I have been trying for hours."

"I am on a mission, sir. It isn't always possible to respond to constant messaging."

The man glared into the monitor, and Isla squirmed in her seat. How rogue was this man?

"I was tasked with a mission. I understand the First Wife is missing, but I can do nothing from where I am."

"She's been found," the general said, his expression unchanged.

"Alive?" Isla asked, but she knew the response before she asked.

"This is more complicated than you could imagine," the general went on as though Isla hadn't spoken. "We need you here to help with this."

"Explain it," Calder demanded, and she wondered if he understood how the ranking system worked.

"She's been dead for some time. Months."

Isla shook her head, remembering the kind woman with her hand wrapped around her wrist. She looked at the place that would have scarred from Calder's knife if Alice hadn't used her humming skills. Isla let out a slow breath.

"Any sign of the imposter?" Calder asked, possibly thinking along the same lines as Isla.

The general shook his head. "We'll find her."

"No," Calder said. "I would guess she is long gone."

"What do you know?"

"Not enough," he snapped, and he pressed the button to end the communication.

"Do you want to return to Hendra?"

"No. I want to find them and stop them from destroying our solar system."

"I think it is more theirs than ours, and we don't have a chance to stop them doing anything."

Epilogue

Alice stood at the end of the examination table in the small lab and sighed. It was a mess. The body before her was a mess.

"They believed it was me?" she asked.

The man standing over the body nodded and mumbled something, his face hidden behind a wide mask and his eyes shining with silver threads that caught the dim light.

"I didn't doubt you," she said. But she had. She wanted to trust. She knew what her place was, where she was destined to be. "They can't announce it though, can they?"

He mumbled something else beneath the mask, and she took it as agreement.

"Island might work it out," she thought aloud. The woman had a much better understanding of what Alice was than she'd expected. Island was more than gifted, more than she thought she might be. "She is safe at least."

"She is with Calder," a voice said behind her, and Alice turned slowly to the tall soldier. He looked serious, staring at the body on the table rather than at her.

"That doesn't worry me."

"No," he said, stepping forward.

"Where did she look?" Alice asked, watching the man study the body.

"Your secret room. She dragged me along to help."

"It was never a secret. Hendra doesn't like secrets. She likes to believe she knows it all, and that she is in control of everything."

The man snorted. Then he covered his mouth, rearranged his features into something of respect and bowed his head to her.

"She serves the people of the Rohendra Complex," Alice said. "Although perhaps not as she understands."

"She appeared worried about you," he said.

"She cares for no one but herself. That will change, or it will no longer matter."

He bowed his head to her and then waved his hand over the body. "What would you have us do?"

Alice ran her hand across the bracelet at her wrist. Hendra thought she knew so much more than she did, and what she did know she had betrayed. "Tell my father that we are coming."

He bowed his head but remained where he was.

"The body stays. You had no connection to it, to her. Don't make it out to be important."

"No, Your Grace," he said swiftly, bowing again.

The laugh that escaped her lips echoed around the small room, and the other man looked at her with open surprise. The soldier smiled, if somewhat nervously, and left the room. The man working over the body removed his mask.

"Is this wise?" he asked.

"You know what we must do."

He nodded, replaced the mask and picked up his scalpel.

Acknowledgements

The team at Deranged Doctor Designs (DDD) for absolutely brilliant cover design work and all the marketing extras. Thank you for your support and clear emails around what was needed from me to make the magic happen.

TWG members for listening and support in all things writing related. Special thanks to Yasmin, for taking the time to read my draft and providing ideas to make the story stronger.

Allison E Wright for wonderful editing work to make my sentences smoother and my intentions clearer.

My parents, Francine and Ken Smith. Amazing, supportive people who I don't thank often enough. Thanks for keeping me grounded and being the best grandparents ever.

As always, Temwa for being my biggest supporter.

About the Author

Georgina Makalani survives life as a servant of the public by hiding in her office at lunch time with dragons, witches, a laptop and a little bit of magic.

For more about Georgina and her books visit her website: www.theflowofink.com